MUSTARD SEED ITINERARY

Robert Mullen lives in Edinburgh. He was born in Washington, D.C., and grew up in Virginia. After studying computer science at George Washington University, he did graduate work at the University of Alberta and became a lecturer at McGill University. His published works include a volume of short stories, *Americas*, which was shortlisted for a Commonwealth First Book award, and *Call of the Camino: Myths, Legends and Pilgrim Stories on the Way to Santiago de Compostela*.

WITHOUT GOING OUT OF THE DOOR,
ONE KNOWS THE EARTH.
WITHOUT PEERING FROM THE WINDOW,
ONE PERCEIVES THE WAYS OF HEAVEN.

Tao Te Ching

ROBERT MULLEN

MUSTARD SEED ITINERARY

MEN OF TALENT SOUGHT!
ONLY SUPERIOR PERSONS NEED APPLY!

Published in Great Britain by EnvelopeBooks 2021
A New Premises venture

EnvelopeBooks
12 Wellfield Avenue
London N10 2EA

Cover design: Stephen Games

A CIP catalogue record for this title is available from the
British Library

EnvelopeBook 5
ISBN 9781838172046

Designed and edited by Booklaunch
WWW.ENVELOPEBOOKS.CO.UK

致玛丽
To Mary

1

CELEBRATION | HEAVEN'S DOME, EARTH'S
OBSERVANCES | THEY SWEEP THE PATH | A FINE
DAY FOR SOME | GRANNY WEN FLIES A BLUE FLAG
| WORDS LEFT UNSPOKEN FALL ON DEAF EARS

It was to be a banner day in Nettle Village, a place of few refinements and little sophistication, and not as a rule given to ostentation. Nonetheless the women had been out early that morning with their brooms, the village dogs had been kept chained and public conveniences had been secured in order that no one, if caught short, would simply squat down in full view of the road on which the guests would at any moment now be arriving. Nettle Village, whose occupants were generally believed to be both prickly and litigious, was being called upon, on that special day, to put its best foot forward.

Po Cheng, the village schoolmaster, had viewed these

preparations from the window of his small, two-room schoolhouse. This would be his first opportunity to observe a country wedding but he was by no means overjoyed at the prospect. His students, by order of Headman Ba, had been sent home early so that they could gather up the village chickens and return them to their hutches before the guests appeared.

He could hear music. Some sort of rehearsal must be taking place. What he could hear was a scratchy recording of the wedding hymn: *We Have Chosen A Timely Day*.

'Just so that everyone,' supposed Schoolmaster Po, 'will know just where to stand until such time as they all end up dead drunk and passed out on the floor.'

What could have been more ridiculous, in any case, than Beauty Ba, the most attractive woman in the village and the daughter of the headman, being married off to a fellow twice her age, with nothing to recommend him apart from the fact that he possessed a cow, and that Beauty Ba—by marrying him—could guarantee that her parents, when they grew old, would always have fresh milk to drink?

But why torment himself? The schoolmaster returned to his desk, where there was a goodly stack of essays waiting to be graded. The assignment had been to give instances in support of a proverb which stated that lengthening the duck's legs would not turn it into a crane, and as luck would have it the essay atop the pile was none other than that handed in by Little Bully Ba, the younger brother of the bride-to-be:

> *I came home from playing football so hungry that I could eat a crane but my mother said that none had passed that day and I would have to eat a duck instead and just leave its legs on the side of my plate … .*

What to make of such a paper? Was such shallow thinking a sign of the times or was it simply to be put down to the high spirits and impatience of youth? Po Cheng took out his Day Book and jotted down a note to himself, a suggestion for a future assignment, namely to explain the meaning of the ancient phrase:

HE POINTS AT THE MOON;
THE CLODS SEE ONLY A FINGER.

A VOLLEY OF firecrackers sounding in Nettle Village's single paved street indicated that the formalities must now have been completed. A visiting magistrate would have been summoned to the village for this purpose by Boss Ba, who had only to crook a finger, so to speak, and things got done.

While such high-handedness might not have been admired by those who believed that times had changed, Po Cheng had to admit to a grudging admiration for the fellow's efficiency and he was therefore in two minds as to whether or not to attend that evening's festivities.

A voice from the doorway of the classroom cut short his pondering.

'Knock! Knock!'

'Ah, Miss Ling. Did you hear all that racket? The Bas, it seems, now have a cow in the family.'

Hers was the other classroom, where she was in charge of the little ones, the infants of the Minnow School, her task being to keep them occupied until such time as they were ready to put aside their toys, wash off their face-paint and attend the Middle School. As always, as her work entailed much crawling around with them on the floor, she was dressed in a wrinkled khaki shirt and baggy trousers.

'A cow, yes,' she agreed, 'but all the same, Colleague,

ought we not to congratulate them? And maybe even join in their dances?'

'Congratulate them? Yes, perhaps, but as for making an exhibition of oneself ... .'

That having been settled, he returned to his grading. The next paper, he immediately recognized from its careful calligraphy, was that of one of the girls in the class. She was, in fact, although small for her age, one of his best students, one who at least attempted to think things through rather than merely putting down the first thing that came into her head, as her essay clearly demonstrated:

A duck or a crane, what difference does it make? Is it not just as important for a duck to be a duck as it is for a crane to be a crane? And would a duck, in any case, not look ridiculous going about on stilts?

The task of a teacher in the Middle School, Po Cheng reflected afterwards as he packed up for the day, was two-fold: with those who were struggling, to teach them to keep their heads above the water, and with those who were more dextrous, to encourage them to make for ever more distant shores. The rest, such as his turning up that evening to congratulate the Ba family on its good fortune, while it may have been necessary, was of another order altogether and so was best described, in his opinion, as extracurricular.

HE COULD HEAR, as he wiped the blackboard and straightened the desks in his classroom that evening, the sound of an orchestra tuning up. That would be the six-piece orchestra which had been hired for the evening and which had arrived earlier from the provincial capital in the back of a pick-up truck. They would be in Granny Wen's place, in the back room of her house, which she ran as an unlicensed wine shop and to which—truth be told—Schoolmaster Po would not be making his first visit.

He also straightened the framed motto on the wall, the latest one embroidered for the school by Madame Ba, the fourth and final member of that tribe:

A POT IS MADE BY HEATING CLAY!

A stern lady indeed was Madame Ba, who kept a sharp eye out for any untoward behaviour in the village and was likely to have her hands full that night if she hoped to keep impropriety in check.

Schoolmaster Po locked the door of the schoolhouse behind him and then paused on the porch to remove a cap which someone had placed on the head of the school's founder. This individual was said to have arrived in the village on the back of a stork, seen that there was no school, built one single-handedly, taught in it for a hundred years and then summoned his stork, mounted it and rode off again, leaving behind a statue of himself which the students had ever since treated as a mascot.

GRANNY WEN HAD hung out a blue flag, signifying that her back-room establishment was open for business. Indeed the place was already bursting at the seams but this didn't prevent the schoolmaster from being spotted by Little Bully Ba, who thrust a brightly coloured 'cocktail' into his hand. Not only wine but also Granny Wen's own illicit spirits were dispensed there, including a 'gin' which she distilled herself from the skins of sweet potatoes.

'You're late, Sir,' the boy complained. 'You're way behind. You'll need to drink up.'

'With pleasure, my boy. But surely one ought to savour slowly what's good in this life?'

'Must you, Sir? Just think what a bad example that would set for everyone else.'

That first cocktail, despite his best efforts, led to a second, and the second to a third, at which point Po Cheng found himself staring at a photograph—no doubt clipped from a magazine—which Granny Wen had pinned up on the wall. It showed a cliff-top monastery, this being a subject which the old woman thought might be of interest to the tourists whom only she and Boss Ba believed would ever turn up this far from any airport.

Out of the corner of his eye, Po Cheng caught a glimpse now and then of Beauty Ba, who was surrounded by a bevy of giggling village girls, and it was easy enough to guess just what it must be they all found so amusing. Those who knew the most would be explaining to those who knew less just what it was that awaited a bride on her wedding night.

As for the bride, Po Cheng had admired the young woman ever since his arrival in the village, but only from afar. Her father, he had come to know, had on various occasions in the past been taken in for questioning by the provincial authorities about this matter or that but had each time been set free again. This was no proof of his innocence, in the opinion of the schoolmaster, but rather a typical case of the little fish going into the pot and the big fish being thrown back into the sea.

Having made his appearance, the reluctant guest then began to edge his way towards the door. He had had, he told himself, a lucky escape. Just imagine, for instance, if he himself had owned a milk cow!

Once outside, he forced himself to walk straight. Some elderly gentlemen, he noticed, had brought chairs out from their houses and were sitting under the village's lone streetlight smoking their long-handled pipes. What he failed to notice was that—when leaving Granny Wen's premises— he had set off in precisely the wrong direction.

'What an idiot!' he thought, upon finding himself not back at the schoolhouse but on the bank of Nettle Brook. 'One misstep at the start, as they say, and a thousand leagues adrift by the end.'

He sat down. He stretched out, taking care to avoid the nettles. Best to have a little rest first, he decided, and to clear his head, and then he could walk back through the village properly, as if he hadn't a care in the world, as if it had always been his intention to take the long way home.

二

2

He was awakened by the voices of strangers: two gentlemen who were evidently not country people and who seemed none too pleased to have been sent to the countryside on some important errand only to find, in Nettle Village, that the inhabitants were all still asleep and lying just where they had dropped the night before.

'What a backwater! Nettle Village! The name speaks for itself.'

'All the better for us then. We can simply cross it off our list.'

Po Cheng sat up and rubbed his eyes. The two were wearing fine silk robes of the type worn in the past by government officials, something which did not surprise him in the least. What better indication could there possibly have been of just how far Nettle Village remained behind the times?

'Begging your pardon, Gentlemen,' he called to them, 'but not so fast. Not all birds, even if they share the same nest, are birds of a feather.'

This, coming from the undergrowth, got their immediate attention. They parted the foliage with some care and so saw before them someone who, while still on the ground, still seated on a tuft of moss, was at least sitting up straight.

'And what manner of bird is this, would you say?' the taller one asked the other.

'A ground-nesting one,' replied the other, sarcastically.

The taller official had a scroll under his arm, which Po Cheng, as the village's schoolmaster, insisted that he should unroll. The two gentlemen exchanged a sly look and then they together unrolled the notice:

MEN OF TALENT SOUGHT!
ONLY SUPERIOR PERSONS NEED APPLY!

So that was it: they were recruiters who had been sent out to round up candidates for the soon-to-be-held Provincial Examinations. There was still time, they assured Po Cheng, if he wished to try his hand, and they were authorized to provide each suitable candidate with sufficient travel money to get him to the provincial capital.

'And just how is one to demonstrate that suitability?' inquired Po Cheng, cautiously.

With a poem. By improvising a couplet in praise of the Emperor's policy of seeking out men of talent even in the most benighted provinces of the Empire.

'Ah,' Po Cheng challenged them. 'So you mean to say that there still is an Emperor?'

'Of course there is. As soon as one dies, another takes his place.'

There was no time to lose. Fortunately, perhaps owing to some distant rainstorm during the night, Nettle Brook, which had until then been a mere streamlet, had now become a river, and this was all the inspiration that he required to produce the following encomium:

A RIVER, HAVING SUMMONED THE STREAM,
THEN TRANSPORTS ITS TRIBUTE TO THE SEA.

This did the trick. Po Cheng was handed a small purse containing the promised travel money, told that there would be a riverboat along soon, and warned to make sure that he was on it.

'Just like that,' he thought. 'Until this, my life had seemed to move at a snail's pace.'

But now, scarcely had the two recruiters gone on their way than he heard what he was at once able to recognize— and never mind if he had never heard one before—as the whistle of a riverboat.

THE BOAT, THE *Dragonfly*, was a dilapidated-looking craft which by no means skimmed over the surface of the water but rather chugged along, already half-submerged in the rapidly flowing river. On its crowded deck, people were zealously guarding their possessions, be they in bundles, boxes, cages or hutches. Riverboats were notoriously unseaworthy and likely to be overloaded, and so the children on board, while they were allowed to run about, all had hollow gourds attached to their arms and legs.

Candidate Po, being unaccustomed to this form of travel, sat still, facing forward, with his back braced firmly against a bulkhead, and willed the boat to remain afloat. As for the examination and the stiff competition which he was certain to face, he remained sanguine. His competitors would no doubt turn up well prepared, having turned the pages of countless books, but how many of them would have faced the even greater challenge, that of trying to pass one's knowledge on to others?

In due course a sign appeared on the riverbank, nailed to the trunk of a tree, and it carried most welcome news, namely that the *Dragonfly* was now approaching the provincial capital:

BRIGHT PROSPECT TOWN WELCOMES
THOSE WHO HAVE WHAT IT TAKES!

One more bend of the river and the town itself appeared, its sprawl of low buildings being dwarfed by the dome of what could only have been the Examination Hall.

'Ah so!' declared Po Cheng, in wonder. 'And what if I've bitten off more than I'm able to chew?'

He allowed the others to disembark first. What if he failed to make the grade? Failed to measure up? Was it too late to take the riverboat back upstream, find the two recruiters and return his travel money?

Then he saw her. The other passengers had already disappeared into the town, leaving just a single figure remaining on the dock, the familiar figure of someone wearing a wrinkled khaki shirt and baggy trousers.

Was he imagining things, Po Cheng asked himself, or was this really Miss Ling? And if it was, what could have brought her to this place? Surely she must realize that in order to be selected as a man of talent, one had by definition to be a man.

And so it was that—out of curiosity—Po Cheng put aside his own qualms, detached himself from the bulkhead and proceeded to disembark.

HOW WAS IT possible? She had given no explanation, merely asked him to follow her, insisting that there was no time to lose and promising to explain everything afterwards. But how could she know the way—without the least hesitation —through that maze of dismal, nameless streets? Could it be that Miss Ling, during all the time that she had been in Nettle Village and in charge of the Minnow School, had been leading a double life?

His suspicions were further increased when they reached a canal, along the length of which was moored a seemingly endless line of brightly painted narrow boats. Not only had Miss Ling been able to navigate her way unerringly through the town but she also knew the way to what was quite obviously the town's Pleasure Quarter.

'It's not much further now, Colleague,' she assured him, setting off on the towpath.

They arrived at a boat much the same as the others, with flower pots on its deck and even a washing line strung between two poles. The door to the cabin was locked but Miss Ling had a key, and Po Cheng, appalled by her apparent duplicity but unable to decide what to do about it, followed her inside.

The cabin was a single long room, furnished with a clothes horse, a lacquered table, a pewter lamp, a terracotta cat, a sleeping mat, a full-length mirror, a chamber pot and a washstand. She too, Miss Ling explained, had crossed paths with the two recruiters, who had unrolled a scroll for her as well:

LUCRATIVE POSITIONS FOR WOMEN!
NOT FOR THE FAINT-HEARTED!

'But surely you didn't fall for that, Miss Ling?'

'Of course not, Colleague. But isn't it usual for a candidate, on the eve of an examination, to spend the night on a canal boat?'

He watched her as she put on some rice to boil. She was right about that old tradition, which had had little to do with concupiscence. The women who worked on these boats, after all, when not entertaining the candidates, were likely to have been entertaining the examiners.

'So then, Miss Ling, let's get down to business, shall we? Just what tips do you have to pass on to me?'

'Just one. I asked around and the women on the other boats all say the same. The most important thing, on a Provincial Examination, is to be concise, so that the examiners won't be too long getting home to their suppers.'

'Ah, yes, their suppers. No need, as the proverb says, to feed dumplings to swine.'

'No need at all, Colleague. You just need to make sure that their meal's not too long delayed.'

SHE HAD LIT a lamp but kept it turned down low. She had work to do, she said, and it would probably take her most of the night. She would do her best not to wake him. Come morning, he would be going up against candidates who had been preparing for the examination for months already and all he could do to prepare himself—at this late date—would be to get a proper night's sleep.

'You take the mat, Colleague. I'll lie down tomorrow while you're at the Examination Hall. That way, the proprieties will have been observed.'

As if anyone else were observing the proprieties! The last thing that the candidate heard that night was the sound of the woman in the next boat cooing invitingly to any individual who passed along the towpath.

'Come and spend the night here, darling, why don't you?'

Scarcely had he closed his eyes that night than he was being shaken awake again by Miss Ling, who, when he had sat up, handed him a bowl of cold rice. He would need something in his stomach, she proclaimed, something bland, something that would sit well and cause no turbulence.

'Turbulence, Miss Ling? What a coy way of putting it.'

She showed him what she had been working on while he slept. Each candidate, she had found out, in order to be taken seriously, needed to appear wearing a robe and with his hair arranged in a topknot. For the robe, she had removed the curtains from several of the boat's small windows, snipped them up and then sewn them back together again into something resembling a gown.

'That was good of you, Miss Ling. But won't I look like a clown?'

'Never mind, Colleague. At least it will get you in the door.'

'And the topknot?'

She did the best she could, as his hair was nowhere near long enough. What Po Cheng saw in the mirror afterwards, to his dismay, was a mere tuft. Those against whom he would be competing were sure to be better dressed, he calculated, and better groomed, and would start the day's race already far ahead of him on the basis of appearance alone.

She saw him to the door. Other candidates, she warned, were likely to appear accompanied by a group of friends banging wooden clappers but he must not let this discourage him. What mattered was not how much noise one made when arriving at the Examination Hall, it was what the candidate had to say for himself once inside.

'But what a fool I am,' she added. 'You'll know all that already. The hen, as they say, ought to know better than to try to teach the rooster how to crow.'

三

3

A Provincial Examination, while only the first rung on the
ladder to perpetual preferment, was not to be taken lightly
and Po Cheng knew very well that others would have hired
fine attire for the occasion in the hope of being placed near
the front of the hall, where the examiners would be most
likely to notice them.

No one, on the other hand (and this included the
examiners themselves), knew just how their decisions were
reached nor how those decisions might be swayed, and
hence the measures taken by the candidates to improve
their chances were taken largely in hope, and Candidate Po's

best hope was that being seated near the back of the hall might be of some fortuitous and completely unanticipated advantage.

The closer that he came to that imposing dome, however, the smaller he felt, and this was not an experience that was new to him. As a hapless schoolboy, he had fallen into the trap of leaving things to the very last minute and so had often found himself on his way—with a churning stomach—to take an examination for which he knew himself to be signally ill prepared.

To his surprise, upon reaching the entrance to the Examination Hall, he once again encountered a familiar figure. That there should have been a doorman controlling access to such an important institution was only to be expected, but the fellow, with his bushy eyebrows and atrocious sideburns, was the very image of the statue which stood on the porch of the schoolhouse back in Nettle Village.

'Not so fast!' the doorman barked, blocking Po Cheng's way. 'You can't just barge in here, not so long as I'm on duty.'

'Barge in? Of course not. I'm here to take the Literary Examination.'

'You should have said so to begin with. Under what name?'

'Po Cheng, if you please. Recently of Nettle Village.'

'Just as I thought: *Found wandering in a country lane.*'

Candidate Po did not bother to correct this as it had probably not been intended as a description, only as a category, and there were already other candidates lining up behind him. Such belligerence in someone so small suggested, furthermore, that it might be the policy in Bright Prospect Town to assign menial jobs—such as that of a doorman—to individuals who were mentally disturbed.

Once through the door, each candidate was scrutinized by an invigilator. When it came to Po Cheng's turn, each item of his clothing was thoroughly searched for hidden notes, along with his ears, his mouth and even the gaps between his toes. What a pity, thought Candidate Po, that this should be necessary, that there should be people who would shy away from the months of study required in order to pass an examination honestly, only to spend an equal amount of time figuring out ways to cheat.

'And this robe of yours?' the invigilator questioned, before allowing him to proceed. 'It seems to have been put together by a committee.'

'It's the latest thing,' Po Cheng prevaricated. 'There's only one person in this whole town capable of doing such detailed work.'

HAVING BEEN ASSIGNED to a mat, the candidate was provided with a cushion, a pair of slippers, an ink stone, a mortar and pestle, some parchment, a writing board, a variety of brushes, foodstuffs for the day, a jug of water and a flag to wave if at any time during the examination he needed to be escorted to the latrine. Every attempt had been made, it seemed, to eliminate physical discomfort and satisfy bodily needs and by so doing permit the true worth of each candidate to emerge.

Hardly had Po Cheng laid out these accoutrements on his mat than a bell sounded. The heavy door of the Examination Hall was swung shut and bolted; a notched taper the height of a man was brought in and lit, so that the candidates could tell at any moment—by counting the remaining notches—just how much time was left before the papers would be collected.

It would be necessary to pace oneself. Many a race had

been lost, but none ever won, on the first lap. Even a strong swimmer, Candidate Po reminded himself, might come to grief, however calm the water, if he did not also know how to float.

The Chief Examiner, a grizzled veteran, by the look of him, of many such examinations, hung up the first signboard:

A BEAR CLAW, ABSENT FROM THE BEAR,
REQUIRES MUCH BOILING

What to make of this? Was it a proverb? A line taken out of context from a poem? A recipe for a meagre meal?

The invigilators were now posted all about the hall and the examiners huddled together, speaking softly among themselves. The candidates on the mats surrounding his own, Po Cheng noticed, were all writing feverishly but this did not trouble him. It was not they but the examiners and their toadies that he would need to outwit.

The giant taper had burned down an entire notch by the time he got to work. He ground some ink and wetted his brush. The best way to deal with that first question, he decided, was to reply to it in the same oblique fashion in which it had been posed:

SEEKING KNOWLEDGE BUT LACKING CERTAINTY:
CLAWS IN FRONT AND PAWS BEHIND.

Several of the candidates had already given up and been escorted, slump-shouldered, from the hall. Another, a rather elderly gentleman, had been expelled for banging his head on the floor in an attempt to recall some word or phrase which—but a few years earlier—he might well have had right on the tip of his tongue.

The rest were still writing furiously, all apart from Candidate Po, who was now sitting up straight, with his hands clasped behind his head, giving every impression, should any of the examiners look his way, of someone who could scarcely wait to see what might come next.

IT WAS NO secret that the first and the last questions in an examination were the most crucial, as it was one's answers to these which even the laziest of examiners was most likely to scrutinize. There was thus a palpable tension in the hall as the final signboard was displayed:

OUGHT ONE TO LEARN
THE WAYS OF MEN FIRST,
OR THE WAY OF HEAVEN?

And this, Po Cheng immediately realized, was a trick question, and that choosing either alternative to the exclusion of the other would at once place him, as it were, at the foot of the class. He had only to pick up his brush and the answer wrote itself:

> *To study the Ways of Men is to ground oneself in the past, in the practical, whereas the Way of Heaven is one's best guide to the future, to what is desirable. How then is it possible to assign priority to either? Are the practical and the desirable not the two legs by means of which men stand upright and go forward?*

What happened next, while difficult to believe, he nevertheless considered to be no more than he deserved. The other candidates, rather than bearing him any evident malice, got to their feet, first to applaud him and then to hoist him onto their shoulders and to carry him out into the street.

'Make way!' they shouted. 'Make way at once! Make way for the First Graduate!'

From his vantage point atop the shoulders of the defeated candidates, he could see that those who had made way for the procession all fell in behind it afterwards. It was therefore a goodly company that finally arrived at the Golden Cockerel Chophouse, where the following banners had been hung out in honour of that year's First Graduate:

HAVING STUDIED THE OLD, HE KNOWS THE NEW!
HAVING LEARNED ONE THING, HE UNDERSTANDS TEN!
OTHERS CONTESTED IT, BUT HE SWEPT THEM AWAY!

THE CHOPHOUSE, BY the time everyone had been seated, was packed to the rafters, with those for whom there had been no room at any of the tables having simply sat down on the floor. First Graduate Po watched in awe as the food being brought out continuously from the kitchen was devoured greedily by the guests, who shovelled it into their mouths as if they feared they might never eat again, and then washed it down by tipping wine into their mouths as if it were water.

'How extraordinary,' thought Po Cheng, 'and all of this in honour of me!'

But then, just as quickly as the restaurant had filled, it emptied again, with guests crawling over one another in their haste to get out of the door. And worse was to follow, when the guest of honour was confronted by a brute of a fellow with a square, pockmarked face, who claimed to be the proprietor of that establishment.

'I hope, Sir, that everything was satisfactory,' the fellow

said, politely enough, 'but isn't it time now that we got down to business?'

So saying he produced a hand-scroll which, when it had been fully unrolled, extended all the way down to their feet.

'As you can see, Sir, everything has been itemized.'

To Po Cheng's amazement, this was the bill for the banquet, and no less amazing was the curious fact that the total which had been run up amounted to precisely the sum of the travel money which had been allocated to him by the two recruiters. And was one not, at this point, permitted to smell a rat? All the same, he might very well have paid up on the spot and chalked it up to experience but for the fact that the purse containing his travel money was still in the pocket of his trousers and they were still back on the canal boat, where they had been draped over a clothes horse.

'See here,' he temporized, 'while I'm not for a moment questioning your accounting, I'll need a little time to read through all this.'

'No, *you* see here!' snapped the pockmarked fellow, menacingly. 'These things are best settled amicably. But should you wish to contest the matter ...'

At which juncture the conversation was cut short by the sound of two loud thuds. The first was the sound of the knuckles of the diminutive doorman from the Examination Hall striking the jaw of the proprietor of the Golden Cockerel Chophouse and the second was the sound made as the brute fell senseless to the floor.

'Allow me to congratulate you,' said First Graduate Po, gratefully. 'That really was a telling blow.'

'A right cross usually is,' acknowledged the doorman. 'No one ever sees it coming. But we ought not to hang around, as the fellow won't be out for long. His sort seldom are.'

4

FLIGHT | HEAVEN'S FULNESS, EARTH'S ACCOUNTING | NO LINGERING, NO TARRYING | ON THE WAY TO WISHBONE MOUNTAIN | SIGNS AND WONDERS | WITH THE PILGRIM, COMES THE PATH

The town was still, silent and plunged in darkness. Having had a fine feed at another's expense, the good people of Bright Prospect Town were now sleeping peacefully. Not so the two fugitives. The doorman, though far from young, was none the less light on his feet and it was all that Po Cheng could do to keep up as they wove their way through the town's deserted streets. Somewhere behind them, it was to be supposed, a posse of angry waiters was likely to be in hot pursuit.

Only when they paused to rest was Po Cheng able to ascertain that the name by which his fellow fugitive was known in the town was Wang Tzu, which was to say, *Master* Wang.

'And just how, if one may ask, did you come by such a grand title?'

'It's a long story,' replied the old man testily, 'and one that I keep to myself.'

Just then, in the distance, a bell began to sound. It was the town's alarm bell, the ten-bushel bell which was rung as need be in order to alert the townspeople to some present or impending danger.

'That's not for us, is it?' inquired the First Graduate, hopefully.

'And why wouldn't it be for us? The fellow who runs that chophouse has accomplices in high places.'

'So how are we going to get away then?'

'By splitting up. Each rabbit to its own hole.'

Upon which the wily fellow simply darted off, leaving Po Cheng planted there and needing to make his own arrangements.

Getting back to the canal was easy enough, as the ditches which drained the town's latrines all ran down to it, but how —in the dark—was he supposed to tell one of those boats of ill repute from all of the rest?

He was still puzzling over this when a light appeared ahead. Someone was approaching on the towpath with a small lantern, someone who he fervently hoped would turn out to be Miss Ling.

'So there you are!' called out a woman's voice which was not the voice of Miss Ling. 'The others are all waiting. Didn't we agree to get an early start?'

She had obviously mistaken him for someone else but he had no good reason to set her straight. Instead he followed her to where the 'others' were waiting, a group of some two dozen individuals of every description, men and women alike, all wearing straw sun hats and all of them milling about nervously, unable to stay still, so anxious were they to be on the road.

'What a stroke of good fortune,' Po Cheng congratulated himself. 'Just when one's luck seems to have deserted one, it turns up again.'

He too was handed a sun hat by the woman with the lantern, and with that his own disguise had been completed, for how better to lie low, how better to make oneself inconspicuous, than to appear as one among many?

THE PARTY OF pilgrims, for that was what they were, walked at first in single file and in silence behind the woman carrying the lantern.

Once the sky began to lighten and the lantern was extinguished, they became more animated and could be heard pointing out, one to another, various unremarkable features of the landscape through which they were passing, believing whatever they saw to be, for this reason or that, propitious for their journey.

'Such enthusiasm,' reflected the First Graduate, not being himself a religious fanatic, 'must be exhausting.'

Simply by listening to their conversations, he learned that they were on their way to visit a certain holy site, Wishbone Mountain, and to pray there in the belief that prayers uttered in the shadow of that strangely shaped peak were certain to be answered. It was of course always perfectly possible when viewing a mountain or gazing up at a cloud to see something which seemed familiar but to place one's hopes in any such resemblance, in Po Cheng's opinion, was to have a wishbone for a mind.

One individual in particular caught his attention. The poor fellow was largely shunned by the other pilgrims, either because he was obviously a rustic or perhaps because he was walking bent over, with a heavy wooden saddle strapped onto his back.

'Hot, isn't it?' Po Cheng remarked to him. 'And my guess is that it will get even hotter.'

'Which is no less than we deserve,' the fellow opined.

'But you seem, if one may say so, to have taken the law into your own hands.'

'Say what you like. None of the others will speak to me, not even to spout nonsense.'

It was necessary to be discreet. To ask too many questions, or questions of the wrong sort, would draw unwelcome attention to himself, Po Cheng feared, and perhaps even reveal him to the others as an imposter.

'One must not mind others,' he ventured. 'Which of us, after all, has not done things in the past of which to be ashamed later on?'

'You're right about that. In a moment, for instance, of inattention … .'

The fellow lowered his voice before continuing. The saddle on his back, he then related, was there by way of a confession. His own offence had been to beat his horse to death one evening, after having fallen off it, when returning home drunk.

'How unfortunate,' commiserated Po Cheng. 'A thing like that could happen to anyone, taking into consideration that he had drunk too much.'

What bothered him was that they had by this time walked a long way since leaving Bright Prospect Town but there was as yet no sign of any hills in the distance, much less of the sacred peak which they were meant to be seeking; but as none of the others showed any concern over this, the First Graduate saw fit to keep his own impatience to himself. Someone who had to ask how much further it was to

Wishbone Mountain, he concluded, might well be thought to have had no business going there in the first place.

HE WAS, HE began to worry, despite his best efforts, in danger of losing track of time completely. Had he been walking for hours, for instance, or for days? Was it the sameness of the landscape that was to blame or was he in fact becoming just what he had pretended to be—just one among many, just one pilgrim more? Still there was no end in sight and nothing by means of which to get his bearings, not until, beside the path, a large signboard suddenly appeared:

PERPETUAL AWE VIEWING POINT!
BY NO MEANS TO BE MISSED!

Just beyond were the remains of a stone rampart, with a ladder up which the pilgrims at once began to scramble, each giving out, upon reaching the top, a suitable expression of appreciation.

'Ooh!'

'Aah!'

'Ah so!' exclaimed Po Cheng, out of genuine amazement.

How was it possible? The town from which he had fled, and which ought by now to have been well out of sight, was still clearly visible and appeared to be little more than a stone's throw in the distance.

All the same, he decided, his best chance was to continue on in the hope that whatever had been slowing him down would also hinder any pursuers.

He waited anxiously while the others took rubbings of the inscriptions left by earlier visitors in the stone of the ramparts. How shallow people were becoming, he mused, being by now in a thoroughly bad temper. How sad that people no longer had any ideas of their own and so went about collecting those of others.

The path after that began to rise, although the fugitive could not discard the possibility this might be a misconception bought about by his having recently climbed a ladder. Then he heard the sound of water running and splashing, and there were more cries of wonder as the party came upon a waterfall, and not just any waterfall but one beneath which a monk was sitting reading but for some reason not getting wet.

Once again there was a signboard:

YOU TOO COULD DO THIS!
(*Inquire at the Rest-and-Be-Thankful Monastery*)

Here the path came to an abrupt end, just at the foot of a steep cliff up which no one could possibly have climbed, as there was not even a bird trail. The pilgrims, rather than becoming dismayed, simply sat down, happy to have a rest, while Po Cheng, who had chosen carefully where to sit, was even able to put his feet up.

A CREAKING SOUND reaching them from the top of the cliff brought the company back to life. The sound was that of a pulley, and a large wicker basket soon appeared, dropped to them from the cliff above.

One by one, the pilgrims were hauled up the cliff-face through the agency of a block-and-tackle, until all were reunited at the top, which was an occasion for much glee and much slapping of one another on the back.

The Rest-and-Be-Thankful Monastery, towards which

they now made their way, was much as Po Cheng would have imagined such an establishment to be.

A wide esplanade brought the visitors to an ornate gate, from where they could survey the magnificent skyline of the monastery with its many fine domes, high towers and shaded porches. Somewhere within those precincts and serving as its heart, Po Cheng anticipated, there would be a fish pond stocked with tame carp, so tame that they would rise to the surface whenever a monk approached, stick up their heads and open their mouths.

The abbot himself, a rotund and jolly looking figure, was waiting to greet the new arrivals and to guide them—first things first—to the monastery's refectory. A refectory, recalled the First Graduate, who had so far eaten nothing that day, was just another name for a facility in which food was served.

'Dear friends,' the abbot addressed the pilgrims, 'all are welcome here, those attracted by the aroma of incense, as well as those drawn by the smell of soup.'

The pilgrims smiled at this pleasantry, as did Po Cheng, although he somewhat sheepishly.

'Here,' continued the abbot, 'we teach that all is illusion but one can attain such an understanding only step by step ... .'

Po Cheng tried not to show his surprise. Had word not as yet reached the monastery? Surely any such notion had long since been discredited, shown to be fallacious and swept away by means of a single, simple counter-argument:

IF ALL IS ILLUSION, THEN ON WHAT DOES DUST GATHER?

But was that not all to the good? If news that all was not illusion had failed to reach the monastery, the First Graduate reasoned, then what chance was there that a report on that unfortunate affair in the Golden Cockerel Chophouse would do so any time soon? And this being the case, could he not now truly put his feet up? Had he not found his rabbit hole?

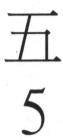

5

SANCTUARY | HEAVEN'S MAJESTY, EARTH'S CONTRI-
VANCES | HIS FOOT IN THE DOOR, OFF COMES HIS
HAT | NEITHER ILLUSORY NOR ALL AS IT SEEMS |
WOE TO THE FISH WHO SEES ONLY THE BAIT

The quarters provided for guests at the Rest-and-Be-
Thankful Monastery could scarcely have been more humble.
The dormitory was bare of any furnishings apart from the
wooden sleeping shelves that had been affixed to the wall.
Guests were tolerated there but not cossetted, and those
assigned to the uppermost shelves had best not have a fear of
heights.

Despite his long walk of the day before, Po Cheng felt
no fatigue, and just as well. No sooner had he finally closed
his eyes than he was awakened by the sound of the pilgrims
jumping down off their shelves in order to get another early
start.

'What morons!' he reckoned, turning his face to the wall.

Contentment, surely, depended above all on being in accord with one's surroundings and not at all on rushing off in the dark in quest of some curiously shaped mountain, some freak of nature. To seek contentment by wandering the world, thought Po Cheng, grumpily, was therefore to wear oneself out unnecessarily.

In return for his meals and a shelf on which to sleep, he readily agreed to collect dew each morning for the brewing of the monks' tea, to sweep the esplanade in case any more guests arrived and to feed their breakfast of breadcrumbs to the carp which populated the monastery fishpond. And what better example could there be—the First Graduate couldn't help pointing out to himself—of someone at one with his surroundings?

As for which gods were revered at the monastery, which immortals honoured, which helpful spirits summoned and which demons exorcized, he left that in abeyance. As for the notion that the world that we think we know is not real but merely a product of our thoughts, he wrestled with this each morning while feeding the fish.

'Are they there or aren't they?' he questioned. 'And the same goes for me.'

Although he wasn't a monk, the carp had nevertheless come to recognize his footfalls and hence to associate that sound with the arrival of their morning bowl of breadcrumbs. He, in turn, had come to recognize the fish and so was able to ensure that each of them—even the most timid—received a fair share of what was left of the monks' breakfast.

'Think!' he then told himself. 'If those breadcrumbs are an illusion, then how can they fill a bowl? And if carp are an illusion, then what gobbles up the breadcrumbs?'

As for his own existence, the existence of someone who turned up at the same time each morning at the carp pond with a bowl in his hand, he took that much for granted. And so too, obviously, did the fish.

THE MONASTERY WAS at once a home and a school for the monks who inhabited it. Many of those who sat ahead of him at the evening meal, Po Cheng noted, were farm boys who had exchanged a lifetime of walking behind a plough for a seat at the table in the refectory. Although decent fellows, they were still high-spirited and somewhat rough-around-the-edges, their favourite prank at mealtimes being to dip their bread into someone else's soup.

Their schooling, which occupied the entire morning, comprised just one thing: meditation on the emptiness and cruel deceits of the world which they had left behind. So as not to be distracted, each was obliged to sit cross-legged in the bottom of an empty barrel but without falling asleep, this prohibition being enforced by the abbot himself with the help of a stout pole and a bucket of icy cold water.

Afternoons were devoted to self-correction, a practice which the First Graduate took great care to observe only from a safe distance. The austerities performed by the older monks—each to his own taste—were really quite imaginative, suggesting to Po Cheng that the faults which they were meant to correct may have been so as well. The novice monks, by contrast, turned it into a competition, with each one, instead of lashing himself with a bundle of nettles, for instance, seeking to land a blow on the back of some fellow penitent.

'Ah, yes,' Po Cheng reflected, nostalgically. 'Boys will be boys, but then most move on.'

His place in the evenings, when the main meal of the day was celebrated, was at the foot of the table. Like the monks he had but one bowl, first to hold soup, and then rice, and which he afterwards rinsed out with the day's final ration of tea.

The soup made in the monastery kitchen was unquestionably quite fragrant but by the time the soup pot reached the bottom of the table, it contained nothing but broth. His portion of rice, similarly, was only what had remained stuck to the bottom of the pot.

'Never mind,' he told himself. 'This is only for now, only until things blow over, and then just wait and see what I make of myself!'

Following the meal, there was a short recess which the boy-monks spent giving one another piggy-back rides, standing on their heads, sticking out their tongues and pulling ugly faces.

'Brothers,' the good-natured abbot then called them back to order. 'Enough of your nonsense for one day. Go to your beds now and beware the lure of vagrant musings.'

'Ah, that old bugaboo,' recognized Po Cheng. 'Masturbation. *Chasing empty pleasures*—as the warning used to be—*enduring endless hells.*'

JUST WHEN HE was becoming accustomed to the monastery and its practices, a new face appeared at the table—at the head of the table seated beside the abbot—and whoever the fellow was, he seemed to have the run of the place. His name was Jade Verity and he wore the robe of a monk but he neither spent the mornings meditating nor did he join the others afterwards on the esplanade as in one manner or another they punished themselves for their lack of progress. Instead, the newcomer was free to roam about, opening and shutting doors, poking his nose into everything, and this was starting to make the First Graduate distinctly nervous.

When not engaged in any other task, such as gathering firewood without damaging any trees or sweeping the esplanade without harming any insects, Po Cheng returned to the carp pond, crouched down and contemplated what it must be like to be a fish. These, being in captivity, did nothing the whole day long, simply lay on the bottom, resting comfortably, just being carp.

It was at the pond that the fellow slipped up behind him and crouched down at his side.

'Don't be alarmed. Carry on with what you were doing, which doesn't appear to have been all that much.'

'I earn my keep,' Po Cheng had the wit to reply, 'so why would I be alarmed?'

'A fair rejoinder. But it's obvious from your robe that you're not a monk, not that a robe alone, of course, makes a monk.'

Was that a hint? Was this fellow with the monk-like name of Jade Verity actually some sort of an inspector? Or perhaps even—and this was indeed grounds for alarm—a police inspector?

'I suppose,' suggested Po Cheng, weighing his words carefully, 'that there's a great deal, in a place like this, for you to keep your eye on.'

'More than you can imagine, and little of it is as it seems.'

He saw the trap. The fellow was clearly trying to trick him into making a confession.

'It's all that talk about illusion,' he agreed. 'How is one to tell what's real from what isn't?'

'It's always possible to tell. This place may call itself a monastery, for instance, but there are boys shut up in barrels here and all manner of riffraff on the loose.'

'Ah so, riffraff. But perhaps seeking to turn over a new leaf.'

'As for you, you're quick on your feet and that should take you far. You'll certainly, in any case, bear watching.'

Was that all? The fellow stood up, as if satisfied.

'One more thing, the world is not illusion, so don't use that as any excuse. The world, you'll find, is error, confusion, miscalculation and an endless succession of unintended consequences.'

THE MONK'S WORK—if he actually was a monk—was now completed, and with his suspicions having been confirmed. He again approached Po Cheng at the fish pond, and the two were crouched there, side by side, for some time and without either one looking up from the fish.

'Just listen,' bade Jade Verity, 'and save your questions for when I've finished.'

It had long been known, he then revealed, that the Rest-and-Be-Thankful Monastery was a hideout not just for fugitive farm boys but for individuals who had found themselves on the wrong side of the law, the most recent offenders being the notorious Plum Village Gang.

'Think about it. A monk is meant to possess only a tooth stick and a begging bowl, so why do you suppose it is that certain of these supposed monks have ill-gotten gains cached under their beds?'

Recognizing that this was a rhetorical question, Po Cheng remained silent.

'It's a pity. Groups of hot-headed individuals who claim to have some grievance or other against the government band together and commit all manner of crimes, some of them quite heinous, as if this were likely to bring about an end to injustice.'

Hence it was necessary from time to time that such delinquents should be winkled out from their hiding places in order that more placid people, people who were prepared to swallow insults and to stomach injustice, could continue to prosper.

'Thus do matters rest,' concluded Jade Verity. 'So do you have any questions or can we get down to business?'

'Just one question. Where do you fit into all of this?'

'Let's just say that I'm at the service of a relevant authority.'

Then the fellow proceeded to pull rank. He would be leaving at first light the following morning, he declared, sternly and it would be necessary for Po Cheng to accompany him.

'So suddenly?' the First Graduate protested. 'Still, I suppose that once I've fed the fish ... .'

'*Before* feeding the fish,' pronounced the monk, categorically.

6

DISPERSION | HEAVEN'S MANDATE, EARTH'S
MANOEUVRES | OUT BY THE BACK DOOR | ALARMS
AND EXCURSIONS | WHAT THE WATER REVEALED |
TO STUMBLE BUT NOT FALL: TWO STEPS FORWARD

The main gate of the monastery was guarded during the
hours between dusk and dawn by a pair of sentry monks
equipped with demon-detecting lanterns, fiend-confusing
mirrors and ghost-detaining ropes.

Hence, rather than explaining their early departure, the
policeman monk and his prisoner—for this was what Po
Cheng took himself to be—left by the small, unguarded gate
used by a local farmer to bring the monks whatever supplies
they needed and to cart off the highly propitious effluent
from the monastery's latrines to spread over his lettuce
terraces.

The reason for their haste soon became apparent. Hardly

were they on their way than the sound of drumming could be heard in the distance, the steady, cadenced drumming which accompanied an army on the march. That would be Ma, Jade Verity explained. Bulldog Ma, General Ma, the fabled bandit-chasing general with his army of bandit-chasing troopers.

'Ah, the relevant authority,' remarked Po Cheng. 'So ours was indeed a timely departure.'

'My work at the monastery was done, if that's what you mean, so why hang about?'

Something still nagged at him. Something about that fellow wasn't quite as it should be, even if it remained difficult to put one's finger on just what that something might be. Certainly the fellow was hiding something, perhaps even hiding it in full view and then employing his cunning to draw attention away from it.

They reached a pond, the crystal-clear water of which sparkled in the morning sunlight.

'Keep watch, will you?' requested Jade Verity. 'It's been days since I last washed.'

The monk removed his sandals and entered the pond slowly, lifting his robe bit by bit as he did so, thus keeping the garment dry while at the same time preserving his modesty. Or it would have done so had Po Cheng not chanced to catch a glimpse, beneath the surface, of what he was able to recognize as a tell-tale discrepancy. Thus was it revealed that Jade Verity was most definitely not a monk, although this did not entirely rule out the possibility of her being a nun.

'Must you stare?' the woman complained. 'I'm old enough, after all, to be your mother.'

Po Cheng averted his eyes until she was back onto the bank, with her robe once more falling safely down to her ankles. Just when he was pondering how he might possibly escape captivity, perhaps by overpowering her, she cut short this train of thought by informing him that he was now free to go on his way, adding that he had best do so sharply, as it would not take long for General Ma to overrun the monastery and remove those elements which ought not to have been there in the first place.

She then handed him a small trowel which she advised him to use to bury his excrements and a bag of acorns for feeding any hungry spirits that he encountered on the road. Lastly, in a motherly fashion, she warned him not to forget the lesson of Little Big-Eyes.

'Little Big-Eyes?'

'Whatever Little Big-Eyes saw, he kept to himself and so enjoyed a long life. Unlike his friend Little Blabbermouth, who didn't.'

SO IT WAS that the First Graduate continued his journey as a party of one and with only a tattered robe on his back to keep him warm. Still it was better than being in custody or being sent back to face the music in Bright Prospect Town, and he took care over where he placed his feet. Excellence in walking—he recalled from another childhood tale—meant leaving no tracks.

He was, however, now victim to certain vagrant musings. He could still see in his mind's eye what he had seen earlier in the water of the pond and this led him to speculate as to whether so generous an undergrowth on a woman was a natural endowment or more likely to be the result of excessive sexual activity.

These musings continued until he reached a forest and found his progress blocked by an unbroken wall of densely packed trees. When searching for an opening, however small, he then came upon the following signboard:

DARK WOOD!
(*Enough said?*)

Nevertheless he found a path. Although perhaps just an animal run, it was well worn into the forest floor and easy enough to follow, even if he had to bend down now and again to avoid a low-growing branch. No forest, after all, was ever quite as dark as one might have imagined it to be beforehand.

He could hear birdsong about him. Also, as it was getting late in the day, a tedious chirruping of insects. Still to come, with the night, would be the call of owls, the howling of wolves and the piteous cry of some smaller, helpless creature which had been caught out of its den. What stopped him from dwelling on such lurid imaginings, however, was a scent in the air. The scent—unless he was sadly mistaken— of a wood fire.

Most likely it was the fire of a woodsman, of a hunter or of a half-crazed forest recluse but no matter. No matter if the person was not in his right mind or even out of his mind altogether, Po Cheng told himself, just so long as the fellow didn't mind someone dropping in on him unannounced and just when he was preparing his evening meal.

THE HUT, AS it had been constructed out of the same material that surrounded it, was barely discernible in the dim light of the forest. Its walls of roughly split logs supported a roof thatched with fern fronds, which overhung the walls like a mop of hair and through which a thin plume of smoke was seeping. There was no door but above the opening where the door must once have been there was still a faded sign:

ASSURED VICTORY BOXING CAMP!

And inside, crouched on the dirt floor beside a small fire of sticks, was the not easily mistakable figure of Wang Tzu.

'So sorry,' Po Cheng apologized. 'No doubt you thought you'd seen the last of me.'

'No one's luck is all bad,' the old man replied, grumpily. 'Perhaps you won't stay long.'

Already balanced over the fire was a blackened pot in which a stew of some sort was bubbling. The stench coming from the pot, Po Cheng guessed, was the same as that coming from the rotting carcase of some unidentifiable forest creature which the old fellow had hung up on the wall—as he explained—to 'age'.

'Don't ask me what it was. I set a trap and that's what got into it.'

That said, he stood up, produced a knife, cut a few more strips of meat off the disgusting thing and dropped them into the pot. He hated the forest, he complained, and had only ever come to that camp in the past in order to train.

'And hence the right cross?' suggested Po Cheng.

'Hence the right cross. There are some things which once learned you never forget.'

There were no bowls. There was no standing on ceremony. When he adjudged that the stew was sufficiently cooked, Wang Tzu removed the pot from the fire and set it down on the packed-earth floor of the hut, equidistant between himself and the unexpected guest. For chopsticks, there were two pairs of sharpened twigs.

'Dig in,' he exhorted the First Graduate. 'Hold your nose,

if you have to. This is a boxing camp, not a chophouse, and a boxing camp is no place for fussy eaters.'

HE HAD BECOME accustomed by now to meals which had no taste. This, he reckoned, was the price to be paid for taking to the road, for going one's own way, for allowing oneself to be guided by one's own lights. One paid in one currency for what one obtained in another. And just as well that he could not taste that stew, not if it tasted as bad as it had smelled while it was cooking.

'You can get used to anything,' Wang Tzu proclaimed, as if reading Po Cheng's mind. He took out a handful of filthy-looking rice, who knew from where; he dropped the rice into the stew pot, added a little water and then put the pot back onto the fire. 'Once you're used to something, you're no longer appalled by it, not in the least, you just die laughing.'

It was while they were waiting for the rice to cook that Po Cheng remembered the fish. He thought of what must have been their confusion that morning when he had failed to turn up with their breakfast and then he imagined the onslaught, the overrunning of the monastery by troopers armed to the teeth with crossbows, maces, axes, horse-whips, bird-nets, hammers … .

In the forest, night had now fallen. Darkness enshrouded the hut, with its feeble fire having been further reduced to just a few glowing coals. Wang Tzu, as soon as he had consumed his share of the rice, lay down, turned his back to the fire, tucked his robe in around him and almost at once began to snore.

'What a strange fellow,' the First Graduate said to himself. 'He's the first thing that I'll need to get used to.'

Meanwhile, as there was no door on the hut, he blocked

the opening where the door should have been with some brush. Whatever sort of creature it was that was hanging on the wall with its entrails exposed, the presence of one such beast in the forest strongly hinted at the possibility of there being another one like it that might well be wondering by now just where its friend had got to.

7

CONTENTION | HEAVENLY SERENITY, EARTHLY
SKIRMISHES | A SYLVAN SETTING | DISTANT
DRUMMING | AN OLD ALLIANCE | THE RULER
REQUIRES A TOOTHPICK, HIS MINIONS FELL A TREE

In return for at least the semblance of a roof over his head,
Po Cheng set about making himself useful. Having risen first
and shaken off the tribe of fleas which had been feeding on
him during the night, he lit a new fire inside the circle of
stones and put some water on to heat in the expectation
than no one with any sense would have taken up residence
in an abandoned boxing camp without having brought
along some tea leaves.

The crackling of the fire caused Wang Tzu to sit up
abruptly and rub his eyes. Seeing that he still had a guest and
recognizing who it was, he proceeded to moisten his fingers
and smooth down his bushy eyebrows and atrocious sideburns.

'You'd best be careful,' he warned, 'when waking up some-one like me. The fists of a boxer are a dangerous weapon.'

Being uncertain how to take the fellow, Po Cheng watched in silence as he took down a stick from the wall.

'This is my shit-wiping stick, so leave it alone. You'll need to find one of your own.'

The old man disappeared out the door with his stick and when he returned after a time seemed to be in a somewhat better mood.

'Business as usual,' he reported, cheerfully, hanging the stick back up on the wall.

From somewhere about his person he then produced a few sadly shrivelled tea leaves which, when introduced to the pot of recently boiled water, scarcely coloured it.

'Never mind,' he dismissed this, taking a sip directly from the pot. 'Just the memory of a steaming bowl of tea, first thing in the morning, can bring someone to his senses.'

Po Cheng was not at all convinced. The brew was completely insipid. Nonetheless he obeyed the old fellow's instructions: he rescued the soggy leaves from the bottom of the pot afterwards and laid them out carefully to dry.

Wang Tzu, in the meantime, having lifted the bottom of his robe from down around his ankles and knotted the ends between his legs, had now taken up a strange stance, one which ought to have been, in the opinion of the First Graduate, impossible to maintain.

It thus came as a relief when the old man, after holding that unnatural position for a time, began to move slowly out of it, as if performing, as in a dream, for instance, some ghostly dance.

'It's called *Tickling the Tiger*,' Wang Tzu elucidated. 'It should be followed by *Baiting the Bear* and then by *Mocking the Monkey* … '

Po Cheng realized at once that these were the exercises which elderly people were to be seen performing every morning in children's playgrounds or public parks in the hope of warding off, for a while longer, some of the woes of old age. And this in turn led the First Graduate to recall— for the mind works in strange ways—an amusing anecdote concerning the king of a city which had for some time been under siege and was unlikely to be able to hold out for much longer.

All of the women in the city were summoned to the main plaza, given brooms and urged to sweep for all they were worth, so raising as much dust as possible to fool the enemy into thinking that reinforcements must have arrived.

NOT LONG AFTERWARDS the delightful morning chatter of unseen birds in the forest canopy suddenly came to a halt and was replaced by the less welcome sound of distant drumming. The old man seemed little perturbed and merely carried on with his exercises, which Po Cheng found strange. Were they not both fugitives and had one of them, an ex-pugilist, not attacked a civilian with a dangerous weapon? How then, if General Ma was still on the march, could Wang Tzu have remained so calm?

'The sound of a drum,' the fellow simply pointed out, 'carries a long way.'

All the same, the drumming continued to grow louder and did so right up until the moment when it suddenly ceased altogether. The explanation, to Po Cheng, seemed obvious: the bandit-chasing forces of General Ma had now reached the entrance to the forest and were bivouacked there for the night.

'Look here,' it was his turn to point out. 'As I was able to find this camp, so will he be.'

'Of course he'll find it but why would he bother? Between the Bulldog and me, it's always been live and let live.'

The menu that evening was much the same as on the evening before. Wang Tzu carved a few more titbits off the anonymous rotting carcass for the stew, added a few slices of an odd-looking tuber that he had dug up earlier when burying his excrements, and then crouched down to wait, presenting the First Graduate with a sitting target.

'So you know that Bulldog person, do you? Maybe you're even old friends.'

'And what if we are? In fact, it would be strange if we weren't.'

They had, after all, grown up only a few doors apart, in the same stinking lane, in the same no-hope ward in the same impoverished suburb of what was generally considered to be the greatest of all great cities, bar none.

'Ah, how interesting. So you began life in the capital, in the Celestial City, right there in the heart of everything, but you're a long way from there now.'

'You needn't remind me. But yes, Ma and I go back a long way. We used to wander the roofs of the city together, stealing eggs from people's rooftop chicken coops.'

But that was before they had discovered boxing. That was before the day that Mosquito Wang and Bulldog Ma, as they had decided to call themselves, knocked at the door of the Forest of Blows Boxing Academy and offered to sweep the floor in exchange for lessons.

Po Cheng had no trouble at all in imagining it: the sawdust on the floor to absorb the blood and the sweat, the stone weights, the sandbags hanging from the ceiling and even the stern motto prominently displayed where no one could possibly miss it:

MAKE AN EFFORT, OR ELSE
MAKE WAY FOR SOMEONE WHO WILL!

THEY WAITED IMPATIENTLY the following morning for the drumming to resume, as this would signify that Bulldog Ma was on the move again, back in the direction of his headquarters. The fellow had a quota to fill, Wang Tzu explained, a quarterly quota of bandit heads which had to be sent on to the capital as a tribute, and hence a proof of his continued loyalty to the Emperor. That business at the Rest-and-Be-Thankful Monastery would have filled his autumn quota, the old man calculated, leaving the Bulldog free now to put his feet up again until winter.

In the boxing camp, it was therefore business as usual. The exercises which he performed each day so religiously, Wang Tzu remarked as they shared their morning pot of 'tea', had been the first thing that the two aspiring boxers had been made to learn before being allowed to throw a punch. Fights were fought in a ring, the newcomers were informed, but were won in one's mind and hence the importance of Spirit Boxing, that form of the sport in which one began by being one's own opponent. Spirit Boxing taught one the ropes, the essentials, and how to give blows without receiving any in return.

'*Against an attack, step back!*' Mosquito Wang could still recite. '*Spotting a weakness, push on!*'

Spirit Boxing was different from prize fighting in another important way, namely that the winner and the loser were one and the same. Both undertakings required concentration, agility, dexterity and accuracy, but this was where the similarity ceased. A prize-fighter, upon entering the ring, sized up his opponent, pulled faces, bared his teeth and made threatening gestures, whereas Spirit Boxing required one to comport oneself as if one's opponent had failed to turn up.

The fourth exercise, *Flight of the Deer*, despite being performed in slow-motion and in place, had nonetheless been believed to boost the boxer's stamina, as it prepared the ground for the many hours of roadwork which the aspirant would put in over the years to come.

'Roadwork!' Wang Tzu enthused. 'Those cold mornings, when I could see my own breath and I knew for certain that I was alive.'

The last of what the Ancients had thought of as the Five Exemplary Animals was the Owl, and so the final exercise, *Gaze of the Owl*, in which a practicant stood up straight, with his arms folded tightly to his sides, like wings, and his eyes surveying the ground before him.

'The posture needs to be held,' the old man described. 'You're a hunter waiting to pounce, ready to swoop at the first sign of a mouse or a shrew.'

THEY COULD BE sure of one thing: it was scarcely credible that General Ma would march his men into a forest and so risk spoiling military formations which had over past centuries proved efficacious. So why had he not moved on? Why were the two fugitives now hearing, from the entrance to the forest, a constant rat-a-tat-tat of axes? Why would Ma have required so much firewood?

Wang Tzu, if he was at all perturbed, showed this only by becoming yet more talkative.

'Those were the days,' he reminisced, 'those days in the boxing academy. The challenge of it, the fatigue, the satisfaction afterwards. We even took to sleeping on the floor at night in order to be the first ones on the heavy bags the following morning.'

'What dedication,' Po Cheng butted in. 'What endeavour.'

Trying hard, however, had been no guarantee of success and in time it became clear that neither of them was likely ever to become a champion. Once let loose in the ring, the Bulldog, although amply endowed with tenacity, never got the hang of ducking-and-diving, and the Mosquito, while able to annoy his opponents, fell short when it came to putting them away. And at the same time, more people were constantly appearing, lining up at the door of the gymnasium in the hope that they themselves might one day become champions.

'Where there's a will, on the other hand,' Wang Tzu declaimed, 'there's always a way, even if it's by the back door.'

If there was no future for them in the Celestial City, where the byword was excellence, there was always the countryside, where excellence was at a premium and a pair of so-so prize-fighters, if they played their cards right, might win a prize every night.

'At least,' the old man qualified, fishing for something in the sleeve of his robe, 'in the months when the roads are dry.'

What he brought out, once unfolded, turned out to be a notice of the sort that tended to spring up overnight in the countryside, having been put up without permission in order to announce some no-doubt fleeting coming attraction.

Hence, as a case in point:

STRAIGHT FROM THE CELESTIAL CITY!
MOSQUITO WANG VERSUS BULLDOG MA!
ONE NIGHT ONLY!

Once again, Po Cheng was easily able to recreate the scene. On the night in question, in some poor nondescript hamlet, a crowd of sorts would gather round a makeshift ring, straining to see, by the faint light of a lantern, the two mismatched figures in boxing shorts. Night after night, in one hamlet after another, the onlookers, having paid their money, could cheer on the smaller fellow and pelt the other with rotten vegetables.

8

DEVASTATION | HEAVEN'S REACH, EARTH'S GRASP |
SIMPLY A MATTER OF SEMANTICS | NO GOING
BACK | A TRULY EXEMPLARY OFFICIAL | A RIVER,
ONCE UPON A TIME | OF WORMS AND WATER

Night after night, Wang Tzu was still boasting when the first
tree fell. Night after night, bout after bout with six rounds
guaranteed. Six rounds and then they were off again with
the purse with the takings, and by the time that the autumn
rains came they were back in the capital, back on Willow
Market Lane with their feet up, sitting pretty.

'WHUMP!!!'

That was the sound of it, of a tree hitting the dirt, and Po
Cheng could feel the ground reverberating beneath his feet.
Only a moment later, a small whirlwind passed through the
boxing camp, carrying off, in its swirl, terrified birds and
displaced insects.

'So!' Po Cheng confronted Wang Tzu. 'Now what do you say? Is that fellow after us or isn't he?'

'I'd say that he must be up to something but there's no need to take it personally.'

There was something else in the air, a slip of paper which was slowly fluttering down and which finally came to rest in the doorway of the hut. The calligraphy indicated that it was an official notice, which in turn suggested that any number of copies may have been printed:

DARK FOREST PROJECT
(*Pushing back the bounds!*)

'And what do you say to that?' the First Graduate demanded, once they had both read it. 'Are we two not sitting on those bounds?'

'It's certainly odd. This is hardly something that the Bulldog, in the old days, would have thought up by himself.'

'*Odd*? Is that the best that you can come up with? If you ask me, we've gone from the frying pan into the fire.'

Various teams of troopers must have been at work. Almost at once the fugitives winced again as a second tree crashed down, further weakening their forest stronghold. Wang Tzu remained crouched beside the cooking fire but he had ceased to tend it and the stew had thus gone off the boil.

'So tell me,' Po Cheng probed, 'if your business with Ma was so lucrative, what went wrong?'

The old man was rocking back and forth now and his eyes were watering, perhaps from the smoke of the fire. The split had come about, he recalled, just as they were preparing to top up their coffers by taking the boxing show back onto the road. Ma was sick and tired, he had claimed, of being the patsy, of being laughed at every time that he climbed into the ring, and then, on top of that, having to spend hours afterwards arguing over the division of the prize money.

'It was a real sucker punch. He was quitting boxing in order to take the Military Examination and become a soldier.'

'Ah,' pointed out Po Cheng. 'But taking into account how things have turned out, ought he not to be congratulated?'

'As if anyone can yet say,' mocked the old man, 'how things will turn out!'

The forest, once the troopers had ceased work for the day, became eerily quiet. Those creatures which had not already fled for their lives would no doubt be keeping to their lairs that night. Po Cheng meanwhile lay wide awake in his own den, beside the cold ashes of a campfire, pondering how things were likely to turn out should there be a further encounter between the Mosquito and the Bulldog and this time with no holds barred. A final and definitive confrontation, the First Graduate imagined, at which he himself—if he knew what was good for him—might do well not to be present.

THERE WERE NO formalities of any sort. The old man remained in his Owl stance, standing as still as a statue and never looking up from the ground as Po Cheng moved past him, picked out the trail by which he had arrived at the boxing camp and set off deeper still into the forest. The world was small enough, he calculated, that they might easily meet again one day but also large enough that they might not.

Being lost, as it might be said, in his own thoughts, the First Graduate had little idea of how long he had been walking, or how far, before he found himself at the lip of a deep ravine, one from out of which sensuous blue vapours were rising. Spanning that frightening gash in the landscape, there was an extremely fragile-looking rope bridge, one made all the more problematic by the weather-beaten sign which was nailed to it:

GO–NO–FURTHER GORGE!

For a time, he remained trapped there, stopped in his tracks, perplexed by the conflicting messages: the presence of a bridge implied that it must indeed be possible to cross the ravine but to do so would be to contravene the clearly-stated warning on the sign.

Something needed to be done. Defacing a sign, he knew, had at various times been considered a capital offence but he could think of nothing else and he had always enjoyed such puzzles, the puzzle this time being—with the help of a little mud—to alter the characters on the sign so that it now read:

LUCKY CROSSING SUSPENSION BRIDGE!

With his first steps, the bridge began to sway and its ropes to creak. The supporting cables would likely be frayed and there were a number of wooden slats missing underfoot. As he progressed, the bridge sagged alarmingly under him, allowing the sinuous blue vapours to lick at his legs. Worst of all, he could no longer make out either rim of the gorge.

'Time to call up the reserves,' the First Graduate said to himself, resolutely. One's self and one's resolve, that was to say, formed a party of two.

THE SOUGHING PINES and the rustling bamboo of the forest

were now behind him and what lay ahead was but a desert, an utter wasteland, empty apart from a few leafless thorn trees whose upper branches still held fast what appeared to be the bleached bones of animals.

'Food for thought,' Po Cheng reflected. 'One could look at this in two ways: either as the beginning of life or as the end of it.'

Having scanned the landscape, he picked out one tree in particular and decided to make straight for it. Once he had reached that tree, he could then pick out another one and so on and so forth. This was but another of his favourite childhood pastimes: connecting the dots in order to create a recognizable image of something which he would not by his own devices alone have been able to draw.

He was heading for a third tree when he saw in the distance what he at first took to be a mirage. Were deserts not known for this phenomenon? Was it not common knowledge that a traveller in the desert, if he became thirsty, was likely to see an oasis ahead, or at least a water hole? What Po Cheng saw, however, was distinct: ahead of him, in the midst of that otherwise lifeless landscape, someone in the garb of a mid-level government official was sitting bent over a teakwood desk.

As the traveller approached, the figure did not disappear; on the contrary, the fellow stood up and proceeded to introduce himself.

'Li Ting, if you please. Sub-prefect Li Ting, at your service.'

'Po Cheng. First Graduate Po, at your service, as well.'

'Excellent. And might I interest you, first thing, in a tour of the town?'

The functionary, who was himself all skin and bones, first pointed out the dry, cracked bed of what had once been the town's river. Still visible on its banks were the packed-earth foundations of an inn, two rival tea houses, a wine shop, a gambling den, a covered market, the town baths and of course, as they returned to where the tour had begun, the town's Yamen, its town hall.

The fellow, Li Ting, sat back down at his desk, which was now all that remained of his former office apart from a hat stand, a bamboo chest and a frayed mat.

'He must sleep on it,' Po Cheng intuited. 'Where else could he sleep? And if it's raining, he must spread it under his desk.'

'Now then,' the sub-prefect inquired, 'just what service is it that you require?'

'Ah so. I really hadn't thought but just what services do you provide?'

'Very few, I'm afraid, for want of custom. It nevertheless remains my duty to expedite the journey of state officials, messengers, postmen, merchants, tax-collectors, census-takers, scholars, monks and any other such seemingly purposeful persons.'

'*Seemingly*?' queried Po Cheng, amused by the fellow's irony.

'Anyone who's not obviously a wastrel, a scallywag, a nincompoop or a poet.'

IF TWO INDIVIDUALS were to set off together and travel any distance in one another's company, each of them would need a good reason for doing so but those reasons did not necessarily need to be the same. Po Cheng was simply anxious to get to the other side of that ruinous landscape as quickly as possible and without getting lost in the process, whereas Li Ting, as the sub-prefect himself professed, was glad of the excuse to stretch his legs.

'I used to make regular tours of inspection,' he explained as he cleared his desk, storing the papers on which he had been working in the bamboo chest and then weighting the top down with a flat stone, 'but it's a good while now since there's been much for me to inspect.'

This had been his first posting, he related as they walked, and he had arrived in the prefecture full of ambition and positively heady with enthusiasm. He had been anxious to fulfil, by dint of hard work and meticulous record-keeping, the promise which he had first shown in school and later on in the Imperial Examinations.

'And it all began so promisingly. The river was full of water, the fields were full of crops and the people were lined up on the roadside with their sun hats in their hands to greet me.'

As a mere sub-prefect, he had been warned, he ought to meddle as little as possible in the affairs of the prefecture, at least for the first few years, but he soon noticed that there were certain matters which required urgent attention. The river, for a start, was badly in need of dredging, as it regularly burst its banks, and this despite being placated each spring with gifts of rice cakes. Hence the first step he took was to summon the water marshals to find out why they had been so remiss.

'They admitted that the river was silted and that the dikes constructed to keep it within its channel had sprung leaks but they denied that it was their fault.'

'So!' declared Po Cheng, his ire having been stirred by the idea of individuals in positions of power not doing their jobs properly. 'So were they water marshals or weren't they?'

'Yes and no. Although in the employ of the government, they were only seldom paid and therefore only seldom turned up for work.'

How fortunate, Po Cheng thought, to have fallen in with that fellow. Had he himself not often wondered why, in government, so little ever actually got done and had he not imagined that the right person, in the right office, could surely have done a better job than the pack of clowns who presently held office?

'I couldn't understand it,' Li Ting admitted. 'Why weren't the people angry? And why, year after year, did they waste all those rice cakes?'

When those living near the river saw that it was rising, they had simply moved onto their roofs, taking along their stoves, their children, their elderly parents and their domestic animals. Some had even made ramps so that the family ox would not be lost to the river.

'It was the hardest lesson that I had to learn: that there was no limit to the people's patience. That they were prepared to put up with any amount of inconvenience because this was what their ancestors would have done.'

The young official had explained to them, argued with them, pleaded with them. Why wait for the government to dredge the river or repair the dikes? Why could they not do that themselves? But always the response had been the same. The dikes leaked because those who had constructed them had failed to propitiate the earthworms which the work had disturbed and the periodic flooding was not the fault of the river—which they themselves propitiated with their New Year offerings—but was rather to be put down to the unrelenting wilfulness of water.

9

CORRECTION | HEAVEN'S SEASONS, EARTH'S ALMANACS
| FROM THAT MUD, THIS DUST | A COMPETENT
AUTHORITY | A HEAD COUNT | IF INNOCENT, DEMAND
JUSTICE; IF NOT, PLEAD FOR MERCY

For how long had they been walking? For hours? For days?
As Li Ting had warned, there was little to inspect, not now,
not any more, and Po Cheng was quite curious by this time
as to how that had come about. As a government
functionary, however, Li Ting was nothing if not methodical
and he told the story accordingly, in his own time, dotting
every 'i' and crossing every 't' along the way.

'A place for everything,' said Po Cheng to himself, 'and
everything in its place, so that nothing gets left behind.'

For the first years, although the danger posed by the
silting of the river was becoming increasingly evident, the
young official had played by the rules. He had done only

what he had been trained to do if some situation threatened to get out of control, he had informed his superior.

'A sub-prefect informs the prefect, who then informs the governor of the province, who will in due course—in theory—inform the relevant minister.'

This meant drafting a memorial, a memorandum, a formal document in which nothing was left to chance, as everything had long since been laid down as to the correct way of drafting such a document, everything from the vocabulary to be employed, the spelling and the punctuation which were deemed acceptable, the shade of ink permitted, the size of one's brush and the preferred style of calligraphy.

'Then, having sent off one's memorial, one must wait patiently for a reply and there are tales of officials who waited for years and others who died in office while still waiting, after a decade or more, for permission to retire.'

'But surely,' argued Po Cheng, 'people in superior positions ought to know that when dealing with water, which has a mind of its own, time is of the essence.'

'That's just what I thought, to my cost.'

Another year, people naturally thought, another flood. Water was simply up to its old tricks. Snow which had fallen in far distant mountains over many months melted in the course of only a few days, thus swelling the river, and people took to their roofs, resigned to waiting for the river to return to its proper channel, as it always did, leaving the fields in which melons, beans, cucumbers, peppers and water chestnuts had always flourished with a fresh coat of loam.

'People came down again from the roofs driving their oxen before them, leading small children by the hand and with chickens under their arms, thinking that they would carry on just as before.'

But that was where they were wrong. People gathered on

the bank, peering down in amazement. Where was the river? How could this have happened? In the mud, at the bottom of the now-empty channel, a few fish were still squirming, breathing their last, but where in Heaven's name had the river got to?

'Ah,' remarked Po Cheng, being unable to think of anything else to say.

'Gone,' Li Ting answered his own question. 'Vanished. Either the river had found a different channel or else it had carved out a new one.'

And that had been but the beginning. No water in the river meant no water in the irrigation ditches, and the soil of the fields, once left without watering, became in no time as dry as dust and mere fodder for the wind.

'At first people carried on. They ploughed their fields as usual that first year, hoping that Heaven, having taken away their river, would make it up to them in years to come by sending more rain.'

Then, after having watched the tender shoots in their fields dry up just as quickly as they had appeared, people had begun packing up their belongings. They dismantled their houses and their paddocks; they dug up their boundary stones and loaded everything onto carts.

'Ah,' sympathised the First Graduate. 'And do you suppose that they were able to find that river again?'

'Who knows? They were decent enough people but not one of them, it's sad to say, would have known how to write a letter.'

THE DEVASTATION OF the land and of the town once sited there had been thorough. Even the roof of the covered market had been removed and so too that of the Yamen, thus leaving the sub-prefect with just a desk and a stool. All the same he had carried on as before, as the penalty for an official who left his post without prior permission was dismemberment, a punishment designed to place great financial hardship on the offender's entire family, Li Ting explained, as by law each of the bodily parts would need to be buried separately.

How long was it since either of the travellers had eaten? They compared notes, with Po Cheng first describing the disgusting stew which had been his fare in the boxing camp, and Li Ting, who was little more than a skeleton, matching this with an account of having to live on a diet of nothing but grubs and the eggs of snakes. Was it not then understandable, when they spotted vegetation growing just ahead of them, that they should throw caution to the winds?

'Brambles!' enthused the First Graduate. 'Bramble bushes! And just look at all that fruit!'

This was no mirage. No sooner had they begun helping themselves to the berries, however, than two large figures sprang from the undergrowth, two men in the uniforms of soldiers.

'Stop right there!' one of the troopers ordered. 'And don't think for a moment about getting away, because we have you surrounded.'

Po Cheng's heart sank. How fervently he wished, suddenly, that he were somewhere else.

'If they ask,' whispered Li Ting, 'just say that we're tramps.'

And might they not well have been? One of them was dressed in what was by this time the merest semblance of a robe, whereas the robe of the other, while of better material and tailoring, was much faded and hung loosely on his shoulders, thus suggesting that it had either been snatched off a wash line or stripped off a corpse.

The sentries, that day, were going by the book. Having brought their captives to a sentry box, they compared the faces of the two 'tramps' with the drawings pinned up on the wall of individuals who—if they should show up—were meant to be detained.

'Well! Well!' declared the lead sentry, bringing his own face uncomfortably close to that of the First Graduate. 'Just out for a stroll, were you? And what about before that? What did you get up to, for instance, on a certain night in an establishment known as the Golden Cockerel Chophouse?'

THE HEAVY WOODEN boots of the trooper crunched menacingly as he marched his prisoner along a gravel pathway. Po Cheng, while trying to keep in step, was nevertheless aware of leafy trees around them, of sculpted shrubs and of carefully tended flower gardens.

'Left! Right! Hop!' barked the trooper. 'And look where you're going, not at your feet.'

What a blunder he had made, Po Cheng realized, once he saw the building ahead. It was a barracks-like structure, it was defended by a pair of catapults and it bore the following motto:

CHASING DOWN BANDITS!
ROUNDING UP FUGITIVES!

Not only had he wandered into what was obviously a garrison town but it was home to the very force from which he had been fleeing, as well as the headquarters of its commanding officer.

'What's that old saying?' he berated himself. '*Drawn like a moth to the flame.*'

The trooper rang the bell mounted beside the door,

which was opened to them by a quite elegantly dressed woman whose features, to Po Cheng's surprise, were not entirely unfamiliar to him.

'That will do,' she dismissed the trooper. 'I've handled much tougher types than this.'

'You again,' blurted Po Cheng once they were alone. 'And what name are you going by this time?'

'This is not the place for impudence. And please address me while you're here as Madame Ma.'

The woman previously known to him as Jade Verity immediately led him down a staircase and into the entrails— as it were—of that edifice. Here they negotiated a long corridor lined on both sides with small doors, each of which was secured by an imposing iron bolt. These he guessed, from the sobbing he could hear from within, were jail cells.

'Those are the real monks,' the woman explained. 'They were prepared, under close questioning, to confess to all manner of things but they'll be released again once they've calmed down.'

At the end of the corridor was a more impressive door, this one without a latch, and that was where they stopped. Her husband, claimed Madame Ma, was a humble man who would have been perfectly happy with a room no larger than a prison cell for an office, were it not for the amount of paperwork with which he had to deal.

'Was he sent here to chase bandits, he's always asking me, or to count them?'

She tapped on the door. Without waiting for a reply, she pushed the door open, shoved the First Graduate inside and then pulled the door closed again behind him. Po Cheng, once having regained his balance, assumed the Owl position, which he assumed to be somewhat similar to standing at attention.

'Po, Sir. At your service.'

'Stand at ease, Po,' ordered a gravelly voice. 'Only a scoundrel pretends to be something that he's not.'

General Ma, Bulldog Ma, was sitting behind a desk piled high with papers, seated in a chair which seemed far too small for him. Certainly he bore all the hallmarks of a prize-fighter, most notably a face which showed signs of having been shattered repeatedly in the ring, with the pieces afterwards having been put back any which way and with no regard for symmetry.

The fellow made a great show at this point of shuffling through his papers, as if he were looking for something, when in fact, Po Cheng suspected, this was just a ruse, a trick to make him start giving answers to questions which he hadn't even been asked.

'Here it is,' said Ma. 'The arrest report. According to the sentry, you bear a strong resemblance to someone wanted for questioning over an affray in a chophouse.'

'An affray?' responded Po Cheng, in mock amazement. 'Isn't it strange how things like this get blown up in the retelling?'

'And yet you turn up before long in a monastery already known to house dangerous criminals.'

The fellow certainly was living up to his reputation: he was nothing if not relentless. So was this what Madame Ma had earlier referred to as close questioning or was there worse still to come?

'And now you show up here,' the general continued. 'Uninvited. In the company of someone who freely confesses to being a vagrant.'

What a relief it was to hear this, what a weight off Po Cheng's shoulders. So Li Ting's strategy had paid off: rather than risk the horrible punishment meted out to an official who had deserted his post, he had pleaded guilty to a lesser charge.

PO CHENG HIMSELF was not yet out of the woods, nor could he be certain of what fate might have befallen Wang Tzu, of whom the general had made no mention. Had the two old foes met again? Had there been recriminations? Had these led to repercussions? And what of the unfortunate members of the Plum Village Gang? Was it not probable that their heads—at that very moment and in some inner courtyard of that very edifice—would be drying out in the sun prior to being boxed up and sent on to the capital?

The general, in a most dramatic manner, then balled up and tossed aside what he had perhaps only been pretending until now was a charge sheet, and sat back in his chair.

'See here, Po, you seem to me quite a sensible chap.'

'How good of you to notice, general.'

'All the same, you really ought to be more careful after this about the company that you keep.'

'So that's the end of it, Sir? I'm to be let off with a warning?'

'With two warnings. You also strike me as someone who intends to make something of himself and that's precisely the sort of individual who poses the most threat to any government and therefore the type of person most in need of being watched.'

With that, the office door swung open again and Madame Ma reappeared to guide him back out along the corridor. The prisoners, hearing fresh footsteps and fearing that they might be those of an executioner, now resumed their piteous wailing.

'They'll be released soon enough,' undertook Madame Ma. 'If not back to the monastery, then back to their ploughs. The trouble with religious fanatics is that you never know where you are with them or they with the world.'

$\dagger$

10

MIGRATION | HEAVEN'S CALM, EARTH'S COMMOTIONS | ONE DOG HOWLS, A THOUSAND FOLLOW SUIT | SEEN BY THE WAYSIDE | A POSSIBLE OBSTRUCTION | RIDING THE WAVES, BRAVING THE WIND

As soon as he saw the sign, he quickened his pace. That sign seemed a confirmation that he was back on course and that any step which he took after this was bound to be a step in the right direction:

ROAD TO THE NORTH

And a fine road it was, having been set above the surrounding countryside on an embankment and running as straight as an arrow for as far as one could see, leaving one with no way to go wrong. Nor would he be alone. All manner of people were on the move and all were headed in the same direction.

One saw donkey-boys transporting immense jars of water, ox-carts piled high with fodder, pony-carts loaded with firewood, dog-carts heaped with fruit and vegetables, even an elderly woman pushing a wheelbarrow full of new-born infants.

'How much,' Po Cheng inquired, purely as a pleasantry, 'for that nice fat one?'

'And how much,' the old woman snapped, 'to get you to mind your own business?'

There were also children alone on the road, walking behind flocks of geese or ducks, and it was indeed necessary to watch where one was going in order to avoid a collision, as well as to guard one's tongue in order to avoid rubbing anyone else up the wrong way.

From time to time, glancing to the side at the landscape through which the road passed, he caught sight of touching scenes, scenes familiar from the illustrations in the books which he had used to carry around with him everywhere as a child, even before having learned how to read. Thus the brickworks, where men were busy making bricks; hence the lotus-gatherers in their round wicker boats harvesting lotus flowers from a lotus pond; hence the mill, with grain wagons arriving at the front and a line of tiny, foreshortened individuals with sacks of flour on their shoulders filing out the back.

He also noted the milestones which marked the progress of the travellers. Every ten leagues, there was a trough at which animals could be watered; when twenty leagues had been covered, one found a well, an inn and a sundial.

'What forethought!' he marvelled. 'What organization! And those who prosper, clearly, are those who aren't afraid to leave home.'

Hence commerce. Hence goods being conveyed from

where they were plentiful to where they were likely to be scarce, and so with every league covered in the direction of the capital, one's goods increased in value. And what was true for the merchant, the First Graduate calculated, must also hold for the man of talent, who also, by leaving home, brought to the market what it was lacking.

SO THOROUGH WAS the organization of that admirable highway and so like-minded those who trod it, Po Cheng noticed, that not a single soldier or policeman was required to keep order, nor was there any need of magistrates for the settling of disputes. All proceeded apace, according to their capacities, with no quarter being asked nor any given, not even to the blind, to the lame or to the elderly, all of whom were expected—just like everyone else—simply to do the best that they could.

Only once did that exemplary procession slow and this was due to roadworks of some sort which were being carried out ahead, supervised by a somewhat corpulent individual in the uniform of a prison guard and brandishing a grappling hook.

'Convicts,' thought Po Cheng. 'And it's probably no more than they deserve.'

A line of men chained together at the ankles and wearing identical sackcloth smocks had been put to work weeding the ditch which ran beside the road. The First Graduate would hardly have given a second thought to such individuals had he not noticed that Li Ting was among their number and that the offence which had brought him to this pass was freshly tattooed on his forehead.

Po Cheng knelt down and pretended to be removing a pebble from his sandals.

'*Useless Vagrant*? But that's outrageous! And of how much

use were any of your superiors when they were called upon?'

'Never mind,' mouthed Li Ting. 'The penalty's only hard labour and it comes with three meals a day.'

Conversation between convicts and civilians was forbidden but Li Ting had already picked up the jailhouse trick of speaking out of the corner of his mouth so that the guards wouldn't notice his lips moving.

'As for the tattoo,' he added, 'it's a perfect disguise. Once having been branded as a criminal, one ceases to be recognized as a man.'

A stern glance from the fat guard with the grappling hook convinced Po Cheng that it was best to move on but Li Ting's predicament remained on his mind. Hard labour was doubtless harder for some than for others, and three meals a day, even if only of gruel, would enable Li Ting to put on weight but was his 'disguise' really as good as he believed? Was an astute observer not bound to notice—as Po Cheng himself had done—that among the gang of convicts at work in the ditch, Li Ting was the only one pulling the weeds out by their roots?

HOW RAPIDLY THE mind moves, flitting from one thing to another, lighting here and lighting there, and as a result being subject to shallow thinking and snap judgments. When Po Cheng spotted a large body of water ahead, for instance, he at once assumed—even though he had not been headed in that direction—that he must have reached the sea and was it any wonder then that he began to see, in the distance, fish jumping, porpoises sporting and the spouts of whales?

Despite its sea-like turbulence, what Po Cheng saw was in fact a river, albeit a wide one, so wide that the far end of the elaborate wooden bridge that crossed it was nowhere in sight. What was in clear view as he approached the bridge, however, was a sign which stopped him in his tracks:

PAY–AS–YOU–GO CROSSING

A toll bridge! He could but stand there scratching his head as people pushed past him, people in all walks of life with their various goods, with their own plans, their own dreams, but never a thought for someone so unfortunate as to have arrived at the bank of that river with no travel money.

'This can't be,' thought Po Cheng. 'It simply doesn't make sense. How could I have arrived here, only to be turned back?'

Then he saw the other sign, this one only barely visible in the tall grass of the riverbank. He parted the grass. The calligraphy was atrocious. Bird tracks would have been more legible. Still, having in his past life been a schoolteacher, he managed to decipher the sign as follows:

CHEAPER CROSSING!
WHY PAY MORE?

A rowing boat was tied to one of the struts of the bridge and in the bottom of it, fast asleep, was a child with a dirty face, spindly arms and—to his surprise—painted toenails.

'Young person!' Po Cheng called out. 'Please wake up. Good fortune has come your way.'

The creature stirred and rubbed her eyes.

'Quickly now. Go and tell your father that he has a customer, providing that the price is right.'

'Go and find your own father!' the child replied fiercely. 'Do you want to cross or don't you?'

The First Graduate studied, by turn, the boat with its

chipped paint, the child and her thin limbs, and the mismatched pair of oars. But then, rather than ask how many times she had rowed across the river before, he decided to begin by negotiating the fare.

'How about this?' he proposed. 'While you're rowing me across, I'll tell you a story.'

'All that work for just a story? And what if I don't like it?'

'Of course you'll like it. It's called *The Great Differentiation*. And unlike money, which is gone as soon as it's been spent, a story's for life.'

From the start, it was evident that the journey was to be an adventurous one. No sooner was the boat free of the bank than it was caught by a strong current, and the small girl, even though rowing for all she was worth, was unable to keep the boat on course. Even supposing that the boat didn't sink and that they were somehow able to reach the opposite shore, they would end up far downstream from where they had set off. All the same, a deal was still a deal.

'In the beginning,' Po Cheng commenced, 'there was only mist ... .'

> *All was still,*   *all was silent.*
> *There was no singing*   *or dancing,*
> *no laughter or tears, nothing had yet been born or died.*
> *Everything remained enclosed within the Cosmic Egg, only*
> *gradually taking form, still coming to be, cohering,*
> *slowly assuming the shape of a hero,*
> *of Pan Gu, the Cosmic*
> *Foetus.*

'*Pan Gu*,' mimed the boat girl, shouting to make herself heard over the roar of the river. 'Never heard of him.'

'Keep rowing then and you will have.'

Pan Gu,
when the
Cosmic Egg
was ready
to hatch,
entered the
world feet first,
and at once began to
walk. He walked ceaselessly,
first this way   and then that,
thereby stretching   the Earth and
creating the Five   Cardinal Directions:
East, West,   North and South.

'But that's only four directions,' complained the boat girl.
'Because he himself was the fifth,' Po Cheng explained.

For a thousand years   Pan Gu roamed the Earth,
expanding its bounds.   No two places would
any longer be the same,   and his constant
wandering had also   dissipated the mist.
Only with his   demise, however,
was his true   greatness revealed.

'His final breath became the wind,' Po Cheng recounted.
'His voice is the thunder, his sweat falls as rain, his moods live
on in the seasons, the growth of his hair resides in grass … .'

But here the story was suddenly interrupted. So absorbed
had Po Cheng been in the telling of the tale, and the girl in
her rowing, that neither saw the bank ahead until the boat
struck it, pitching the First Graduate head-over-heels up
onto the shore.

'Oops,' said the little boat girl, sheepishly.

THERE WAS NO trail now, no path. Underfoot there was only mud, clinging mud, mud which sucked at his feet and his legs as he made his way through a dense tangle of curiously formed trees, each one of which was in the process of being strangled by snake-like vines.

'A cheaper crossing indeed!' Po Cheng reflected. 'Providing, of course, that one has no objection to being dropped off in the middle of a jungle.'

Worse even than the mud which threatened to swallow him, or the green tentacles seeking to wrap themselves around his arms, was a troubling sound coming from the nearby undergrowth, the sound of something which seemed to be following him.

When he sped up, it did the same; if he slowed down, it again followed suit, which he took as convincing evidence that, whatever it was that was pursuing him, it was far more to be feared than a mere wild animal.

He decided to bring things to a head. He stopped suddenly, braced his back against the trunk of a tree and clenched his fists.

'Right!' he shouted out. 'Enough of this! Show yourself! I'm in no mood for hide-and-seek.'

Out of the foliage appeared a figure with a truly frightening face. And as Po Cheng had surmised, the fellow was standing upright.

'I'm Tiger,' the individual introduced himself. 'Or I will be, once I've learned my part.'

'Ah, an actor. But doesn't a tiger, as a rule, move on four legs?'

'Not in the theatre. It's called poetic licence.'

Why labour the point? This feline, Po Cheng immediately realized, would be his ticket out of the jungle and so it transpired. In no time at all, with Tiger to lead the way, he arrived at an encampment in which a small fire was blazing, a handcart was parked and where—strung up between two poles—he saw the following freshly painted banner:

COMING SOON!
THE SMALL FULNESS THEATRE COMPANY
PROPRIETOR: WANG TZU

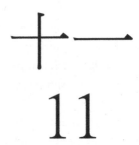

11

FRIVOLITY | HEAVEN'S SOLEMNITY, EARTH'S DIVERSIONS | OLD STAGERS | GETTING THE SHOW ON THE ROAD | MONKEYSHINES | THE LADIES OF PLUM VILLAGE TELL THEIR TALE | A DIRTY TRICK INDEED!

The idea of a theatre company had come to him, the old man claimed, as a result of his having met Bulldog Ma again, in what had once been their boxing camp. The general had turned up at the hut one day to pay his respects and to talk over old times but had claimed to be far too busy to stay for supper.

'Which didn't surprise me,' Wang Tzu added. 'The old devil's up to something.'

'Ah, yes. That Dark Forest Project.'

'Or so he wants us to think. I poked around a bit after that and all he's been doing is building a road.'

'And why would he want a road through that forest?'

'That's just what I was wondering. Especially as it only goes so far and then it simply stops. All the same, I thought to myself, if that fellow's still capable of coming up with a hare-brained scheme at his age, then maybe I should do the same.'

The five actors he had come across in a tavern where they were being held captive until such time as they were able to settle their bar bill, and he immediately cast them—in his thinking—as the Five Exemplary Animals: Owl, Deer, Monkey, Bear and Tiger.

'Of course I had to get them released first but I already had some experience, as you'll know, in settling such disputes.'

Although entertained by Wang Tzu's account of these machinations, Po Cheng was still far short of being convinced of his sanity. How much did the old fellow understand, for instance, of just what was required in order to produce a play?

'See here, isn't it usually the case,' Po Cheng challenged him, 'before recruiting any actors for a play, to know just what play it's going to be?'

'I was just coming to that. What I didn't know until now was when the final piece was going to fall into place.'

'Ah, the final piece. Well if you're counting on me to write a play for you, you're barking up the wrong tree. I wouldn't even know how to begin.'

'That may be but there'll be no need for you to begin. Everything's already in place apart from a few lines of dialogue, which you could no doubt knock off in no time at all.'

Po Cheng, while he couldn't help but admire the old man's guile, was also wary of it.

'Agree to one thing,' he told himself, 'and he'll ask for ten. That's the way these fellows operate. Once they get you by the ear, they have you.'

All the same, if it was just a matter of putting a few words into someone else's mouth, how hard could it be? Might he not even turn out to be good at it? He promised Wang Tzu that he would give the matter some thought but in fact what he ended up thinking about was what it would be like should his efforts bear fruit and the play be a success and he be called up onto the stage afterwards to take a bow, thereby acknowledging the plaudits of an admiring public.

THE FINAL MEMBER of the Small Fulness Theatre Company was a sprightly woman called Widow Wen. She had been discovered by Wang Tzu in a field where she was lifting potatoes, and she had agreed that the company could make use of her handcart providing that they took her along as well. It was she to whom the actors owed their animal costumes, and Wang Tzu his own, which was that of the ringmaster of a circus, and it was she, once the performances began, who would take tickets.

'Start with Monkey,' she advised Po Cheng. 'He's fun-loving and that's what people most like to see. Maybe it's different in the city but country people don't want to return home from the theatre sad.'

Monkey was easy-going, exuberant and energetic but his energy was diffuse. Unlike a camel, for instance, or a water buffalo, his strength could not be harnessed; his force was instead similar to that of a volcano, which could be put to no useful work but simply needed from time to time to be vented. If the pace of a performance started to flag, on the other hand, Monkey could be counted on to belch, fart or even quit the stage altogether, and go on the prowl through the audience as if in search of the crimson hindquarters of a female in heat.

Wang Tzu's instructions had been clear. Theatre pleased the public by presenting it with pleasing illusions, as well as plenty of knock-about, skulduggery, double-dealing and dirty tricks. One must give the public what it wanted, that was to say, until such time as it learned to want something better.

So rickety was the platform on which the company gave its premiere performance of *The Monkey Expediency* that it was all the actors could do simply to keep their balance. All the same, tickets had been sold and the show had to go on. So it had gone on, and Widow Wen, who also kept the books, was able to report afterwards that the proceeds taken had exceeded the amount which it had been necessary to pay out in bribes in order to get permission to perform in the first place.

'So there's enough left over,' Monkey boasted, 'thanks to me, for a round of drinks!'

Monkey's expediency, the play had made clear, was mockery. This was his means of gaining safe passage through a world which was fraught with danger. The script had hence called for him to show up the other animals, taunting and ridiculing them, which naturally they resented, and above all Tiger, who failed to see the humour in his having been made the butt of anyone else's jokes.

'It's impossible,' he complained. 'How can I be expected to play my *own* role? How can I appear to be bloodthirsty, if no one takes me seriously?'

'Just be patient,' Po Cheng urged him. 'Wait until you see what happens to that ape in *The Tiger Expediency*. We'll need to put up a notice that children can attend only if accompanied by an adult and seated a safe distance from the stage.'

THE TROUBLE WITH actors, according to Wang Tzu, was that they were all conceited. Each believed that he possessed a talent for mimicry superior to that of anyone else and that nothing was therefore too good for him. Actors, as a result, never ceased acting and when not performing on a stage spent their time either bickering among themselves or complaining about the accommodation.

Po Cheng, after the success of his first two plays, had no reason to complain. A proper roof over his head, a cooked meal, warmed wine, and once a week—with the payment of a firewood fee—a good long soak in a hot bath, was as much luxury as anyone deserved, and if this was to be seen as suffering, then how better to suffer than to suffer for one's art?

Nor did he mind the early mornings or the forced march which was often required in order to get from where they had performed only the evening before to where they would be performing again that very night.

One day the company received a strange request. The tables were to be turned. Rather than giving a performance, they were being asked to attend one. And a further surprise awaited the troupe upon its arrival at the village by which it had been hired:

PLUM VILLAGE
(*Birthplace of the famed
Plum Village Gang*)

The drama that night was to be played out beneath the village catalpa tree, where a courtroom of sorts was awaiting them. Benches were in place for the actors, who would form a jury; an armchair had been brought out for Wang Tzu, whose role was that of the Visiting Magistrate; and Po

Cheng, as the Court Clerk, had been provided with a stool.

He needed to write quickly, he found, in order to get everything down. One by one the women of the village came forward with their stories, with their accounts of what they all described as a shameful occurrence and of its sad aftermath.

And if certain details differed in their different accounts, was this not in their favour? Did it not indicate that they were not merely repeating something which they had earlier cooked up between them?

The official had turned up one day in a fine carriage, on that they were all agreed. He had been well-dressed and well-spoken—just the sort of son of which any mother would have been proud—and when he introduced himself as the new famine commissioner, everyone naturally assumed that his job in the government must be to *prevent* famine.

The more of this that he heard, the more convinced Po Cheng became that he was not hearing it for the first time. Was corruption really rife and were dishonest government officials then not the exception but rather the rule?

Having won the villagers' trust by praising their plum orchards and by accepting a cup of the plum brandy for which the village had long been famous, the official then produced a scroll and unrolled it to reveal a painting of a truly horrifying little creature which he claimed was a plum beetle, an insect with three distinct heads and therefore even more voracious than a locust.

Until now the actors had sat in silence but this was too much. Never mind their past bickering, they now leapt to their feet as one, flushed with the unmistakably human trait of moral indignation.

'Outrageous!' roared Tiger.

'Scum of the Earth!' growled Bear.

'Guilty as charged!' shrieked Monkey.

'Not to be countenanced!' declared Owl, sententiously.

Only Deer, although on his feet along with the others, remained at a loss for words. Only Deer, with his large round eyes. Only Deer, whose expediency was watchfulness.

WHEN THE HULLABALLOO had calmed down and the jury was once more seated, the hearing continued. The only way to eradicate the plum beetle once and for all, according to the commissioner, was to deprive it of its favourite food and the government was therefore offering to pay for any plum orchard which was uprooted and replaced with a mulberry grove, twice what the orchard had been worth, and hence everyone would benefit.

'But some more than others,' calculated Po Cheng, even as he continued to record the proceedings. 'More mulberry trees equals more leaves for the court silkworms, which in turn adds up to more silk for the robes of the courtiers and the gowns of the palace ladies.'

It was painful to sit there and listen to the women, each in her own words, describing how foolish they had been to swallow that nonsense about beetles having more than one head. Be that as it may, they must have thought at the time, if the government was so foolish as to offer them twice as much money for their land as it was worth, why not accept the offer?

At first they had tended the mulberry saplings. Why not? Just in the meantime. Just while they were waiting for their funds from the government to arrive and then they would do exactly as they pleased, perhaps even move closer to the sea so that they could watch the waves rolling in and out.

The final act wasn't hard to predict. One had only to

look around to see that while there were no longer any plum trees on the surrounding terraces, no mulberry trees were growing there either, only wild grasses. Which grasses were of little use, the women testified, apart from the weaving of baskets such as the baskets which they had once used when picking plums.

The final act occurred on the night that they finished off the last jar of plum brandy remaining in the village. The mulberry saplings had grown before their eyes into trees but without a penny of the money owed to them for the land having yet turned up, and the men of the village had taken matters into their own hands, dishing out to the now-hated mulberry trees the same punishment that had earlier befallen their beloved plum trees. Then, knowing that there was sure to be a price put on their heads, they had all gone off to become bandits.

It was impossible to say after this recital whether it was the members of the Small Fulness Theatre Company who were consoling the widows of Plum Village or vice versa. Po Cheng was still seated on his stool putting the finishing touches to his transcript when one of the women approached him, one to whom the traditional accolade of 'round in front and round behind' was certainly applicable.

'Would you mind my sitting in your lap?' she asked.

'Not greatly,' replied Po Cheng.

He put aside his writing paraphernalia, making space for her. Not knowing what he was meant to be doing with his hands, he used one to support her back and with the other began stroking her hair. She, for her part, started purring like a cat.

'You must miss your husband terribly,' he said then, not meaning anything untoward by it.

'That goes without saying,' she replied. 'We were a once-in-a-lifetime couple and that's quite rare these days.'

'I'm sure it is and you're to be congratulated for it.'

'That's good of you to say, Sir, but now he's gone and lost to me forever.'

'And you to him, dear lady. And you to him.'

十二

12

AMBITION | HEAVEN'S GRANDEUR, EARTH'S
PRETENSIONS | A FISH LEAPS FROM ITS POND, IT
HOPES TO REACH THE OCEAN | FULL SPEED AHEAD
| THEY LOOSE THE MONKEY OF THE MIND

For how much longer, Po Cheng had begun to ask himself,
could that continue? Was this his destiny? Was the writing of
action-packed farces all that he had been born for? Was it
any excuse that night after night, in village after village, the
performance was sold out in advance and that those without
tickets, rather than miss the performance, could be seen
watching from the branches of trees?

He was, in any case, losing patience with the actors.
Monkey, although already popular with the public, would
often garble his lines deliberately just for the sake of getting
an extra laugh, and Tiger, in order to grab more attention for
himself, would return to the stage after the end of an already

successful performance and deliver his most telling lines all over again as an encore.

Mushrooms, for another thing, were starting to appear in the fields, which was a sign that autumn was on the way. Performances by the Small Fulness Theatre Company would before long be getting fewer and further between and the entire company would therefore be faced with tightening its belts. The first thing to go, Wang Tzu had hinted, would be the extra expense of a firewood fee, as excessive bathing, for a company of strolling players whose performances were generally given out-of-doors, was a luxury which could surely be done without.

The final drop in the bucket came one morning when Po Cheng discovered that, in addition to more mushrooms, copies of the following government notice had sprung up during the night:

IMPERIAL EXAMINATIONS!
SEEKING MEN OF TALENT!
DOES THIS MEAN YOU?

Why would it not mean him and how would he ever forgive himself in later life if he allowed this opportunity to slip by? So why not chance his arm? Why not, when invited to do so, make an effort to stand out from the crowd?

He broke the news to the others as gently as he could.

'I'll never forget you,' he promised them, 'or the free-and-easy life that we've shared.'

As might have been expected, Owl was the first to come up with a reply.

'What will be, will be, and very seldom will it be what one was hoping for.'

'And so say all of us,' seconded Tiger.

It was too much for Monkey, who suddenly commenced racing back and forth, shrieking at the top of his lungs. Monkey had until then played his role only for laughs and Po Cheng found this new behaviour unsettling. Were these unearthly shrieks intended as an alarm call? As some simian war cry? Monkey, in either case, was plumbing new depths.

The day was warm and such a frenzy could not be sustained for long. Monkey, exhausted, came back to his senses and for a moment he appeared to be about to take a bow. But the fellow had yet to learn when enough was enough and now took his tail in one hand, put on an idiot grin, approached the departing member of the company and concluded what had been a truly virtuoso performance with a double somersault turned in mid-air.

A NARROW TRACK brought the lone traveller back to what had previously been known to him as the *Road to the North*. He may have strayed from it for a time but he was now picking up the thread again, even if the road, in his absence, had received a new name:

IMPERIAL HIGHWAY!

All the better, judged the traveller. No more hit and miss, no more vacillations. Surely on so splendid a thoroughfare—and one with so few exits—he would have his mind only on his destination and any lingering doubts would have no purchase.

Splendid it might be but it was also congested. Whole families were on the move, the womenfolk bent double under loads of firewood, rushes, bedding and cooking pots, while their menfolk supported shoulder poles, so balancing a stove on one side with an armchair on the other, a sack of charcoal with a child, or a sheep with an ageing parent.

'And when they've reached the Celestial City?' Po Cheng puzzled. 'Just where are all of these folk supposed to sleep?'

But this wasn't the time to worry over that. As he himself had nothing to carry, the First Graduate was able to walk at a rapid pace, passing any number of more encumbered travellers. Only when he had reached the capital could he begin preparing for the examinations which would determine whether he would become someone of influence and therefore be of some future use to those who, at that moment, were too heavily burdened.

In due course the city walls appeared ahead and then the city's intricately carved Southern Gate and, within the gate, an inevitable customs post.

'Purpose of your visit?' demanded the official in charge.

'The highest, if you please, Sir. Self-improvement.'

'And your luggage, I suppose, will be following?'

Having been warned by Wang Tzu of the reception which he was likely to encounter, the candidate was able to skirt this first obstacle with a token payment of a few small coins, which at once vanished into the wide sleeve of the customs officer, who in return made no further reference to Po Cheng's obvious lack of visible provision.

Wang Tzu's instructions were that he should next seek out the Willow Market and then proceed along Willow Market Avenue until he reached Willow Market Lane.

Having accomplished this, Po Cheng then found himself before the door of a somewhat shabby-looking edifice bearing the following carefully polished placard:

CELESTIAL HARMONY LODGING HOUSE.
ROOMS FOR ASPIRING SCHOLARS
(NO OTHERS NEED APPLY!)

The elderly gentleman who came to the door could hardly have appeared more scholarly himself. He was holding an open book and wearing a robe of the sort said to be held together by ink stains. His name was Lü and he did indeed have a room to let but only to someone with references.

'Well there's this fellow Wang,' the First Graduate mentioned, hopefully. 'It seems that he used to be a boxer ... .'

'Mosquito Wang? Of course I remember him. What a time people had, back when he was young, keeping that little devil out of their henhouses.'

The room was reached by means of a creaking staircase and it contained only the bare necessities, these being a brick bedstead, a writing table, a wobbly stool, a single book shelf and—on the back of the door—a hook from which to hang one's spare clothing.

'And the funds?' queried Po Cheng, hesitantly.

'A mere detail. Nothing to make a fuss over. I'll keep track and you can pay me when you leave.'

So it was settled, and once he was alone Po Cheng studied the room more closely, thinking about the many months during which it would be his home. From the bed in which he would be sleeping, it was but a single stride to the reading table and but one stride more to the room's single window, which looked down on Willow Market Lane and from which the shutters had been removed, he noted, thus preventing the aspiring scholar—should he ever wish to —from shutting out the morning sun.

THE WRITING MATERIALS which he required he obtained on Willow Market Avenue from the All-Needs Stationery Shop, along with various guides and primers and sample papers purported to have been submitted by successful candidates in the past. Once again, no funds changed hands:

his account was simply chalked onto the wall behind the counter of that establishment, to be settled at such time as Candidate Po emerged from the Examination Hall with the rank of 'proven talent' and with a post waiting for him somewhere in the government.

Next he visited the vast and bustling Willow Market. The Imperial Examinations were not due until spring but those with stalls in the market seemed only too happy to extend to him the credit necessary to get him through autumn and winter, and Po Cheng thus obtained, with no further outlay of funds, an all-season cap, a pair of warm slippers to wear when reading and several essential items of underclothing.

'At this rate,' he calculated, feeling a little guilty, 'I'll soon be a wealthy man and without ever lifting a finger.'

Nevertheless he continued his shopping. Under that one roof, in addition to what he had come to buy, he also encountered all manner of things which—had he been left to his own devices—it might never have occurred to him that he might need. On a single aisle, for instance, he could have had his fortune told, his tea leaves read, his horoscope drawn up or his dreams interpreted.

'I'll need to come back later,' Po Cheng found himself repeatedly apologizing, 'when I have more time.'

'That's all very well,' said the dream interpreter, 'but you mustn't leave it too long. Dreams are best interpreted while they're still fresh.'

He couldn't resist pausing for a moment at the stall of a matchmaker. On display were portraits of a considerable number of quite attractive young ladies and the matchmaker was prepared to draw up a contract for any one of them right then and there. For the contract to become binding, however, the groom-to-be would need to obtain at least the minimum passing grade on the Spring Examinations.

'Ah so,' deduced Po Cheng. 'Thus the popularity of spring weddings.'

Having explored the Willow Market, he then raised his sights. The Willow Market Ward was but one of the dozen wards which made up the district of the Celestial City known as the Southern Suburb. Finding one's way was in theory simple, as the streets all ran East/West and the avenues North/South.

The beginner, in order not to become lost, therefore had only to think of the city as an immense game board and himself as one of the counters.

What somewhat compromised the good order of the game board, however, was the river that ran higgledy-piggledy through the city, oblivious to the very existence of streets or avenues. The world of such a river, Po Cheng imagined, would encompass only docks and piers, boats of every description, and perhaps here and there a drawbridge.

When passing through the Southern Suburb, the river passed under Magpie Bridge and it was there that the First Graduate paused on his way back from the Willow Market and where—despite himself—he began to experience second thoughts.

'What if I'm wrong?' it occurred to him. 'What if all this is indeed merely illusion?'

What if he had miscalculated? What if he were merely repeating mistakes already made to his cost in the past? What if, like so many others who arrived in the Celestial City determined to make a big splash, he succeeded only in getting a good soaking?

ON THE GROUND floor of the Celestial Harmony Lodging House was the kitchen, Landlord Lü's study and the room in which the old gentleman slept surrounded by his books. Of the three rooms on the floor above, one was empty, one was inhabited by Po Cheng and the third was let to a curious individual who called himself Student Pang, although there was little to indicate that the fellow spent much time studying, as he was always on his way out somewhere and seldom reappeared before the small hours of the morning.

'To each his own,' Po Cheng reflected, charitably. 'Although he's clearly no swot, he might all the same turn out to be a fine fellow.'

He was soon presented with an opportunity to find out. One evening when Student Pang was on his way down and Po Cheng just coming up from the back garden latrine, they met on the staircase.

'Well, well,' said Pang, 'so you do sometimes leave your room.'

'And you, it seems,' retorted Po Cheng, 'seldom do anything else.'

'Truce. We're neighbours, after all. I was just on my way to the Green Monkey, so why not join me?'

'The Green Monkey? But isn't that a tavern?'

'Call it what you like but it's a real institution and you ought at least to give it a try.'

The Green Monkey Tavern might also have been called notorious. It was where the stallholders from the Willow Market were said to meet their 'wholesalers', the latter being individuals who came and went not through the city gates but through tunnels which they themselves had dug through the city's walls.

Student Pang led the way to what he referred to as his 'usual' table. This, like all the other tables, was merely an upturned barrel but it had the advantage of being near to a log fire which was burning in one of the tavern's several large fireplaces.

'And how did you come by such a snug nest?' queried Po Cheng.

'Not by reading the *Ten Classics*, if that's what you think, or ploughing through the *Ten Thousand Commentaries*.'

A jar of spiced wine was set before them together with two drinking bowls and for a snack there was also a plate of pork crackling. And just as before, Po Cheng again noted, no money had changed hands.

'Seriously speaking,' Pang went on to say, 'it won't matter a fig to the examiners how many books you've read. They're experienced at what they do and can tell at a single glance whether someone's from a respectable family or from one that's barely scraping by.'

The fellow, Po Cheng told himself, was almost certainly exaggerating. Moreover, if he knew that much about the examiners, then it was most probably because he had taken the examination himself in the past and perhaps even on multiple occasions but had so far failed to pass.

'So you're saying that the answers don't matter either?' Po Cheng challenged him. 'In that case, why go to so much trouble searching the candidates for hidden notes?'

'Is that what you think?' mocked Student Pang, signalling to a waiter with the empty plate for more pork crackling. 'Do you really believe that they expect to find hidden notes when they search between a candidate's toes? They just want to know if his feet stink.'

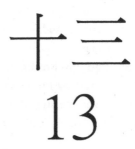

13

CASTIGATION | HEAVEN'S ORDER, EARTH'S SANCTIONS
| AN OBVIOUS CASE OF NEEDFUL CORRECTION? |
THEY GATHER IN GREAT NUMBERS | THE CROOKED,
STRAIGHTENED; THE BEREAVED, CONSOLED

His day began just as it did for the birds nesting in the packed mud of the city walls: with the booming of the Thunder Drum.

What roused the sleepers was also a signal to the carts and wagons waiting at the gates to enter the capital now that the Celestial City had come back to life and was once more open for business.

From his bed Po Cheng went straight to the window to await the arrival on Willow Market Lane of the woman from the Fresh-Daily Bakery with her basket of steamed buns. Only an ancient sage living in a cave somewhere in the mountains, or a monk sitting under a waterfall, would have considered it possible to commence his day's reading on an empty stomach.

The first text that a candidate was expected to master was *The Classic of Mountains and Seas*, a compendium of ancient beliefs, superstitions and delusions. Only by revisiting the blind alleys down which people in the past had been lured, the argument went, could one hope to avoid the impasses of one's own times.

Even after having had his breakfast, the candidate was from time to time distracted by noises in the lane below: by the bell of a tinker, the tin whistle of a rag-and-bone man, the plaint of a blind beggar or the ditty of a street barber:

> *Off with the whiskers, away with the stubble:*
> *It's the smoothest cheeks which get the most kisses!*

Maybe so but first things first. Spring might be a long way off yet but the more time that one had to prepare for an examination, the more rapidly that time was likely to pass.

His midday meal he took in the kitchen of the lodging house with Landlord Lü, who was himself a retired official and a stickler when it came to routine and to punctuality. Each morning Lü went out to shop and returned with something delicious, such as snapping turtle soup, candied crabs or pickled sea urchins.

Lü, when shopping, was nevertheless easily blown off course and Po Cheng, when descending from his room in anticipation of a tasty meal, might find the old gentleman not at the stove but seated cross-legged on the kitchen floor varnishing some shabby-looking book of the sort sold on street corners, out of wheelbarrows, by individuals who may well have been housebreakers.

'Is it that time already?' Lü would ask, genuinely

surprised. 'Would you mind just frying yourself some noodles? This book needs to be protected from cockroaches.'

How could one be angry with such a sincere individual? Po Cheng, rather than complain, simply got out a pot, put in some oil and fried up sufficient noodles for a meal for them both. Scholars, after all, whatever their origins, ought to be seen as a clan of their own.

THE BOOK WHICH Student Pang had open when Po Cheng joined him at his habitual table in the Green Monkey had the intriguing title of *Revealing Heaven's Destiny*. No sooner had the First Graduate sat down than a drinking bowl appeared, without his even having to ask, along with a generous portion of crackling.

'So, Pang,' he remarked. 'You've become studious as well. It must be my good influence.'

'And the influence is mutual. The waiters hop to it now when they see you.'

The book in which Pang had been immersed was a diviner's manual. On its cover was a portrait of the night sky, a sky replete with dots of light, and all that was necessary in order to know Heaven's will and so to get things done, Pang explained, was to connect the dots.

'Suppose,' he argued, 'that someone wants to dig a well or to bury a loved one ... .'

'Well if it were me,' interrupted Po Cheng, 'I'd use a shovel.'

'Of course you would but where would you dig?'

Pang, although seldom in his room at the lodging house, could not be said to be idle, not entirely. He was working as a wind-and-water man, a geomancer, someone who by observing the lay of the land, the alignment of the stars and which way the wind was blowing, was able to predict, for any given site on Earth, if a well sunk there would ever run dry or a grave be likely to flood.

'But what if all that is pure nonsense, Pang? Won't people be getting cheated?'

'And what if the examinations are a nonsense? Won't you be getting cheated?'

These were murky waters, Po Cheng reflected. Waters in which, as the saying went, carp could not be distinguished from bream. Yes, people might be cheated but would people dig wells at all if they were not first led to believe that water would be obtained as a result?

'Just tell me this, Pang. Do you believe that this wind-and-rain business actually works?'

'If you mean does it pay, of course it does. And I could even cut you in on it.'

'Cut me in? What a curious expression. Isn't that how criminals talk?'

'What if they do? The facts are the facts and in case you haven't noticed the days are starting to close in. Autumn, after all, for a wind-and-rain man, is the busiest season of the year, so are you in or are you out?'

AUTUMN IN THE capital was the season of falling leaves and wind-borne snow. The awnings which had sheltered the streets in the hotter months had been taken down and the news coming out of the Inner City was that the ageing Emperor (whose name it was forbidden to mention) had begun wearing padded clothing and that the court was following suit. And so too, Po Cheng noted, Landlord Lü, who had taken to wearing a scarf when he went out, even though the coldest months had yet to arrive.

Autumn was also, by definition, the season for the dreaded Autumn Executions. Student Pang, along with every other wind-and-water man in the Celestial City, had been pouring over his star charts and an almanac in anticipation of what was to come, as the mortal remains of those to be executed would need to be buried before the ground froze. Po Cheng, meanwhile, was still trying to decide if he was in or he was out.

Surely it was shameful to benefit financially from the misery of others? Pang's retort to this was how could it be shameful when the police benefited from arresting suspects, judges and juries profited from finding them guilty, jailers received a salary for keeping them locked up, and so on and so forth, right down to the executioner who was simply doing his duty, and the guardsmen who were on hand to hold back the crowds. And as for those who took charge of the corpses afterwards, Pang argued, they were no worse than any of the others. They were simply stationed at the end of the line.

They set off in good time on the day of the executions, taking Willow Market Avenue, Donkey Street, Filial Piety Avenue and Sustained Endeavour Street. Despite the early morning start, the best vantage points were already taken by the time the pair reached Great Redemption Square, which the First Graduate, for one, thought to be no bad thing.

'Don't worry,' said Pang, who also seemed a little nervous. 'Our man is down to be strangled, so there's unlikely to be any blood.'

A platform had been erected in the middle of the square and a squad of Imperial Guardsmen were in position, with shields and broadswords at the ready, in order to keep a passage open for the prison wagons. Hoods obscured the faces of the condemned but dangling from each one's neck was a placard spelling out what had brought him to this pass.

'*Killed a man in a bar fight*,' Pang pointed out. 'That's our fellow.'

The unfortunate brawler was dragged forward, brought centre stage and made to kneel down. The executioner, an imposing figure with bulging arms, approached from behind, looped a wire round the neck of his victim and without further ceremony yanked hard on the wire with both hands, bringing the matter, mercifully, to a quick conclusion.

Po Cheng, although it was surely only his imagination, felt as if he too had a wire around his neck.

'And are we meant to believe, Pang, that strangling that poor devil has put an end to wickedness?'

'Probably not but who knows how much wickedness it might deter?'

In any case, they had a contract to fulfil. The wire was removed from the neck of their client and between them the two friends dragged the poor wretch off the platform by his feet. From the crowd came, in equal measure, hoots of derision and cries of indignation, before which, to Po Cheng's relief, the Imperial Guardsmen stood firm.

PO CHENG SOUGHT to gather his thoughts. Things were what they were and in the face of this one ought perhaps to bear in mind that such things had in the past been even worse. Criminals had in earlier times been crushed with rollers, placed between two planks and sawn in half, as well as skinned alive and forced to watch as their hides were stuffed with sausage meat. Given these antecedents, might one not celebrate strangulations and beheadings as being almost humane?

Their client had left behind two ageing parents, a wife and three small children. Although surely grieved by the loss of their son, the elderly couple were seeking to entertain their grandchildren by speaking to them through the mouth of a hand puppet.

'Where's your daddy off to? He's off on a journey. Wave bye-bye to daddy, little ones.'

A trip was indeed on the cards. No one executed for a crime committed within the walls of the Celestial City was permitted to be buried within those walls. A suitable site would need to be found outside the city, amidst the haunts of bears and wolves, and it was Pang's task to locate one consonant with the nature and the practices of the deceased. Po Cheng, as Pang's assistant, went to work at once gleaning the necessary information.

'Please forgive the intrusion,' he began, politely, 'at a time like this …'

Her son, the mother of the deceased recalled, had from an early age shown every sign of having too tender a heart. Many a time he would come home from school without some article of his clothing, having given it away to a child more in need of it.

'And not just that. He not only did his own homework, he did it for other boys as well.'

'Ah,' thought Po Cheng, making a note. 'So he was bullied as a child.'

The wife, when it was her turn, described her late husband as the most caring of men and the most devoted of fathers. His only flaw, she agreed with her mother-in-law, if it was a flaw, was the unusual goodness of his heart.

'That was his undoing, Sir. It was the sight of so much suffering and cruelty in the world that, in the end, drove him to drink.'

That was half of the job done. Student Pang could now negotiate for a suitable plot of land and Po Cheng set to work on an epitaph. It was a fine line to walk, neither praising the deceased too fulsomely for sentiments upon which he may not have acted, nor taking him too severely to task for deeds which he may have been powerless not to perform.

Everyone, fortunately, was well satisfied with what, after no little thought, the First Graduate was able to come up with:

A GOOD MAN,
A CARING MAN,
HE TOOK TO DRINK,
AS A WARNING
TO OTHERS.

14

ARTISTRY | HEAVEN'S GLOW, EARTH'S REFLECTIONS | A FISHERMAN'S GUIDE | LUSTING AFTER THE SOFT AND THE SUPPLE | WHY THE ROOSTER CROWS | NEAR NEIGHBOURS, PAIRED PRACTICES

Was there anything worth knowing about the Celestial City that Student Pang didn't know? The best bait to use when fishing for catfish in the quarter's stagnant and filthy canals, Pang recommended, was a nice fat grub, and the best grubs were to be found on the Thousand Flower Embankment, where the night soil collected throughout the city during the hours of darkness was dumped first thing every morning.

'It comes down to how you look at things,' Pang pointed out. 'A grub, after all, is just a worm and a fish is no less of a fish for having whiskers.'

Autumn was by now shading over into winter. Great flocks of birds were to be seen passing over the city and

fishing on the canal would soon become ice-fishing. Po
Cheng had paid a first visit to the Money-for-Old-Rope
Pawnshop, coming away with a nearly new pair of gloves, a
worn leather jacket, and a winter cap with one of the ear-
flaps hanging by a mere thread. Best to be prepared and he
soon took to donning this apparel as soon as he left his bed
in the mornings.

'What a fright!' Student Pang declared, having burst into
Po Cheng's room one morning without knocking. 'Are you
thinking, if the exams don't pan out, of seeking work as a
scarecrow?'

'And when did you last see this hour of the day?' Po
Cheng retorted.

'Not recently, I grant you. But something's taking place
today—and not far from here—which may well bear
looking into.'

Only when they were on their way did Pang reveal what
was up. Just a few short blocks away, in a perfectly legitimate
establishment and with the full knowledge of the police, a
young woman calling herself Precious Pearl was going to be
posing that day in a state of disarray.

'Ah, in disarray?' Po Cheng queried. 'So you're expecting
to see her undressed?'

'Maybe not entirely, as she's just arrived in the city and
may still be somewhat shy.'

The establishment in question was on Great Renown
Street and immediately recognizable by the brightly painted
sign in the shape of an artist's palette which was suspended
by two hooks above its door:

THE FOREST OF BRUSHES
ACADEMY OF ART

They were met at the door by the director, a short, pudgy fellow called Chan, who, in return for a small viewing fee, showed them to a bench.

'Art, gentlemen,' he then warned the two viewers, 'as practised on these premises, is no mere entertainment, so please remain seated at all times.'

The students were already in place at their easels, forming a semi-circle in front of a still-vacant stool, at the foot of which a number of potted plants had been artfully arranged, thus suggesting that the model who was about to pose for them should be portrayed as a woman taking her ease in a garden, without knowing that she was being overlooked.

Scarcely had the two friends made themselves comfortable than the model—who must have been changing her clothes—appeared from behind a screen, causing Po Cheng to suck in his breath. She was wearing a blue satin jacket embroidered with small yellow birds, which was set off nicely by a pair of black, form-clutching, silk trousers. There could be, however, in the mind of Po Cheng, no doubt that the person now going by the name of Precious Pearl was, in fact, none other than Miss Ling.

NEVER BEFORE HAVING visited an art academy, Po Cheng could not be absolutely certain what he was witnessing. He certainly found it odd the way that Director Chan went about arranging Miss Ling's pose—so familiarly and with so much laying on of hands—as if he himself were the artist and she his medium.

'Now then,' he ordered, once he was satisfied, 'remain still. Don't move a muscle until I say so and if you must breathe, do so discreetly.'

With that, the students were loosed on her. Their heads

bobbed up and down, up from their easels to Miss Ling in her garden and then back down to their paintings-in-progress. Now and then someone would hold up his thumb and peer past it in order to obtain, Po Cheng supposed, a truer measure of this or that facet of Miss Ling's anatomy.

'Just wait,' Pang whispered. 'Another week or two and less of her will be left to guesswork.'

Director Chan, meanwhile, couldn't remain still. He moved from easel to easel making derogatory and sarcastic comments, leaving a goodly number of glum faces in his wake.

'So you think that you can paint, do you?' the fellow ranted, left and right. 'Well think again! Art seeks the artist and not vice versa.'

Student Pang had soon had enough of this bullying and excused himself but Po Cheng stayed on, rooted to the spot, until Director Chan became fed up as well and declared that the class was now over for the day. The First Graduate, at this point, shot Miss Ling a glance and received a look instructing him to wait outside while she changed back into her own clothes.

Indeed it was the Miss Ling of old who reappeared, the one wearing her usual wrinkled khaki shirt and baggy trousers. How surprised he had been, Po Cheng confessed, to have run into her again, and in the garb of an actress or a sing-song girl.

'Needs must, Colleague. What's important is that, if two people are meant to meet again, then they will. And what's more, I had something that belonged to you.'

So saying, she produced the small purse containing his travel money. Simply by feeling its weight in his hand, Po Cheng was able to ascertain that the funds within had not been touched. Hence he was also being repaid for the trust which he had first placed in her back in Nettle Village, when he had hired her to look after the little ones in the Minnow School.

'So, Miss Ling, tell all. How did you manage things on that canal boat?'

'It's good of you to ask, Colleague, but in fact it was all quite straightforward.'

She had waited on the boat for several days in the expectation that he might return at any moment from the Examination Hall. Each morning an 'accountant' had turned up at the door to collect her 'rent', which she had paid him using her own funds. Then, upon hearing about the scandal at the chophouse and that those responsible for it had fled the town, she had decided to set out in pursuit.

'You might not be overjoyed to see me, I thought, but the money was sure to come in handy.'

'Indeed it will, Miss Ling. Or do you prefer *Precious Pearl*?'

It was a courtesy name, she explained, a name taken as a courtesy to her parents, to prevent them from finding out that their daughter was working as a model for men to gawk at. To save them from the humiliation of it, as her parents were quite old-fashioned and—had they known—might have gone off and committed suicide out of shame at ever having given birth to such a daughter.

WHY WOULD HE not have been glad to see her? Had she not already proved herself to be trustworthy, resourceful and considerate of her parents? It was, at the very least, incumbent upon him to take her under his wing, so to speak, but how was he going to convince Landlord Lü, a life-long bachelor, that the presence of a woman in the Celestial Harmony Lodging House was not going to disrupt the smooth running of that household or to distract its most promising resident from his studies? For it was clear that, like many another retired official, Lü had been seeking just one thing in his later years, namely to foster a new talent and so to leave behind, when his own time on Earth was done, a second Lü.

'Here's what to say,' suggested Student Pang. 'Tell him that she'll help out with the cooking. A woman's touch, in the kitchen, is never likely to go amiss.'

Would that be sufficient? Might the old gentleman not take this as a criticism of his own cooking? Po Cheng, meanwhile, was meant to be tackling the imposing *Classic of Rites*, this being an exhaustive—and exhausting—treatment of the various recondite religious practices of the Ancients. Scholar Lü, who was a great believer in the motivational power of mottoes, had posted the following exhortation on the kitchen wall:

RITUALS MARK THE SEASONS;
RITES STRAIGHTEN THE RANKS

And could two not play that game? Knowing now just what was required, the First Graduate also knew where it could be obtained. Anyone who failed to find what he was looking for in the Willow Market, after all, had either not looked properly or else had not known his own mind.

So a second motto soon appeared in the kitchen of the lodging house, on the wall above the stove where Landlord Lü—even though he was somewhat short-sighted—could hardly have missed it:

IT'S NOT FOR THE SUN
THAT THE COCK CROWS,
IT'S FOR THE HEN!

The matter had been well-judged. Understanding at once just what point was being made and realizing that he had been out-flanked, Lü threw his arms up as a sign of defeat.

'Well,' he conceded, 'since you put it that way … .'

NO ONE COULD have denied that Precious Pearl, once having been installed in the last free room of the lodging house, was pulling her own weight and not just in the kitchen. In the evenings she grilled Po Cheng on what he had read that day, taking him to task for any material which he may have skipped, for it was well known to be the case that the questions most likely to come up in any examination were the very ones that one had thought it safe to ignore.

This meant, on the other hand, fewer evenings sitting before a log fire in the Green Monkey.

'Since you've become so fond of mottoes yourself,' Student Pang complained, 'here's another one for you: *The hair of a woman, when plaited, can tether an elephant.*'

What his study of the rites of the Ancients was demonstrating to Po Cheng, meanwhile, was just how far people had been prepared to go to appease beings which did not exist and therefore could not possibly have harboured any animosity towards—or felt any fondness for—the human race. The most mundane of occurrences as a result had been taken as secret signs, as hidden harbingers of what was to come, and hence the seemingly inborn human tendency to go off on wild-goose chases.

'And can you give an example,' Precious Pearl quizzed him, 'of such confused thinking?'

There was, for instance, an account of how a cow had been seen, during a thunderstorm, riding on the back of a man. This was interpreted as an ill omen and a great number of cows ended up beaten to death, unnecessarily, before further investigation revealed that what had been observed was not in fact a cow hitching a ride on the back of a man but merely the cowherd taking shelter from the rain.

'Well chosen,' Precious Pearl proclaimed. 'Full marks to Candidate Po!'

At first they had sat apart, Po Cheng at his work table and Precious Pearl on a corner of his bed, but winter was taking hold, they could see their breath in the air, and in order to keep warm they now sat side by side on the bed with a quilt draped over them.

'I've been thinking ... ,' Precious Pearl said tentatively one evening when the time had come for her to return to her own room.

'Yes, I know,' seconded Po Cheng. 'Me as well.'

They were not children. They could not have claimed later, should there be an accident, that they had been unaware of the facts of life. It was thus essential that they not allow things to spiral out of control.

'Perhaps,' suggested Precious Pearl, 'if we're not too shy, we should each, before we snuggle up, perform a solo practice.'

'Thereby admitting to a familiarity with such practices,' Po Cheng pointed out.

'Well, I'll let the cat out of the bag, if you will.'

They undressed back to back. It was not so easy, once they were both stretched out in that narrow bed, for one not to stray too soon into the territory of the other but they kept to what they had agreed: not to embrace until, working apart, they had both spent. Not until Po Cheng had had his eruption and Precious Pearl her rainbow.

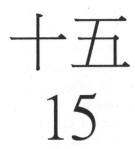

十五

15

OBSERVANCE | HEAVEN'S MAGNIFICENCE, EARTH'S
MACHINATIONS | GAZED AT BY OTHERS, WILL HER
BRIGHTNESS BE DIMINISHED? | THE LITTLE
LUMINARY | A CRANE CALLS IN THE NEW YEAR

The sound of the Thunder Drum in the mornings rudely awakened them both and there could be no lying in, not even on the coldest mornings.

They muttered those pleasantries typically exchanged by a couple who had shared a bed, after which Precious Pearl padded off to her own room to apply the make-up appropriate for someone intending to spend her day at leisure in a garden.

The book now lying open on Po Cheng's work table was *The Classic of Poetry*. While not required to produce a poem himself, he would need to be conversant with poetry. A candidate would need to distinguish between the profound and the trivial in poetry, between the deep resonance of a spring rhapsody on the one hand and the tawdriness of a mere love lyric on the other.

'But even a poet surely,' Po Cheng complained to Scholar Lü, 'is entitled to seek a mate.'

'Of course,' the old gentleman agreed. 'But he ought to do so in his own time.'

Not surprisingly, Lü had little time for living poets, whom he described as over-excited individuals of uncertain provenance, residing in cellars, garret rooms and rooftop chicken coops. They thrived, he claimed, on disorder; they ignored the norms, turned their noses up at tradition and were the purveyors of a fearful pestilence.

'Pestilence?' Po Cheng prompted. 'What sort of pestilence?'

'That of unbridled wilfulness.'

The First Graduate, thanks to his experience with the Small Fulness Theatre Company, had some notion of what was meant by 'artistic temperament', which in addition to wilfulness also incorporated a tendency towards pretension.

Take, for instance, the motto displayed on the wall of the Forest of Brushes Academy:

1. TO ACHIEVE GREATNESS, TAP THE DEPTHS
2. TO TAP THE DEPTHS, ESCHEW THE ORDINARY
3. FOR MERE ACCURACY, TAKE A RUBBING

A rubbing indeed! And was that not just what Director Chan was doing each time that he set about readjusting one of Precious Pearl's poses? And why, for that matter, was it necessary for her to pose with her hair down or in such tight trousers and—worse still—without all of the buttons on her jacket done up properly?

'Because I'm alone,' she explained. 'In a garden. Thinking myself to be unobserved.'

'So it's just in order to get into your role?'

'I'm no longer aware that anyone's watching. And as for Director Chan, he's a perfectionist and what others might see as youthful breasts or as well-turned legs, he sees only as curvature.'

WHILE NO LONGER a regular at the Green Monkey Tavern, Po Cheng had instead become a not-infrequent visitor to the premises of the Forest of Brushes, where he was no longer required by Director Chan to remain seated. Rather he was able to wander about with his hands clasped behind his back, peering over the shoulders of the would-be artists as they worked and even offering now and again what was intended as a useful comment. Once a teacher, always a teacher.

One student in particular piqued his curiosity, one who was smaller than the others and who sat apart from them, protected by a screen from their gaze. The boy spoke to no one and once seated at his easel never glanced up at the scene which he was meant to be painting, nor did Director Chan ever approach him to criticize his work. From Precious Pearl, Po Cheng learned that the boy was referred to by his fellow students as the Little Luminary and that he was dropped off in the mornings and picked up again in the afternoons by someone in a two-horse carriage.

Student Pang filled them in on the rest. The two-horse carriage was the conveyance used by the First Concubine, a certain Lady Yao whose son—whose title was indeed the Little Luminary—was in fact no less than the current heir apparent.

'For want of any other candidate,' Pang explained. 'And

despite the Emperor having sampled in his day, rumour has it, every third woman in his realm.'

Like a bee or a butterfly, he had disported himself with the fairest flowers in every garden in the land but only to end up empty-handed, childless, with no little bundle of joy to bounce on his knee, and afterwards to be taught to follow in his father's footsteps. Not until a common prostitute, a back-alley beauty, was smuggled into the Inner City one night inside a hemp sack. Not until then, so the story went, was the Son of Heaven's seed at last able to germinate.

'So proving,' added Pang, facetiously, 'that the Emperor, despite his exalted position, was in his heart of hearts a man of the people.'

The woman in question had been rewarded with the title of Lady Yao, and her brother, until then a mere water marshal, was now Marshal Yao, the head of the secret police, and as such was the only individual in the Celestial City who was allowed to go about masked.

'But that makes no sense,' Po Cheng pointed out.

'No it doesn't,' agreed Pang. 'He sticks out like a sore thumb. All the same, the idiot thinks that he can remain incognito if he never wears the same mask twice.'

THE HEAVENS HAD not ceased turning and preparations were soon under way throughout the capital for setting aside the old year and welcoming in a new one. The news from the Inner City was that the Court Astrologers—in their white smocks and wise-old-bird caps—had ascended to the top of the Star-Gazing Tower, where they would await a cloudless night, one suitable for viewing the night-lights of the heavenly firmament, and so be able to descend again afterwards with word about the year to come.

Classes in the Forest of Brushes had meanwhile been

suspended, with the students having instead been put to work producing New Year's Pictures. These portrayed peasants, woodcutters, charcoal-makers, lotus-gatherers, weavers, women reeling silk, watermen, butchers, bricklayers: in short, all manner of people performing all manner of tasks and—most importantly—all doing so with cheerful faces.

Being temporarily at liberty, Precious Pearl set to work helping Landlord Lü return the Celestial Harmony Lodging House to tip-top condition for the start of another year, beginning by putting down poison for the cockroaches and other disgusting insects that populated the many unregistered lanes and nameless alleyways which—as in any great city—had sprung up in the capital during periods of lax government.

Po Cheng, from the window of his room, watched the two of them setting off one morning for the Willow Market and saw them returning some time later burdened with all manner of foodstuffs, all to be used, on the eve of the new year, for the preparation of a celebration feast. Old Gentleman Lü, in addition to everything else, had a crane under one arm, which Po Cheng found that evening hanging from a hook on the wall in the kitchen, still alive, with its beak tied shut and its eyelids sewn closed.

'I know that it seems cruel,' Precious Pearl admitted when they were preparing for bed, 'but Lü says that it's traditional.'

'Traditional to torture a crane?'

'To have crane soup on New Year's Eve. And for that, dear friend, you need a crane.'

They no longer undressed back to back. Perhaps it was playing with fire but they liked looking at one another before they got under the quilt. Being naked together for a moment in the soft light cast by Po Cheng's small oil lamp could hardly have been called depravity, they told themselves, and might even have been considered to be in good taste.

THE YEAR WAS all but at an end. Word had come from the Inner City that the aged Emperor, supported by two sturdy Imperial Guardsmen, had successfully performed the Great Exorcism, thus ridding the Celestial City of devils, demons, fox spirits and hungry ghosts. Elsewhere in the city, a long queue had formed outside the Money-For-Old-Rope Pawnshop, where people were pawning their winter clothing in exchange for funds with which to redeem clothing better suited for the warmer months to come. This curious custom, according to Student Pang, was known as 'taking a brick from the East Wall to repair the West Wall'.

On Willow Market Lane, all was ready for a grand celebration. The insect corpses had been swept up, sweet-smelling herbs had been placed in the latrine, and an intoxicating aroma was coming from the kitchen, where the poor crane—prior to going into the soup pot—had been force-fed with aromatic spices.

Lü did not have to call them twice. Rather than arrive empty-handed, the three friends had clubbed together to purchase a New Year's Picture for the house, one portraying a quite respectable-looking old gentleman hard at work with a feather-duster, dusting his books. And they had chosen, for the caption which ran down one side:

EXCELLENCE EVEN WHEN OUT OF OFFICE!

'What a fine choice!' responded Lü, appreciatively. 'Out of office but without, one hopes, having entirely outlived one's usefulness.'

Student Pang was then sent down to the cellar with instructions to bring up what he found there and what he returned with was a large earthenware pot sealed with mud. Lü himself set about removing the cobwebs and breaking the seal, after which he carefully extracted the wax plug and used a ladle to fill four drinking bowls with a rich crimson liquid smelling strongly of fruit.

'To the Son of Heaven!' he pronounced, raising his bowl.

'To the Emperor,' endorsed the others, somewhat less enthusiastically.

The crane soup with which that evening's banquet began tasted just as good as it had smelled. On the stove, meanwhile, other pots were on the go and some were piled several storeys high. It would be the sort of meal from which one might get up thinking that there would be no need to eat again for the rest of one's life.

Before that, however, Landlord Lü refilled their drinking bowls and announced that the next order of business was to be a round of matching toasts. Each, in turn, was to make a toast, keeping as closely as possible both to the style, and to the sentiments expressed, by the one before. They drew straws and Pang began:

Student Pang: *To each as merited, a just and timely reward!*
Candidate Po: *Success and prosperity, wherever it is merited!*
Landlord Lü: *Success as merited, prosperity within measure!*
Precious Pearl: *Joy beyond measure, and perennial good cheer!*

Neither in the Southern Suburb—nor it was to be presumed in any other suburb of the Celestial City—were any tears shed that night for the year that was passing. All hopes, instead, were now placed in the year to come, with strings of firecrackers being set off throughout the city to mark the transition and to frighten off any remaining household sprites.

Such enthusiasm! Such good cheer! Such a racket! But this was not, after all, Po Cheng reflected, just a matter of turning a new page in the almanacs. There might still be ice on the canals and the wind might still be from the North, but they were also celebrating the imminent turning of the seasons, away from the dark and gloomy days of winter, towards a bright and boisterous spring.

十六

16

Winter's grip had been loosened, allowing spring to hang out its banners. In the Southern Suburb with its many warehouses and granaries, sparrows were toiling, flying low with twigs and bits of grass in their beaks, so becoming fair game for the squealing, moon-faced children who sought to catch them in their hands.

What joy! What exuberance! Less welcome to Po Cheng, who was now in the final stage of his preparations for the Spring Examinations, was the constant caterwauling of the quarter's cats.

'Live and let live,' recommended Precious Pearl. 'Put

some candle wax in your ears. Without that racket, after all, where would more cats come from?'

What remained was to prepare himself for composing—on the day of the Literary Examination—an eight-legged treatise on a topic which would not have been announced in advance. Scholar Lü, who would also have been faced with that daunting task, could still recall the topic assigned to him:

THROUGH WHICH EYES DOES HEAVEN VIEW EARTH:
THOSE OF THE SOVEREIGN OR THOSE OF HIS SUBJECTS?

And he still dreamt from time to time of getting up to hand in his paper, Lü claimed, only to find that the ink had faded and that the treatise was now too faint to read.

'Life is unforgiving,' declared Lü, 'and made up of things which can never be put behind us but we must continue on regardless.'

The first leg of the treatise was restricted to just two sentences, declarative sentences, and both of a similar length. The challenge was to present, as concisely as possible, an overview of the position that one intended to take, with the choice of position being less important than the concision.

'So one might just as well argue that up was down?'

'Theoretically you could,' Lü agreed, 'but I wouldn't advise it.'

The second leg, which might run to as many as five sentences, was for developing the argument of the first leg, and exceeding that arbitrary limit, Lü warned, would identify one as a novice, as someone who was indecisive or as a windbag.

The middle four legs, which formed the body of the treatise, were for unfolding one's argument, providing a rationale for any measures which one was advocating, anticipating possible criticism of those measures and dismissing such criticism as vacuous.

The seventh leg was for seeking allies. By quoting from the Ancients, citing passages from the *Ten Classics*, and recounting incidents from the lives of the Immortals, one might at once shore up one's own position, reveal the breadth of one's learning and demonstrate an ability to make use in one's own work of the work of others.

The final leg of the treatise was to be used for invective. Here the candidate was free to ridicule those who might not agree with his previously stated suppositions, his reasoning or the conclusions at which he had arrived. Humour was therefore permitted, and interrogative sentences, just so long as they were at the service of irony or sarcasm.

That evening, as the weather was fine, Po Cheng set off for a walk beside the river with Precious Pearl. The river rushed past them, being still swollen with snow-melt from the Western Mountains, which it was carrying away in the direction of the Eastern Ocean.

'Well there's no reason to be nervous about a mere essay,' Precious Pearl was saying. 'Whatever the topic turns out to be, simply say what's in your heart.'

'But what is there in the human heart, pray tell, which goes about on eight legs?'

There were entertainers performing on the riverbank: weightlifters, pole-climbers, sword-jugglers, acrobats, contortionists, all competing to draw a crowd, and wherever a crowd had gathered there were also vendors of Spring Rolls and individuals selling saucy pictures of Spring Lovelies caught in the act of shedding their winter furs and woollen undergarments.

'You're right of course,' said Precious Pearl. 'The heart doesn't do sums, only the mind does.'

There was within the human heart, so to say, all that one might wish for and more besides, but not arithmetic.

HE WAS FED up with so much preparation. From the window of his room he could see that the sky over the city was full of kites, and at the other end of each string there would be someone who had never passed an examination in his life but was to all appearances none the worse for it.

So Po Cheng himself had taken to spending the final hours of the day in the Forest of Brushes, waiting for Precious Pearl to finish work and wondering how much longer—now that the warmer weather had arrived—she could get away with merely undoing another button on her jacket.

The Little Luminary, Po Cheng noted, still showed no interest in her. The boy never looked up at the figure seated before him, not even now that one of her breasts was precariously close to being on view. The little fellow did give a start, however, when he sensed the presence of someone behind him.

'Don't worry,' Po Cheng assured him. 'I know nothing about art. I wouldn't even claim, as do most people, that I know what I like.'

One glance was nonetheless sufficient to reveal that the boy could certainly draw, which put him head and shoulders above most of the other students. What he was drawing— not from life but out of his own head—was some sort of monster, some creature with wings like a bird, a reptile's tail, webbed feet and an equine face.

'My, my,' Po Cheng ventured. 'And how does a nice boy like you come to imagine something so frightening?'

The boy, seemingly pleased at this assessment, reached down for the school satchel at his feet, and one by one produced a whole series of similar pictures, all in the same style and all being of monsters.

'Ah,' thought Po Cheng. 'He must have seen those on a wall scroll or a frieze or in the Imperial Sculpture Garden and he would no doubt, at first, have been terrified by them.'

This could only be guesswork, as the boy refused to speak. Perhaps he was forbidden to converse with commoners. Precious Pearl confirmed later that from the time the boy arrived in the morning until he was picked up in the afternoon, he never opened his mouth. Nor was there any need for him to do so, as his colours were ground for him beforehand by Director Chan, food and drink were brought to him directly from the Inner City, and none of the other students dared come anywhere near him.

'And who wouldn't be pleased with such a student?' remarked Po Cheng. 'One who simply gets on with his work?'

'But aren't you taking a risk?' Precious Pearl warned. 'What if there's a secret policeman hiding among the students, one whose job it is to guard him?'

'How strange. Where did you get such an odd idea?'

'From the book that I've been reading during my breaks. It takes my mind off things.'

She showed him the lurid cover. It was a novel called *Death Stalks the Purple Lotus Pavilion* and it smelled strongly of mould. The story began with a government official having been murdered in a brothel, and the reader was thereafter left with the task of figuring out who had committed the crime before the detective assigned to the case could do so.

'That's all very well,' Po Cheng scoffed, 'but how can you bear to handle such a book when you don't know who was handling it before you?'

'And what's the difference, dear friend? You and Landlord Lü wash your hands before picking up a book and I wash mine afterwards.'

HE WAS DETERMINED this time that he would look the part. His hair had grown sufficiently by now for a proper topknot and he had been fitted for a cap and gown at the All-Needs Stationery Shop, where if all went well he would soon be in a position to settle his account. And why should it not go well? Why, after so many months of polishing, should he not outshine the mere reflected brilliance of those whose fathers —and fathers' fathers before them—had succeeded in passing an Imperial Examination?

It was when leaving the stationery store with that new garb under his arm that the candidate spotted a carriage waiting, a two-horse carriage with its door already thrown open.

'Get in!' commanded a stern but definitely feminine voice.

An introduction was scarcely necessary. Who else could this be if not Lady Yao, whose brother Marshal Yao headed the secret police? The former back-alley beauty may no longer have been any great beauty but her tone of voice, as well as the expression on her face, marked her out as being an individual of iron-clad determination.

'Shall we get right down to business, candidate? It seems that my son has taken quite a shine to you.'

'How flattering, Your Ladyship. Although he's never said anything to me about it.'

'I'm sure he hasn't. The difficulty which arises is that you're a complete stranger.'

'True enough, Your Ladyship. But there are strangers and there are strangers.'

'Indeed, but how is one to tell the difference?'

He would need to beware, Po Cheng realized. For a woman in Lady Yao's position—one to which she had ascended by means of an act committed in the dark—a quick mind and a sharp tongue were of the essence and she would no doubt make short work of anyone who sought to thwart her.

'Your son, I believe, is an only child,' diagnosed the First Graduate, 'and quite possibly given to inventing imaginary friends. Hence his having taken so quickly to a stranger.'

'Be that as it may, what's been done with that boy can't be undone and under no circumstances are you to encourage him to believe that he could ever become a great artist.'

'But I said no such thing, Your Ladyship. Art itself will choose who is to serve it.'

'Do you think so? A great deal of nonsense, that's what I think, is said about art.'

Her intonation, when proffering that opinion, was such as to indicate that the interview was now at an end, and she emphasized this, when Po Cheng did not get up at once, by reaching across him to open the carriage door.

'I trust, Candidate Po, that we understand each other and I mean this for both our sakes, as I'm not the sort of woman who, if someone does her a favour, is ever going to forget it.'

ALL OVER THE Celestial City, for each and every one of the candidates, time was now running out. It was the evening before the Imperial Examinations were scheduled to commence and on Willow Market Lane, Po Cheng was trying on his gown. The books over which he had toiled had all been put back on their shelves, leaving him with only what—once put to the test—he would still be able to remember.

'Of course you'll remember,' declared Precious Pearl. 'A handsome fellow like you, and in such a fine gown. Up with Candidate Po and down with the rest!'

How could he have come that far without her help? All the same, only he would be admitted to the Examination Hall, to be searched and scrutinized, on the assumption that every candidate, if not kept under constant surveillance, was sure to attempt to cheat. And after all of that, when the marks were given out, if he had not succeeded, he would have to bear, alone, the shame of having let them both down.

These concerns were cut short by the sudden sombre tolling of the Thunder Drum. Was there a fire? Had the river overflowed? They rushed down the creaking staircase to the kitchen, where they found Old Gentleman Lü already in tears.

'It's the death knell,' sobbed Lü. 'I heard it once before, when I was still a child. That was the last time an emperor died.'

Student Pang returned early from the Green Monkey and he had more news. The Emperor had fallen ill shortly after consuming his favourite dish: horse liver and onions. The liver had been eaten raw but still warm from the heat of the creature from which it had only a few moments earlier been removed.

'How sad for everyone concerned,' Po Cheng remarked, sombrely.

'And for the horse as well,' Precious Pearl reminded them.

The streets, Pang reported, were full of people wandering about aimlessly, as if sleepwalking, all with nothing to do and nowhere to go. Notices would have been prepared in advance—and hence had gone up within moments of the Emperor's demise—banning all entertainments, all shows, all forms of gambling, any sort of athletic contest, group singing, kite flying and exercising in public. Also, Pang revealed, a warning had been issued to keep an eye on the elderly and to prevent them, by all possible means, from committing suicide.

'And we should keep a watch on Old Lü,' Pang suggested. 'Just for a few days. Just to be on the safe side.'

'But why?' argued Precious Pearl. 'Lü, in his entire life, probably never exchanged a single word with the Emperor.'

'Because it's enough,'—it was Po Cheng who answered her question—'in the case of a sovereign, simply to know that he exists.'

So it was agreed that they would take it in turns to check up on Lü from time to time. Sensible or not, the old fellow was a creature of habit, and set in his ways, and so might choose—rather than to throw in his lot with a new devil— to try his luck in the Life Beyond with the one that he knew.

17

INTERREGNUM | HEAVEN'S SONS, EARTH'S SOVEREIGNS
| STAGNATION | IT GROWS ON THE RIVERBANK |
SOME SEE IT ONE WAY, OTHERS BEG TO DIFFER |
BAMBOO IS REPAIRED, AS USUAL, WITH BAMBOO

No expense had been spared. The deceased Emperor had been placed in his tomb standing upright, in a hunting chariot, with his favourite dog and a pet monkey beside him. In train had gone a camel, a rhinoceros, a cook, a barber, a dancing girl and the physician who had immediately rushed to His Highness's bedside but had failed to revive him.

'As an official,' Landlord Lü expounded, 'one never imagines that one will ever be in a position to mourn one's sovereign. One rather hopes that the opposite might one day be the case.'

Po Cheng, while feeling sorry for the old gentleman, nevertheless had good reason to feel sorry for himself as well. Given the parlous situation of the country at that moment, the Imperial Examinations for which he had been so painstakingly preparing had been set aside, postponed indefinitely, with the candidates having been instructed to return home, to continue with their studies there and to keep out of trouble until such time as they were summoned back.

So now what? He felt as though he had once more been set adrift. On the one hand, an immense weight had been lifted from his shoulders but at the same time a carpet had been pulled out from under his feet.

'Never mind,' recommended Precious Pearl. 'We'll get by somehow. And who knows, we may well look back on these days as having been the happiest and most carefree of our lives.'

They tried simply walking the largely deserted streets but there was little joy to be had from this, as they encountered the same police notice on the door of every shop that they passed:

ESTABLISHMENT CLOSED
UNTIL FURTHER NOTICE
BY GRIEF!

They also spent more time in bed together but only to come up against another wall. They teased, they toyed with one another, their former solo practices having evolved into shared practices, but this was no time, they agreed, to be throwing caution to the winds.

'Surely this won't last forever, dear friend,' predicted Precious Pearl. 'At least one hopes not.'

Landlord Lü, meanwhile, had returned to being his old self again and was seemingly resigned to the fact that the next occupant of the Peacock Throne was likely to be either a woman or a half-grown boy. Evidence was the new motto which he had nailed to the wall in the kitchen:

ALLOW EVERY STEP
TO BECOME AN ARRIVAL!

The knock on the door of the room which Po Cheng was now quite openly sharing with Precious Pearl came just when she was reading to him from *Death Stalks the Purple Lotus Pavilion*. Although by no means expected, the visitor was not for that reason unwelcome.

'Pardon the intrusion,' apologized Wang Tzu, 'but I don't suppose you'll mind if I unroll my mat here for a night or two.'

Precious Pearl, who would have heard much by this time of the old rascal's exploits, at once made him feel at home. Having assigned him to a place on the floor, she then slipped out, descended to the kitchen and soon returned with a plate of snacks, not wishing any guest of theirs to go to sleep on an empty stomach.

'Much obliged,' acknowledged Wang Tzu, digging in. 'Meals, lately, for entertainers, have been few and far between.'

'And if people don't stick together at a time like this,' Precious Pearl replied, 'when will they ever catch up with the other animals?'

Po Cheng could not help but admire how she was able to turn what might have been awkward into a mere inconvenience. When it was time for going to bed, she first said that she would count to three; next, having extinguished the lamp, she got out of her clothes, climbed into the bed in which she had become a fixture and pulled up the quilt, all before Wang Tzu's possibly still sharp eyes had time to become accustomed to the dark.

THERE WAS NO mystery behind Wang Tzu's sudden appearance back on Willow Market Lane. With all entertainments having been banned and therefore no bookings in prospect, the Small Fulness Theatre Company had fallen on hard times and been forced to disband. With all of their costumes having been seized by the landlord of an inn in lieu of payment, the actors—whom Po Cheng knew only as Owl, Deer, Monkey, Bear and Tiger—had gone their separate ways, leaving the Widow Wen to return home with her cart and Wang Tzu once more at loose ends.

'What bad luck,' sympathized Precious Pearl. 'As a theatrical impresario, I suppose you once had the world by the tail.'

'Only to be left holding nothing but the tail, dear lady.'

As the city's markets were nearly bare by now, Wang Tzu showed them where on the riverbank they might find edible plants. Once they had got the hang of this, they spread out, and so returned afterwards with wild chives, garlic, celery, ferns, plantain, mugwort, mallow and cocklebur, all of which went into that evening's soup.

'Tomorrow,' promised Precious Pearl, 'I'll try for a rotten cabbage. That, at least, ought to be possible to chew.'

Landlord Lü had spent that day scavenging for news. Lady Yao, it was now known, upon realizing that the Emperor was on his way out, had bent over him with a handkerchief in order to catch his final breath. There were conflicting versions, however, of just what she had done with the aforementioned handkerchief afterwards.

'The last breath,' Lü expounded, 'was once believed to contain the soul of the deceased, and given that someone still believes that, there might be two reasons why they would wish to possess it.'

Firstly, as Lady Yao's supporters claimed, she might merely wish to employ the handkerchief as a talisman, as something which, in the form of an undergarment, her son could wear in constant contact with his skin. Or she may already, as her enemies alleged, have set fire to the handkerchief in order to avoid the possibility of her being revisited later by a vengeful ghost.

'Who knows, in such cases, what to believe?' pronounced Lü. 'Not knowing the water, it's best to keep one foot on the bank.'

The official investigation into the events surrounding the Emperor's untimely death had uncovered nothing untoward. The liver consumed by His Late Highness had been taken from a living animal and served without a sauce and could therefore not possibly have been poisoned. This did not, of course, satisfy those who had their knives out, as it were, for Lady Yao, who argued that the investigation ought not to have been undertaken by her own brother.

'Factions!' the Old Gentleman snorted. 'They're the bane of government.'

The law of succession was unambiguous. Regardless of who the mother might be, the boy was his father's son. The fruit came from the tree, not from the basket. Nonetheless, and regardless of what it was that was under discussion, opinions on it all too often turned out—in government—to be divisible by two.

THOSE WHO TOILED within the confines of the Inner City did so in mysterious ways, out of sight of the populace as a whole, who could but await patiently the outcome of those dark proceedings. So it was announced, but only in due course, that all was well again, that normality had been restored, that the Little Luminary had been installed on the Peacock Throne, that Lady Yao had been named the Lady Regent and that the new reign which was commencing had been designated as the *Era of Protracted Prosperity*.

Overnight the Celestial City came back to life. By morning the police notices on the doors of the shops had all vanished, torn to bits, as Po Cheng imagined, by a populace which had grieved for long enough and as a whole didn't greatly care who was now on the Peacock Throne, just so long as someone was, and that life as they had known it could go on.

And go on it did. The markets were once more buzzing with activity, entertainers were once again performing on the riverbank, and on the river itself, and easy to pick out amidst the barges, were the usual, garishly painted pleasure boats, with their brocade sails.

'*Protracted prosperity*!' mocked Student Pang. 'Business as usual, I'd call it. The rich will carry on getting richer and the poor, by comparison, poorer.'

'Why not wait and see?' suggested Precious Pearl. 'Might prosperity not perhaps turn out to be contagious?'

The first of the current residents of the Celestial Harmony Lodging House to benefit from the new era was Wang Tzu. He would no longer be a burden to them, he announced one evening, as he had obtained a post as a doorman at an establishment called the Blue Heaven Pavilion, and included as part of his remuneration was a bed on the premises.

'And you're aware, I suppose,' said Po Cheng, disapprovingly, 'that the Blue Heaven Pavilion is a brothel?'

'I'm aware of what I'm aware. My post is on the door and it's my job to keep out the riffraff.'

Of course they wished him well in this new undertaking. Saying goodbye to a guest was always difficult and Precious Pearl, in order to delay their farewell, asked Wang Tzu how —after being a boxer—he had then come to work as a doorman in the Examination Hall in so forlorn a place as Bright Prospect Town.

'You may well ask, dear lady. It was all on account of a scoundrel called Bulldog Ma, who had been posing at the time as my best friend … .'

Part of the story Po Cheng had already heard. Ma, having wearied of putting on a ridiculous boxing show each night, had decided to take the Military Examination and become a soldier, and poor Wang, rather than be parted from his childhood friend, had decided to take the examination as well but only to be turned away at the door.

'For insolence, dear lady. For having imagined that I was tall enough to be a soldier.'

'How unfair,' agreed Precious Pearl. 'Surely you might have come in handy for something?'

But Wang's luck had not been all bad. Having been refused entrance to the Examination Hall, the ex-pugilist had ended up instead with the job of refusing entrance to others. They all smiled at this, savouring the irony of it.

'Just one more thing,' Precious Pearl persisted. 'How did you come by the title of "master"? Is that not generally reserved for individuals in possession of esoteric knowledge who go about disturbing the peace?'

The old scallywag didn't answer at once. Had she managed to corner him? Their guest carefully rolled up his mat and then secured it with a cord.

'It is an embarrassment to have to say so myself, dear lady, but I could spot with just a glance what it would have taken an entire company of examiners all day to discover. And no ifs, ands or buts about it afterwards. I could send someone packing simply by raising my eyebrows.'

'A happy attainment indeed,' Precious Pearl conceded, 'for a doorman.'

'And the Chief Examiner must have thought so as well. I can still recall, in fact, exactly what he said to me.'

'Then by all means, esteemed guest, let us in on it.'

And hence, as recalled by their departing guest:

Excellent work, doorman. Carry on. You're a real master, Wang, at what little you do.

THE MYSTERIES OF the Inner City, fortunately, were not completely mysterious to Old Gentleman Lü. The government was being reconstituted, beginning with the lower echelons, which meant that distant relations of the Yao family would be coming out of the woodwork in every corner of the Empire and all descending on the capital to stake their claims.

'Like pigs to the trough,' paraphrased Lü. 'It's a vulgar expression but apropos.'

The higher the position, the more difficult the decision. To whom were favours owed; from whom were they likely to be needed in the future? Complicating matters was the cancellation of the Imperial Examinations, which meant a dearth of new graduates, a shortage of fresh faces, of individuals with untapped potential and of impeccable character who sought office in order to be useful to others and not merely with an eye towards feathering their own nests.

'Individuals as yet untainted,' Student Pang commented, 'by the actual practice of government.'

The names of those newly appointed to government

appeared each day on the city's noticeboards and the list was read religiously even by those who had no reason in the world to imagine that their own names might appear on it.

'Perhaps,' suggested Pang, 'they're hoping for a misprint.'

How demoralizing it was to read those lists! With so many undoubtedly incompetent people being appointed to the government, Po Cheng agonized, what chance did anyone of true worth have of getting a foot in the door, much less a seat at a desk?

Goods of all sorts were once more reaching the city from the countryside. Even farmers were in line for prosperity and without having to wait for their names to appear on any list. A farmer simply got up in the morning and went to work, Po Cheng imagined, and when his work day was over he penned his ox, gathered in his chickens, scratched his pig behind the ears, whistled for his dog, greeted his children affectionately and climbed into bed afterwards beside his wife with only one thing on his mind.

These idle and somewhat bad-tempered musings were interrupted by Precious Pearl, who returned from the street with her face flushed and out of breath. Had she been in a race? Had someone been chasing her?

'Shall I tell you straight out, dear friend,' she gasped, 'or would you like to try to guess first?'

'I'm in no mood for riddles, so please speak plainly.'

'Well for a start, my parents may well end up being proud of me after all.'

'It couldn't happen to a nicer person. Proud of you for what?'

'Proud of me when they find out that I've been exchanging sexual favours with no less a personage than the next commissioner of the Southern Suburb!'

18

ALLIANCE | HEAVEN'S PROMISES, EARTH'S PRACTICES
| NO MERE PASSING FANCY | A GANG OF TWO | AT
HOME ON GOVERNMENT ROW | HE SWINGS THE
SATCHEL, SHE TAKES POSSESSION

As a commissioner, Po Cheng learned from Landlord Lü, he
would be on a salary of five hundred cash a year, plus a
house on Government Row, a travel allowance, three new
robes, logs in the winter and a cake of ice during each of the
three summer months. The old gentleman, however, also
issued him with a warning: a commissioner who set up
house with a 'wife' to whom he was not in fact married
would be asking for trouble.

'My own experience in such matters is limited,' Lü
conceded, 'but what's generally spoken of as marital bliss, if
carried out beyond the bounds of matrimony, is liable to be
labelled as carnality.'

They wasted no time. Neither the bride nor the groom had to be dragged to the altar, nor was there in fact any altar, merely a magistrate seated at a desk before whom the couple stood and made their vows, each testifying to a love that was sincere and promising to watch the other one grow old.

For the celebration, Student Pang had reserved a corner of the Green Monkey Tavern. There were streamers, banners, a choice of barley or sorghum beer, and a veritable mountain of sun-and-moon cakes. The greatest surprise of the day was when Wang Tzu arrived, having brought with him, from the Blue Heaven Pavilion, an all-girl bell-and-whistle orchestra.

The bride's whole-body sash had been prepared by the students of the Forest of Brushes Academy. Once put in place by Director Chan, the sash fell from Precious Pearl's left shoulder down to her right hip, and she pirouetted several times so that everyone could admire the pair of love-birds painted on the front as well as the motto which had been stencilled on the back:

GIVEN TO PO CHENG BY HEAVEN!

Pang, as the Master of Ceremonies for the day, had duly provided the couple with a Pillow Book, a manual which would guide them through that part of the ceremony which was to take place in private, in an upstairs room of the tavern.

'My word!' exclaimed Precious Pearl once they were alone. 'What explicit illustrations!'

'Indeed,' agreed Po Cheng. 'One wonders, moreover, whether such practices are even possible.'

'Or only possible, perhaps, with prior training.'

The first instructions were for the male, for whom the

recommended rhythm was four short thrusts followed by a deep one. This sequence was to be repeated as many times as was necessary, with the male—if he was a gentleman— holding back his own ejaculation until he had heard the female's five sighs.

'So will you do the counting,' asked Precious Pearl, facetiously, 'or will I?'

They had to laugh again the next morning when they realized that Student Pang had at some point slipped away from the party which was continuing on the floor below, and placed the following notice on their door:

MAN AT WORK!
DO NOT DISTURB!

GOODBYE, GOODBYE! HAVING packed up their modest possessions and loaded them into a handcart, they had then to say farewell to the Celestial Harmony Lodging House. Glancing back from the end of Willow Market Lane, they could see that Landlord Lü was still watching them from his doorway, with his hands tucked in the sleeves of his robe, but had he himself not predicted this? Every step that the newlyweds took after this was indeed going to be an arrival.

Together they pushed the cart along Willow Market Avenue, up the slope of Magpie Bridge, and then down the other side, leaving behind the hovels and the garrets of the Willow Market Quarter, with its smell of latrines and its rutted, pounded-earth streets. And how much easier it was to roll a cart—they couldn't help but notice—over neatly cut and carefully laid cobblestones.

Government Row was lined on both sides with modest but well-kept houses, each with a wicker gate, a garden, a fish pond and a cage containing a songbird in its front window. All very peaceful, Precious Pearl observed, all very tasteful.

'If you get bored,' Po Cheng suggested, 'you can always take up a hobby.'

The house which had been assigned to them appeared to have been vacated in some haste. Not only had the previous occupant left all manner of possessions behind but the poor bird in the window had simply been abandoned and was lying dead in the bottom of its cage. In the kitchen, food had been left to spoil, suggesting that the whole place was in need of a thorough cleaning, even if Po Cheng, had it been his decision alone, might nevertheless have preferred to commence their new life together by unpacking his books.

'I'll get started scrubbing,' Precious Pearl proposed, 'if you'll go for water and give that poor bird a decent burial.'

'Ah. And where's Funeral Director Pang when we need him?'

On Willow Market Lane a single well had sufficed for all and sundry, whereas on Government Row—perhaps in order to prevent some deranged individual from poisoning the entire government in one fell swoop—each of the households had a well of its own. The well supplying the household of the Commissioner of the Southern Suburb was a small wooden structure almost completely overgrown with ivy. While picturesque enough, the well did not inspire Po Cheng with any confidence and he stood there for some time staring down into its dark depths.

'Where's that water?' sounded his wife's voice from the house.

'On its way, my dear.'

He lowered the bucket cautiously until he heard a splash. Using the rusty crank, he then drew the bucket back up slowly, taking care that it didn't bump against the sides and loosen anything that might have been clinging to them. There were any number of tales, he seemed to recall, of individuals who were not so scrupulous when drawing water from a strange well and who were appalled afterwards by what they found in the bucket.

HE HAD BEEN advised by Old Gentleman Lü that he ought not to be dismayed when he discovered, upon taking up his first post, that he was already six months behind in his work. This simply made it all the more imperative that he arrive early and leave late; then, even if unable to recover any lost ground, he might hope by means of long hours and unceasing effort to avoid falling any further behind.

The robe of a district commissioner was green with brass trimmings.

'What an imposing husband!' Precious Pearl pronounced, approvingly. 'But you'll need to take care, because green shows the lint.'

His slippers were also green and so too was his satchel. Everything had been laid out the evening before and he was therefore able to set off from Government Row that first morning properly dressed and in good time, even if still munching on his morning cake.

The Yamen, the suburb's fortress-like seat of government, was at once a courthouse, a jailhouse, a library, an archive, a consulate, a beehive of small offices, a warren of corridors, and host in its many over-crowded waiting rooms to any number of distraught, desperate, despairing and quite possibly dangerous complainants. And how could it have been otherwise when the Southern Suburb was by some distance the least prosperous of the city's suburbs and so the most prone to contention, minor litigation, petty jealousies and the making of mountains out of molehills?

The new commissioner, as he sought his office that first morning, found the corridors congested with clearly displeased individuals including but not limited to: office seekers, timeservers, careerists, sycophants, persons passed over for promotion, wives of husbands who had deserted them, husbands of wives who had gone home to their parents and people who had simply come to the wrong floor.

The first thing that he noticed when he reached his office was that there was a bell mounted on the wall, and he at once rang it in order to find out what it was for. Within moments he was joined there by a large, square-jawed individual who introduced himself as First Secretary Chow.

'And now that I know how to summon you, Chow, what's your function in this madhouse?'

'This and that, Your Excellency. I keep an eye on things.'

'In which case, First Secretary, you can perhaps inform me of the circumstances surrounding the precipitate departure of my predecessor.'

'I could, Sir. But why not let the sleeping dog lie?'

'Because the fellow left a mess behind on Government Row, that's why, and perhaps he did the same thing here.'

'Quite frankly,' the First Secretary confided, 'the poor fellow wasn't up to the job and when he found out that he was being replaced, he took it badly.'

'Please go on, Chow. I'm all ears.'

'He was disconsolate. He remained at his desk until everyone else had gone home for the night, and then he killed himself by swallowing venomous spiders.'

'At *this* desk, Chow? The very desk at which I'm at this moment seated?'

'You needn't fret, Excellency, not over the spiders. I myself carried out a search afterwards for any that might have escaped.'

THERE WAS MUCH to learn, starting with the division of labour which existed within the Yamen. In order to deal efficiently with the myriad matters which arose each day in the Southern Suburb, responsibility was delegated to a small army of clerks, each of whom had his own tiny cubbyhole of an office and his own circumscribed sphere of interest, his own private preserve upon which no other clerk would have dared to poach. Not even the Commissioner himself, as a result, could have expected to obtain any useful information pertaining to roofs and chimneys, for instance, from the clerk in charge of cellars and drains or vice versa.

In Po Cheng's own office, in addition to numerous drawers and shelves, there were three capacious baskets on the floor beside his desk, each already full to overflowing. According to the labels affixed to them, these baskets held, respectively, documents relating to *Affairs Awaiting Assessment*, *Affairs Out To Consultation* and *Affairs Under Advisement*. Such fine distinctions, applied to what was more broadly speaking merely unfinished business, reminded the Commissioner of something which he had heard once about the Northern Barbarians, namely that they required some half a dozen terms in order to say all that needed to be said about snow.

Also on hand under the roof of the Yamen, with its generously overhanging eaves, were countless scribes, copyists, hall porters, door porters and runners. These last-named individuals—who took pride in going about bare-legged all year round—were there to ensure that any directive emanating from the Yamen was distributed in a timely fashion throughout the streets and avenues of the suburb, as well as down its every lane and alleyway.

With so much to be seen to within the Yamen, it could not help but be a relief to Po Cheng, when he returned to Government Row in the evening, to find that Precious

Pearl, far from being idle, had been occupied with making that little house their own. The garden had been weeded, peonies had been planted, and there was once more a live canary in the birdcage.

'Excellent!' Po Cheng congratulated his wife. 'Only our books on the bookshelves, our clothes in the wardrobe, and foods of which we ourselves are fond in the pantry.'

The days may have been long for them both but they were still young and it was not uncommon, after their evening meal, for one or the other of them to suggest an early night, albeit with no intention of going straight to sleep. As they were now man and wife, there was no longer any need to hold back or for any measured practices apart from those recommended in the Pillow Book.

Every coming together of the Male and the Female, according to that exemplary work, ought to be a full conjunction, one consonant with the interplay of night and day, the constant turning of the seasons and the continued presence, under Heaven, of something rather than nothing.

In the course of human couplings, they read, it was essential for each yin note to resonate with each yang note, and in practice, and with a little goodwill, this was easily enough achieved. Initially the yang, the male force, might be allowed to come to the fore, after which a rest was quite often taken; following on from this, in order for the yin, the female force, to predominate, and the balance of the Cosmos to be restored, it was then just a matter of turning the pancake.

十九
19

GOVERNANCE | HEAVEN'S HOLD, EARTH'S
CUNNING |HE TIGHTENS THE REINS | HOW ONE
CONSULTS A SUPERIOR | A STRANGE FISH INDEED!
| THE SON OF HEAVEN PUTS HIS FOOT DOWN

Before anything else it was necessary that the Yamen itself should be up to scratch.

It was scarcely surprising that amidst all of the coming and going in the corridors there should be evidence of various lax procedures and corrupt practices but Po Cheng was dismayed to find that these were not in fact the exception but the rule.

Wherever he cast his eye, he found dark efficiency to be at work, which was to say, that shameful system which enabled those with the means to pay a 'surcharge' to expedite their business, while leaving those without such means to cool their heels in a crowded waiting room, or to spend hours down on their haunches—and in tears—in the corridor outside someone's office.

'This simply won't do, Chow,' the Commissioner informed his second-in-command. 'We're here to serve all of the people and not just those who are prepared to tip well.'

'Of course everyone needs to be served, Excellency, but in what order?'

The obvious place to begin was with the door porters. It was their responsibility to ensure that all those entering the Yamen did so in a calm and dignified manner but their own threatening and high-handed behaviour had the opposite effect, as it produced unnecessary anxiety and fostered unseemly grovelling.

'Door porters are a law unto themselves,' Chow agreed, 'but you can't just dismiss them. People would then enter the Yamen willy-nilly.'

'All the same, Chow, we have to start somewhere and we'll begin with their motto.'

What was not said in so many words, experience taught, could be just as persuasive—and perhaps even more so—than what had been ever-so-painstakingly spelled out. In the case of the door porters, the motto which they had the gall to display, and where no one seeking to enter the Yamen could fail to notice it, read as follows:

FOR THE WHEEL TO TURN,
IT NEEDS TO BE OILED!

Language was a powerful tool but at the same time really quite flexible. By altering only a few characters of the offending motto, Po Cheng was able to deliver a warning not just to the door porters but to everyone else on the payroll of the Yamen:

IF EACH MINNOW STEALS A PITTANCE,
HOW MUCH WILL THE WHALE STEAL?

Word of this was likely to be disseminated by the hall porters, whose own corrupt practice entailed escorting clients from one office to another by the longest possible route, so 'earning' for themselves a handsome gratuity.

The copyists too would benefit from having their sails trimmed. Although of higher rank than the porters, they were equally venal and perfectly willing—should it be made worth their while—to read 'guilty' and write 'not guilty', to miscopy 'culpable' as 'capable', or, with the touch of a brush, to turn 'Ching' into 'Chang'.

Better educated still were the clerks, who from their cubbyholes controlled the flow of information so essential to the ongoing business of the Yamen. How unfortunate if even a clerk might be suborned, as was commonly believed, and induced to discover a document not previously known to have existed or, conversely, to be unable to locate one that was right under his nose.

It would nevertheless be a mistake, the Commissioner was warned by his First Secretary, to try to take on the clerks, as they were not the sort of individuals who were easily cowed.

'They stick together, Your Excellency. They may appear to be timid and retiring but should danger threaten they'll simply switch around the nameplates on their doors.'

THE DAYS WERE growing shorter but so too, strangely, were the nights. Scarcely would Po Cheng have covered the canary's cage with a cloth, extinguished the lamp and climbed into bed beside his wife, than the Thunder Drum would sound and another day would have commenced.

There was no hiatus, no time for rest, as each day followed hard on the heels of the one before, leaving the Commissioner to wonder, at times, as he was crossing Magpie Bridge, whether he was coming or going, on his way to the Yamen or on his way back to Government Row.

Autumn was in the air again and preparations for it were everywhere under way. Autumn, he read in the copy of *Monthly Ordinances* which First Secretary Chow had left on his desk, was the season of flowing essence, of cool winds and white dawns, of hairy creatures, of setting traps for eels, of fish swimming upstream, of south-flying birds and of insects stopping up the entrances to their holes with mud.

Inside the Yamen, he was no longer feeling his way and so had begun to put brush to parchment and compose his first memorial, a memorandum addressed directly to the Lady Regent. He described how, for three seasons of the year, boats and barges and even sea-going ships arrived each day in the Southern Suburb to deliver their cargo to the quarter's many warehouses, granaries, cellars and silos. A great number of sturdy people with broad backs and weight-bearing legs—and all wearing flat caps—were required to unload these vessels and naturally those people required accommodation, and so had developed the suburb's many narrow lanes and pestilent alleyways.

> *In summer, Your Ladyship, in such accommodation, it's difficult to sleep owing to the heat, the dust and the voracious mosquitoes; in winter, one is kept awake by the whistling of the wind under one's door and the crackling of the paper windowpanes.*

He knew whereof he spoke. He himself had experienced such hardships, albeit while at the same time running up a bill at the All-Needs Stationery Shop, the Ready-in-a-Jiffy Noodle Bar and the Green Monkey Tavern.

> *What's more, there's no work to be had in the winter. Entire families feed only on scraps and on dregs scraped from the bottom of empty wine barrels. Well might it be said of our otherwise splendid city, Your Ladyship, that the poor are its pigs.*

Only at this point, when taking stock of what he had written so far, did the Commissioner realize that he was in fact composing that memorial in the form of an eight-legged treatise. Did this not prove the point that there was nothing, once learned, which might not one day come in handy?

He struggled for a time with the final leg, the one in which interrogative sentences were permitted. One ought to close a memorial, just as any other treatise, with something likely to stick in the minds of all who read it:

> *And should one fall behind in one's rent, even by so much as a single day? Is it fair for the door of one's house to be removed, so permitting children, domestic animals and the aged to wander off, and allowing thieves to enter at will? Ought even one's swine, Your Ladyship, to be held in so little regard?*

NOTHING GENERATED MORE complaints from the residents of the Southern Suburb than did the tricks played on them in the district's fish markets, tricks such as sewing the head of a fish which was dear onto the body of a fish which was not, one which, with its proper head attached could have been had for a pittance. Such allegations, the clerk charged with investigating such matters argued, were most likely to be the work of troublemakers, malcontents or people who were mentally ill.

'As if only disturbed people,' thought Po Cheng, 'expect not to be cheated!'

The Commissioner, as a lesson to the clerks, announced that he would look into the matter himself and he wasted no time in doing so. He paid a visit that very day, while still in his robe of office, to one of the markets in question and announced that he wished to purchase a fish with the body of a carp and the face of a bream.

What consternation! What a commotion behind the counter of that establishment!

'But sir, Your Excellency,' someone managed to babble, 'no such creatures exist.'

'Precisely! So please make sure that none ever turn up here again in the future.'

He had not gone far afterwards before he realized that he was now being followed. Even after increasing his pace, he could still hear the footsteps just behind him.

'Slow down, can't you?' a familiar voice pleaded. 'There's no need to run me ragged.'

Li Ting! Three meals a day at the government's expense had enabled the fellow to put on a bit of weight since their last meeting but he still bore on his face—even if it was now slightly faded by the sun—the tell-tale tattoo of a convict.

'What gives, Li? Time off for good behaviour?'

Not exactly. Amnesties had been handed out to mark a new era of government but as none had come his way, Li Ting admitted, he had found it necessary to employ his own previous experience as a government official in order to forge one.

'Good work, Li. And you couldn't have appeared at a

more propitious time, as I'm very much in need of someone like you.'

'That's good of you to say, Commissioner, but with this face … .'

'With just that face! If people look away rather than acknowledge you, so much the better.'

For keeping an eye on things within the Yamen, there was First Secretary Chow, who was turning out to be a real bloodhound when it came to sniffing out corruption, and who better than Li Ting for keeping an eye on affairs outside the Yamen? Respectable people might well look at him askance and give him a wide berth, whereas less law-abiding individuals would no doubt welcome him as one of their own.

'You'll be worth your weight in gold,' Po Cheng assured Li Ting. 'You'll be the eyes in the back of my head.'

Worth his weight in gold but all the same—they were agreed—it would be best, in order not to arouse any suspicions with regard to his appointment, if he commenced on a porter's salary.

WINTER, AS DETAILED in the *Monthly Ordinances*, was the season for shelled creatures, for burrowing animals, for windblown snow, for protecting tender plants, for redeeming one's padded clothing and fur-lined caps, for moving the chairs of the elderly closer to the fire, and for bored children to be made to cut out paper snowflakes. Winter was also the season, that was to say, if precautions were not taken, when children were in danger of falling through the ice on the river.

Po Cheng, with winter now knocking at the door, was still awaiting a reply to the memorial which he had sent off some months earlier to the Lady Regent and he was hence greatly heartened when a runner arrived with the news that Her Ladyship wished to see him immediately on a matter of the utmost urgency.

'Ah!' he gloated. 'So she's finally read it, and the rest will be history.'

A sedan chair was waiting to convey him to that gate of the Inner City reserved for officials of low-to-middling rank. A well-manicured walkway then took him to the Bright Hall, an immense edifice capped with a magnificent, incandescent dome.

'No filthy canals or rowdy markets here,' he noted, so as to be able to describe the Inner City to Precious Pearl afterwards. 'No feral cats or snarling dogs, no beggars, tramps or untidy children.'

From without, the Bright Hall took his breath away. Upon entering, however, he at once observed that its brilliance was achieved by means of but a single oil lamp, the trick being that the walls were lined with mirrors, each one of which not only reflected the light cast by the lamp but also enhanced it and directed it upwards into the dome.

'Come in, Commissioner,' Lady Yao greeted him. 'I'll be brief, so you needn't go to the trouble of being seated.'

It was the boy, she complained, her son, the Little Luminary. Far from being grateful for all that she had done for him, he was already bored with sitting on a throne and welcoming the seasons, which he was declaring to be, in any case, unnecessary.

'Boys will be boys,' Po Cheng sympathized. 'That's what distinguishes a son from a daughter.'

'Perhaps as a rule,' retorted the Lady Regent, 'boys will be boys, but not the son of Heaven!'

Until now His Small Highness had led a sheltered life and so been largely unaware of the brutal realities of other people's lives but Lady Yao had a plan by means of which that could be changed. It was time for the Little Luminary to be introduced to the people, in her view, and the people to the Little Luminary.

'What's required is a tour. A Grand Tour, needless to say.'

'An excellent plan, Your Ladyship. And needless to say, I wish you well.'

'You'll do more than that, Commissioner. The boy put his foot down. The Son of Heaven, he says, will go on the Tour only if you come as well.'

This was clearly not a request but an order. All the same, no tour could take place before spring, the season in which —among other things—the roads dried out.

'And my memorial, Your Ladyship?' Po Cheng hazarded.

'Yes, of course. And what was it that you called it?'

'*Defeating Poverty, Deflating Privilege*, Your Ladyship.'

'Indeed, and let me give you a word of advice. In the future, when championing the cause of the poor, you would do well to bear in mind on whose toes you might be stepping.'

20

ARTIFICE | HEAVEN'S LIGHTS, EARTH'S ILLUMINATIONS | LEAVING IT TO CHANCE WON'T DO | ALTHOUGH SEPARATED, THEY GAZE UP AT THE SAME MOON | A CLAY COW LOWS, A WOODEN HORSE WHINNIES

With the first sign that winter was waning, there was a sudden rush on all things green: green flags, green clothing, green parasols, as if spring had never before followed winter, and people had therefore been taken completely by surprise. Spring, as characterized in the *Monthly Ordinances*, was bright and expanding; it was the season for plants to blossom, for birds to nest, for dormant creatures to return to life and for moles—upon emerging from their dark burrows—to be transformed into quail.

Inside the Yamen of the Southern Suburb, the iron fetters of the prisoners incarcerated there had been loosened and every second individual being held on remand had been released. Of those set free, however, a good number had subsequently been re-arrested, on compassionate grounds, having been found wandering the streets aimlessly and with no idea of where their next meal was going to come from.

Li Ting's first report was on the subject of rumour-mongers, who had not ceased spreading the story that the death of the late Emperor had been brought about by foul play. Even if the Emperor's last meal of raw liver had not been poisoned directly, it was argued, might not someone with access to the royal stables have poisoned one of the horses, little by little, knowing that the poison would in due course come to be concentrated in the animal's entrails?

Preparations for the Grand Tour were meanwhile proceeding apace. A new Royal Carriage had been ordered to replace the one now buried in the Royal Necropolis, and a team of horses matched as to colour and gait had been selected to pull it. Less happily, a list had been posted of those who were to be included in the Royal Entourage, and several of those whose names did not appear on the list, according to Li, had thrown themselves into wells.

'What's that old saying?' Po Cheng heard himself saying. 'That to make an omelette, one must first break a few eggs?'

Things were falling into line. Road menders had been sent out from the capital to put right the damage done by winter's frosts and spring's floods, and to rebuild, if necessary, any roads which had been washed away completely. Accompanying them were stonemasons, whose job it was to replace the milestones which people had carted away to use for shoring up their walls.

Whatever information reached him during the day, the Commissioner was in the habit of passing on in the evening to his wife. Their practice, before enjoying their own meal, was to stand side by side in front of the birdcage, feeding the canary its evening meal seed by seed, and comparing notes on any occurrences of which either had become aware.

'And Marshal Yao hasn't been idle either, far from it. He's been clearing away all troublemakers living along the route.'

'How presumptuous,' Precious Pearl remarked. 'What a nerve that fellow must have.'

'It's called protective custody. It's in order to save them from their own worst instincts.'

He hid nothing from her, nor did she begrudge him her opinions. There was also a plan in place which called for any village which had been rebellious in the past to be evacuated entirely on the day that the Imperial party was expected to pass through it.

'And what way is that, dear husband, to show the sovereign to his people?'

'It's called keeping the peace. Rebellious people will be carted off for the day but the idea is to replace them with other people.'

'What a song and dance!' pronounced Precious Pearl. 'Moving some people out only to replace them with others.'

'With more congenial people,' Po Cheng clarified.

GOODBYE, GOODBYE! THE day had come, and they said their farewells at the wicker gate in front of the dear little house on Government Row.

The peonies would soon be in flower but Commissioner Po had other things on his mind that day. He had been summoned from his cosy home—and this ought not to be forgotten—by no less a personage than His Small Highness the Son of Heaven.

'How hard this will be to bear,' predicted Precious Pearl. 'We must try not to forget each other.'

'If absence makes a heart grow fonder,' Po Cheng assured her, 'then mine will surely burst.'

He noticed, when crossing Magpie Bridge, that the river was still in spate. And was this not also the case in government, beneath the surface of which unseen currents also ran? Currents so powerful, he imagined, that even the strongest swimmer was at their mercy and could but wait— once having chosen to enter that stream—to discover where, in the end, he would be cast up.

His assigned place was not inside the Royal Carriage but atop it, aloft, beside the coachman, who was a somewhat surly looking fellow but nevertheless greeted the Commissioner with a complicitous smile.

'Never mind, Your Excellency. One gets a better view from up here and there's nothing worse on a long journey than being cooped up with a crabby child.'

So they were off, leaving the Celestial City behind them, and how pleasant it was, on that superb spring day, to breathe the country air again and to be free of the carping of those who complained that the Tour would be far too costly, that it would accomplish nothing, and how, in any case, could it be called a 'Grand' Tour, given that they themselves had been excluded?

Even a hard seat on such an occasion was better than none, and how peaceful to hear only the clip-clop of the carriage horses. Eventually, however, the sound of dogs barking warned that they were now approaching a village and that it was time to get down to work.

'Guardsmen!' Lady Yao called from the window of the carriage: 'Front and centre!'

The procedure had been carefully rehearsed. A company of Imperial Guardsmen armed with long bamboo poles was to enter the village first in order to police the crowd which would no doubt by this time be lining the road. The Little Luminary, meanwhile, was also receiving his orders from the Lady Regent.

'Remember what we practised. Sit up straight, smile, wave and appear to be enjoying yourself.'

And all of this for what? All of the preparations, all of the expense, and if that first village was any indication of what was to follow, they might as well have saved themselves the trouble. The carriage moved through the village at a walk, and Lady Yao, by the time it reached the other end, was livid.

'Am I to understand that that's a crowd?' she raged. 'Three filthy children and a mangy dog?'

The procedure would clearly need to be changed and the officer in charge of the guardsmen was so informed. Upon approaching the next village, a company of guardsmen would again be sent forward with bamboo poles but their orders had been altered: their task would no longer be to take control of a crowd but to round one up.

THE BOY, THE Little Luminary, remained, for the most part, a puzzle. It was impossible, for instance, to tell how old he was or why he spoke to no one apart from his mother, and then only in a whisper. Was he afraid of being overheard? What did he have to say that needed to be kept secret or that anyone else might possibly have wanted to overhear? Why, for that matter, would he not have preferred to sit atop the carriage, closer to the horses—boys being boys—rather than remain cooped up inside beside his mother?

'Give him to me,' suggested the surly coachman, 'for just one week and not even his own mother would recognize him afterwards.'

'Not much chance of that,' remarked Po Cheng, 'although it's good of you to offer.'

There was on that first day of the Tour, after the daily quota of villages had been visited, a curious interlude. The coachman was ordered by the Lady Regent to leave the road and pull up beside a rice paddy in which a dozen or so quite stunning young women were bent over planting the most delicate of shoots. Even more surprising was that, as soon as they realized that they had an audience, they at once burst into song:

BEND AND STRAIGHTEN, STRAIGHTEN AND BEND;
WHEN WILL THIS MISERY EVER COME TO AN END?

It was a fine performance, delivered in what appeared to be a real rice paddy, of what for all Po Cheng knew might be a genuine work song, but the women, with their sweet singing voices, were surely not what they seemed.

'Who but an actress,' he pointed out to the coachman, 'before turning up for work in a rice paddy, would have gone to the trouble of shaving her legs?'

'And who cares if they're actresses?' demanded the coachman, belligerently. 'Aren't actresses all the more likely to be free-and-easy?'

Awaiting the party at the end of that first day's progress was the Travelling Pavilion, an immense marquee whose many chambers would provide the members of the party—taking into account their respective ranks—with all the comforts of home. Po Cheng, once established in a chamber suited to a district commissioner, set to work at once writing a letter to his wife:

The show is now on the road, my dear. Today the Little Luminary was exposed to the people for the first time, and vice versa, with mixed success ... .

He had to write quickly, before the final courier of the day set off from the Travelling Pavilion for the capital. He said nothing about the actresses or about their reputation as being free-and-easy, lest this occasion unnecessary alarm:

> *Tomorrow the boy will face his first test, when he's invited to plough the first furrow on what is to be a field of sorghum, something for which he has been practising for several weeks apparently, in one of the Inner City flower gardens, using a toy trowel … .*

A gong sounded in the distance, signalling the courier's imminent departure:

> *It remains but to hint at what cannot be said in so many words, my love, in a letter which may be perused by others. Namely, as you will in any case know very well by now, just what else is on my mind when you are!*

EACH NEW DAY commenced within the Travelling Pavilion with the sound of the court eunuchs going about their morning chores. Fires had to be lit and water heated for the Little Luminary's daybreak ablutions; clothing suitable for both the season of the year and the day of the week would meanwhile have been ironed and laid out so that there would be no last-minute confusion—or tantrums—over just what the Little Luminary would be wearing when he exited the pavilion and came beneath the gaze of Heaven.

Grooms each day examined the horses and tackle, looking not just for any wear-and-tear but also for any damage brought about by misuse, carelessness, inattention or maliciousness. Beaters armed with probes and pitchforks would be sent ahead to inspect the roadside ditches on that day's route and a forester with a powerful crossbow to shoot down any birds of ill omen which he found nesting in the surrounding trees.

For breakfast there were trays of buns still warm from the kitchen, and steaming buckets of tea, but there was no hanging about. Anyone who fell behind during the course of the Tour, the Lady Regent had proclaimed, would be *left* behind. So it was assured that taking to the road early each morning would be the same motley train of coaches, sedan chairs, buggies, sulkies, hay wagons and dog-carts.

Only the house eunuchs remained behind, their task being to dismantle the Travelling Pavilion, sweep up any debris and fill in the latrines. Then they would race ahead in order to prepare another encampment, one identical in every detail to the one of the night before, thus lulling the travellers into believing that they were, and would remain, no more than a single day's journey from the capital.

The actresses meanwhile created another sort of illusion. Each day they appeared someplace along the route, although never in the same role twice. Now they were to be seen picking mulberry leaves and now dyeing cloth, weaving mats, reeling silk, doing their washing on a riverbank or digging for clams. There was nothing at which an actress would baulk, Po Cheng concluded, just so long as she got noticed.

And what would the boy conclude when he saw through this deception? When he realized that these weavers, these pickers, these washerwomen, were the same women every time, and all engaged in what was essentially the same task, albeit with innumerable changes of clothing? Might he not, for instance, be tempted by the consoling—but surely erroneous—belief that *all* was illusion?

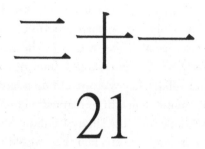

21

PERSEVERANCE | HEAVEN'S CONSTANCY, EARTH'S
CAPRICES | ADVISEMENT: IT PAYS TO TRIM THE SAILS
| WHAT THE CAT DRAGGED IN | THE CONFESSIONS
OF LADY YAO

The Imperial party was in actual fact now a great distance
from the capital, expenses would as a result be spiralling, and
what had the Lady Regent to show for it? Had any hearts,
for instance, as yet been won over? Ought then the
Commissioner to remain aloof and simply enjoy the
landscape stretched out before him or ought he rather to
follow the ancient tradition which required that an official,
in the interest of good government, offer useful advice, if he
had any, to the sovereign of his day?

He waited until her son was otherwise occupied—
watching attentively as the actresses stretched up to pick figs
—before ever so cautiously approaching the Lady Regent.

'Please pardon the intrusion, Your Ladyship, but I've been giving some thought to what benefits might accrue from our making a few economies. Letting a few people go, for a start.'

'And just what benefits do you see accruing from that, Commissioner?'

'There will be fewer mouths to feed, for one thing. And a smaller party will raise less dust.'

The actresses, Po Cheng argued, would be only too pleased to be sent back to the capital, as they had been complaining for some time now of over-exposure: so much time spent under a hot sun, they feared, was ruining their complexions.

'Very well then, and who else?'

What need was there for acrobats or weight-lifters, or for a dog-cart full of clowns whose antics the Little Luminary had long since ceased to find amusing? And what about the court ladies—the poor things!—who were suffering agonies as a result of being improperly dressed? Although it had been spring already when the party set out from the Celestial City, those fine ladies had packed only padded vests and woollen undergarments, thinking that—beyond the walls of the capital—it would still be winter.

'It's clear that you've been keeping yourself busy, Commissioner. But could we at least retain the eunuchs?'

'Half of them, Your Ladyship. The other half came along just to keep the first half company.'

Lady Yao was nothing if not decisive, and it was a greatly diminished force which set out the following morning from the Travelling Pavilion, one consisting of only the Royal Carriage, a supply wagon, the mobile kitchen, a portable smithy and a rolling latrine.

Also following, but well back, was an additional

conveyance, or at any rate one which Po Cheng had not previously noticed.

'Ah,' he remarked to the coachman. 'A mortuary wagon. So that's not just a myth?'

No it was not. The Lady Regent and her son, before leaving the Celestial City, the coachman revealed, had been measured up for coffins, just in case, the boy having been told that he was being fitted for a new set of clothing.

'A sensible precaution, I suppose,' the Commissioner concurred. 'Any number of things might come to pass on the road and one's rank would no longer be any protection.'

'And what about us?' demanded the surly coachman. 'Where are our coffins, if rank will cease to matter?'

'An interesting conjecture, my dear fellow. But as for me, I can't imagine that I'd mind much, one way or the other, what became of my remains.'

'Well I would!' contradicted the coachman. 'Life is bad enough, and death is likely to be even worse, so why must one be submitted, in between, to being picked apart piece by piece by crows?'

THE MUCH-REDUCED royal party, as it was moving faster, was also covering more ground and people were now lining the roadside of their own accord in order to wave cheerfully to the diminutive Son of Heaven as he passed. These were simple people, who rather than ape the dress or customs of the city had stuck to their own ways. Hence the men still wore tortoise shells for their head covering, and the women sedge caps. Commissioner Po, in a letter to his wife, described the situation thus:

> These people have had no previous contact with the government, have neither asked for nor expected any favours

from any such entity and hence have as yet to be let down. Being so far away from the stove, as one might say, they have not yet had their hands burned.

Even by a fast horse, letters from the Travelling Pavilion now took several days to reach the Celestial City and so were somewhat cold comfort for anyone anxiously awaiting news of an absent loved one. Precious Pearl, writing to her husband from their once-shared abode on Government Row, summed this up with a poem:

SHE YEARNS FOR HIM IN THE NORTH,
AS HE PINES FOR HER IN THE SOUTH.

A communication of another sort reached the Commissioner but not in the pouch of a government courier. The document bore signs of having passed through many hands prior to its being handed to its intended recipient surreptitiously by a shifty-eyed individual with the tell-tale tattoo on his forehead of someone once convicted of being a swindler: *Not to be trusted!*

It was a report from Li Ting chronicling recent events in the capital. The prolonged absence of the Lady Regent had brought a number of rats out of their holes, it seemed, and Marshal Yao had taken it upon himself to order a clamp-down. The benefit of the doubt had been suspended and anyone seen to be stepping out of line was immediately taken into custody and obliged to attend remedial classes in civility.

Li was nothing if not thorough and had done his homework on the subject. Such highhandedness on the part of the police was not unprecedented, he reported, but had been employed in order to still dissent in past times as well, under the rubric of: *Sweeping away dust before it can settle.*

Po Cheng, while disturbed by what was taking place back in the capital, had no choice but to keep his thoughts to himself. The Travelling Pavilion, after all, was no more than a glorified tent and its walls were thin. Government was not, moreover, all clear sailing: how could it be when not everyone ever wanted to go in the same direction, and ought one then to be surprised, when in government, if one was left, on occasion, not knowing whether to laugh or to cry?

SOMEWHERE ALONG THEIR route, there had ceased to be any road signs. What need was there for any, Po Cheng speculated, when there were no longer any junctions and therefore only two directions in which to travel, either in the direction in which they were heading or else in that from which they had come?

Nor were there any milestones, nor any need for them, he further supposed, as the people now to be met with seemed perfectly content to continue living out their lives in whatever village or hamlet they had chanced to be born and therefore had no need to know how far it was to anywhere else.

The road itself had by now been reduced to little more than a pair of ruts, and so sparse must have been the traffic that small vegetable gardens had here and there been planted in between those ruts. It was on the whole a bucolic scene, one which suggested to Po Cheng both the simplicity with which the first peoples on Earth had lived, as well as the conceivable outcome of some great cataclysm which would return said peoples to just such said simplicity.

For the Little Luminary, mercifully, what had begun as a somewhat tedious chore now turned into a really fine adventure. His attitude changed when an old man appeared one day in the middle of the road and stopped the carriage horses dead in their tracks simply by pointing a finger at them. Before any of the guardsmen could react, this clearly mad fellow approached the Royal Carriage, reached in through the open window and presented His Small Highness with what he claimed was a numinous mushroom.

There was no concealing the boy's joy at this gift. Unable to get him to give it up afterwards, Lady Yao at least succeeded in getting him to wash off the soil that was still clinging to it. And this was just the start: there were many such deluded individuals about and the boy was soon in possession of a fox with two heads, some dragon bones, a finger drum, phoenix droppings and a large egg to which an old woman was said to have given birth—at the cost of her own life—after having inadvertently stepped into an immense footprint.

As there were no longer any palace ladies about to look after the Little Luminary in the evenings, that task now fell to Po Cheng, who watched with great interest as the boy brought out his collection of artefacts—which was increasing day by day—and proceeded to organize them into what the casual observer might well have seen as a mere procession but to the former schoolmaster seemed to indicate the boy's attempt to understand those strange objects and perhaps even to create a taxonomy.

The longer that it went on, the more certain Po Cheng became that this was more than just a game. The boy was never satisfied with the arrangement of the objects, however they were aligned, and so kept rearranging them, exchanging one with another, nor was this surprising given that such disparate items surely defied any definitive ordering.

Once a teacher, always a teacher, and Po Cheng could not leave this alone. Perhaps he was reading too much into what he saw as the Little Luminary's attempt to impose order on what was by its very nature disorderly and confused, but might the boy not move on from this, if given proper instruction and encouragement, and one day become, for instance, a world-renowned ethnologist?

There was also the problem created by His Small Highness's stubborn silence, the source of which remained a mystery. So what prevented Po Cheng, as a commissioner, and as he now had the ear of the sovereign, from putting an oar in? Could he not suggest to the Lady Regent that her son's somewhat tardy development might be sped up if he were permitted to converse more freely with others?

'Tardy?' Her glare was a thing to behold. Anyone of lesser rank than himself, Po Cheng imagined, might have been dissolved on the spot. 'As in turning up late for school?'

'A student turning up late for school, Your Ladyship, usually arrives with a note.'

'Yes, of course. A note from his mother. Taking upon herself, I suppose, all of the blame.'

Lady Yao, once she had calmed down, described the Little Luminary as having been a cheerful child to begin with, one who had indeed spoken freely to everyone. The palace ladies in particular had doted on him, as had the court eunuchs, and no mention was ever made of how long he seemed to be taking to grow up.

'It was just one of those things,' the Lady Regent hastily added. 'There are, as everyone knows, no hard-and-fast rules. Some boys might shoot up outrageously but not all do.'

The Little Luminary had grown at his own pace, remaining cheerful and talkative throughout. As the only child at court, he had on the one hand been fussed over and on the other spared any onerous comparisons, until one day when a young ruffian climbed over the wall of the Inner

City and was discovered by the Little Luminary in the act of stealing cherries from the Imperial Cherry Orchard. Words had been exchanged, according to Lady Yao, and the future Son of Heaven, who had until then encountered only adults, had come off much the worse.

'Not even I know just what was said, only that it had something to do with his voice not yet having changed.'

'Ah, his voice had yet to break. And that's been stuck in his mind ever since?'

'Precisely. So will that do for a note, Commissioner?'

TRUTH BE TOLD, he would miss the Travelling Pavilion with its copper lamps, animal-shaped braziers, silver salvers, teak furnishings, silk screens and delightful hanging scrolls. All the same the time had come to call a halt, to declare the Tour to have been a signal success and to return to the Celestial City with all haste and with all flags flying.

To celebrate the successful culmination of the Tour, the Lady Regent packed her son off to his bed early and ordered that a decanter of cherry brandy be brought out from the stores. She then sat herself down on the travelling replica of the Peacock Throne and kicked off her slippers.

'I hope you don't think this an imposition,' she then addressed the Commissioner of the Southern Suburb, 'but would you mind terribly, as you've sent almost everyone else home, rubbing my feet?'

These were not the dainty, slippered feet of a palace lady, useful only for tripping lightly over parquet floors. These were sturdy feet, somewhat swollen feet, but nonetheless still serviceable, if need be, for walking over stones or trudging through mud, and this lent credence—to Po Cheng's mind —to the story which Lady Yao then proceeded to tell of her own humble beginnings in the countryside.

'Poverty was all that we knew. Just imagine, my dear Commissioner, an entire family supported by a vegetable patch scarcely larger than a tablecloth, not that any of us would have known at the time just what was meant by a tablecloth.'

She paused while their two cups were filled with cherry brandy from a heron-neck decanter. Many a night, Lady Yao recalled, she and her brother had gone to bed hungry and dreamt of sitting down to a tasty meal, only to find when they awoke that it was their bedclothes which they had been gnawing on.

So they had made no objection when informed by their parents that they had been sold to a recruiter and were to be taken to the capital and taught a useful trade.

'In fact, we were excited. All of those people, and all of them on their way somewhere … .'

Po Cheng nodded in recognition, remembering his own first impression of the Celestial City. The brandy, meanwhile, had been going down a treat, and Lady Yao herself, without bothering to summon a eunuch, refilled their cups.

'The place to which we were taken was called the Early Spring Teahouse, and that was when we started to become suspicious. Rather than being given food straight away, as we had expected, we were instead given baths.'

It was, and it wasn't, a teahouse. It was a teahouse on the ground floor and another establishment altogether on the floor above. The new arrivals, after being scrubbed down and scented, were at once put on display and allowed to eat only after completing what was considered—in such a shameless establishment—to be a good day's work.

'Both of you?' queried Po Cheng. 'Your brother as well?'

'And have you never heard, dear Commissioner, of the pleasures-of-the-back-courtyard?'

How had they survived such humiliation, such degradation? By closing their eyes, answered Lady Yao, and thinking of food. So it came to pass that having become hardened to practices which, had they remained in the countryside, they would in all probability never have imagined, they themselves later turned their hands to the lucrative business of finding girls for teahouses and teahouses for girls.

'One never knows,' reflected the Lady Regent, who was perhaps by this time a little tipsy, 'just how things truly stand. Just what will turn out to be advantageous and what won't.'

'But that night, Your Ladyship, when you confronted the Emperor, as it were, in his own lair … .'

'No need to remind me, not that I've ever denied it.'

That notorious night when she had been smuggled by her brother into the Inner City to conjoin with the aged and still childless Son of Heaven, and was able to provide him afterwards—by dint of sheer determination—with what Heaven itself had until then denied him.

'You have my sympathy, Your Ladyship. Not everyone finds so many obstacles in their path. But you know what people say.'

'People say many things, Commissioner, most of which is sheer nonsense.'

'About a river, isn't it?' Po Cheng, too, was beginning to have trouble keeping his thoughts in order. 'About how a river, for all its twists and turns, eventually finds its way to the sea.'

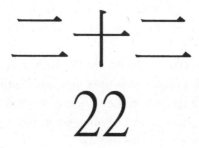

22

PROLIFERATION | HEAVEN GRANTS IT, EARTH NOURISHES IT | OF MINGLED ESSENCES | BROUGHT FORTH BY SUSTAINED EFFORT | A FOOT-LONG CHILD WRAPPED IN THREE FEET OF CLOTH

Although difficult to weigh or to measure, there was nevertheless considerable reason to believe, in the case of the Little Luminary, that the Tour had done him a power of good. While it was too much to ask that he should have become talkative again overnight, he was now the custodian of objects which were neither toys nor souvenirs, not mere personal possessions but rather relics, markers, items indicative of the mentality and beliefs of peoples who—metaphorically speaking—still dwelt a long way from the fire.

The boy's intention now, according to Lady Yao, was to use one of the palace ovens to try to hatch the giant egg from which he had, ever since receiving it, become quite inseparable. As for the Son of Heaven having grown taller on the journey, as she sought to maintain, Po Cheng thought it more likely that the little fellow had simply ceased to slouch.

The undertaking, in any case, had not been the utter disaster that many had predicted and perhaps had even hoped that it would be. The Lady Regent's enemies had thus been confounded, and Po Cheng, as he once more crossed Magpie Bridge, could look forward to relaxing that evening in an armchair which bore his own imprint.

As soon as he turned into Government Row, he saw his wife waiting for him at their wicker gate. The peonies may have been beyond their best but Precious Pearl appeared perfectly radiant, as if she had only at that moment burst into bloom.

'My dear husband,' she said softly, touching him lightly on the arm.

'The same,' he teased. 'But there's no need to create such a scene.' Only when they were inside the house, and with the door closed behind them, did they embrace. It seemed to Po Cheng, however, a somewhat awkward embrace and Precious Pearl almost at once broke it off.

'What is it?' asked the Commissioner. 'What's happened? We weren't like this before.'

'No we weren't but you had best sit down. I might have told you in a letter but I thought that it would be better face to face.'

Po Cheng sank into his favourite armchair, which did indeed fit him like a glove. 'There. I'm sitting comfortably, so you can now speak frankly.'

'And what a relief it is to do so! In your absence, dear husband, nature has taken its course and we must therefore prepare to welcome a little lodger.'

While they had not planned for this, neither had they

done anything to prevent it. What was most to be desired, both had tacitly assumed, was what occurred naturally, according to the way of things and consonant with the will of Heaven, and any plans were therefore best made afterwards, once the signs were clear.

The book which Precious Pearl had chosen in the Good Physician Pharmacy—and which was now to become their bedside reading—was entitled *Making Way for the Newcomer* and its first suggestion was that the prospective parents should remind themselves of just what it was that had attracted them to each other to begin with and so had brought them to this pass.

'Well,' began Precious Pearl, 'it didn't hurt, I suppose, that you were going to be on five hundred a year.'

'As for me,' Po Cheng in turn recalled, 'it was the way that you spread your rice out on your plate to cool before you ate it.'

'If only I had known! Who but a shallow person could have found a thing like that endearing?'

'All the same it's the truth, and it's still true. I could hardly think of anything else all the time I was away.'

IN THE YAMEN of the Southern Suburb, nothing had changed: the same documents were still awaiting attention, the same matters still pending and whatever business had been left unfinished at the time of the Commissioner's departure remained so.

The Grand Tour had not come cheap and the debts run up by the government in order to fund it meant that there were unlikely to be any funds available for anything else anytime soon. Hence the already hard-pressed residents of the suburb were to be left with no choice but to tighten the ropes with which they held up their trousers.

'All the same,' commiserated First Secretary Chow, 'it's good to have Your Excellency back at the helm.'

'That's good of you to say, Chow, but what price a helmsman if the ship's becalmed?'

His next meeting with Li Ting took place under one of the arches of Magpie Bridge, where they were unlikely to be overheard. In addition to making a clean sweep of dissent within the Celestial City, according to Li, Marshal Yao had taken advantage of his sister's absence to settle a number of old scores and his first target had been the city's brothels.

'And high time too, Li! What excellent news.'

'It might have been,' the former sub-prefect hedged, 'if any brothels had actually been shut down but it appears that they've merely been placed under new management.'

How pleasant, after the cares of the day, to return to Government Row in the evening and resume work on the preparations which were by now well under way for welcoming the newcomer. What had until then been Precious Pearl's sewing room was to be converted into a nursery, which meant painting the walls a cheerful colour, pasting up pictures of smiling animals and installing a fish-shaped cradle, as fish were known for the care which they took of their young.

They still made love. Not every night but sometimes, and somewhat less vigorously than before. On other nights, as the manual recommended, they lay side by side and spoke to the child of what lay ahead: autumn would be for rolling about in dead leaves, winter for fashioning snow animals, spring for flying a kite and summer for running about bare-legged.

'And if you're a boy,' Po Cheng promised, 'I'll teach you to whistle through your teeth.'

'And if you're a girl,' intoned Precious Pearl, 'I'll need to teach you not to.'

IN THE SOUTHERN Suburb, which was illuminated after dark only by the dim light of its all-night markets, carp were still being sold as bream, mutton as lamb and cats as rabbits. However hard he was willing to work, Po Cheng could not be everywhere at once or anywhere all of the time, and hopeful girls from the countryside were still being lured to the city by unscrupulous recruiters in the belief that they were to be employed as actresses, only to find out, when they arrived, that all of the actress positions were already filled.

No such shady practices, fortunately, disturbed the peace, by day or by night, on Government Row. In the Po household, the nursery was now ready for the newcomer, who would find there, as well as a fish-shaped cradle, a music box, a tiger's-head cap, the clay figure of a child riding on the back of a sea-horse and a pair of colourful wooden dragonflies. Also, mounted on the wall, compliments of Old Gentleman Lü, was what would be—as it was for all newcomers—the child's first motto:

LONG LIFE!

As the time to give birth drew near, the manual warned, the prospective parents of a first child were apt to become anxious about the outcome, and by dwelling too long on just what would need to be accomplished they might come to convince themselves that childbirth was in fact quite impossible. In such cases, the author recommended, the husband and wife should separate and the husband be sedated until such time as the procedure had been completed.

At the first sign that it might be time, Wang Tzu was summoned. He arrived from the Blue Heaven Pavilion, as had been agreed, accompanied by a midwife, or rather by someone who he introduced as a midwife but who Po

Cheng recognized at once as being none other than the Widow Wen, whom he had last seen taking tickets for the Small Fulness Theatre Company.

Not wishing to spread alarm, Po Cheng kept his doubts to himself until the two women had vanished into the kitchen and slid the door shut behind them.

'What's the meaning of this?' he then confronted Wang Tzu. 'Didn't you say, when that theatre company of yours broke up, that she had gone back to growing potatoes?'

'And so she did,' agreed the old man, nonchalantly. 'But then she decided that she couldn't live without me, and who was I to say any differently?'

'A touching story, but how dare you pretend that she's a midwife?'

'Calm down. She's learned on the job and where better to get her hands dirty than in a brothel?'

What was done, was done. Although far from satisfied, Po Cheng had no choice but to accept that Widow Wen—even without formal study—was likely to know a few useful things about a woman's inner apartments.

'Of course she does,' Wang Tzu concurred. 'And you can add to that all the time she's spent lifting potatoes without bruising them.'

HOW MUCH LONGER were they to be kept waiting? Commissioner Po passed the time anxiously pacing the floor and thinking back to all of the lists which he and his wife had made. Was there anything that they had forgotten, anything which they ought to have done but hadn't? Was that why it was taking so long? Now and again he interrupted his pacing to press his ear to the door of the kitchen in the hope of hearing something which would reveal just how far things had progressed.

'Settle down, can't you?' complained Wang Tzu. 'Wearing out the floorboards won't help any.'

The manual, which Po Cheng by this time knew by heart, had said something similar. The chief responsibility of the husband during the time that the wife was in labour was not to get in the way. A woman, it went on to say, was not a tender plant which required cossetting, despite what was widely believed. A woman was actually quite hearty.

This led the Commissioner to change the subject. Who better to provide the information which he was eager to obtain concerning the 'new management' of the Blue Heaven Pavilion, after all, than the doorman of that institution?

'It's true,' Wang Tzu confirmed. 'The fellow drops by every night to check up on things.'

'And that business about the masks?'

'That's true as well. He's wearing a different mask every night and I've got to pretend that I don't recognize him.'

What doubt could there be? Marshal Yao, the brother of the Lady Regent, the uncle of the Son of Heaven and the Chief of the Secret Police, was involved up to his neck in what one might be forgiven for thinking should have long since become a thing of the past.

At this point, however, a sudden loud cry coming from the kitchen brought Po Cheng's mind back to more immediate concerns. Whether it had been a cry of pain, of surprise or possibly of triumph, he was unable to say, but that ceased to matter once the kitchen door slid open and Widow Wen appeared, smiling and holding a small but well-wrapped bundle.

'Sincere congratulations,' she pronounced. 'It's a boy, Sir, and on your very first try.'

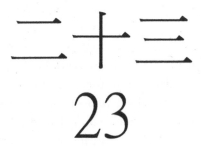

23

ENTRENCHMENT | HEAVEN'S PLAN, EARTHLY
PREFERENCES | PREDOMINANCE OF THE SMALL |
NOT BY ANY OTHER NAME | ALL ABOUT BRIDGES |
IT SEEKS THE FLAW

The first person to pay a visit to the newest member of the
Po family was Student Pang, who arrived in the sparkly robe
and matching slippers of a diviner, as this was no mere
courtesy call.

Pang was there to size up the newcomer and fit him
with a name and he went right to work, lifting the still-
bundled-up infant from the fish-shaped cradle in order to
give him a good going-over.

'Excellent,' Pang pronounced. 'An eye to each side and a
nose in the middle. A really top-notch specimen.'

He had brought along a star chart, an almanac and an
abacus but he began with just a length of string, using it to

measure the child's limbs, the width of his shoulders and the distance between the tip of his nose and his navel.

'Best not to leave these things to chance,' he explained. 'A poorly chosen name risks leaving the child open to ridicule.'

'And where did you learn that?' questioned Precious Pearl.

'In school,' replied Pang, without taking offence. 'It must have been on a day when I was paying attention.'

He then made a few calculations. His fingers flew over the beads of the abacus with the dexterity of a market trader or of a bookmaker taking bets on the annual Dragonboat Races. Choosing a name which tallied with the child's attributes, he went on to explain, would enable the new-comer to go from strength to strength and perhaps even to live up to the expectations of his parents.

Once he had finished doing his sums, Pang consulted the star chart and then the almanac, guided in this by the season, the suburb and the time of day of the boy's birth. The situation facing the child was likened by Pang to that of an athlete whose success or failure would depend not just on his physique and his prowess but also on the state of the game at the moment of his taking to the field.

Much to the relief of all concerned, the name which resulted from all of this rigmarole was 'Wu', a name which conjured up not only strength but also resistance and a refusal to run with the crowd.

'Address him as Little Wu to begin with,' Student Pang recommended. 'Then, once that starts to embarrass him, you can call him simply Wu.'

No sooner had the couple seen Pang out than they rushed back to the nursery and knelt down on either side of the cradle in order to put the seal, so to speak, on what had been done.

'Hello, Little Wu,' Precious Pearl cooed, maternally. 'It's so good to have you with us.'

'And the same goes for me as well,' Po Cheng seconded.

Not long after this another visitor appeared at their door, Old Gentleman Lü, who had brought a gift for the child to mark his naming day. It was—and they had to laugh—a book bearing the title of *The All-Under-Heaven Encyclopaedia*.

'I know it's rather soon,' Lü apologized, 'and you'll probably need to turn the pages for him … .'

The elderly scholar and lifelong bachelor was quite reluctant to visit the nursery but he was unable to resist Precious Pearl's prodding. He stood beside the cradle peering down, with his arms folded behind his back.

'But he's so tiny! How hard to believe that he'll one day be reading Confucius or puzzling over Mencius.'

Or, as the proverbial man unfamiliar with cherries was said to have remarked: 'What small apricots!'

NOTHING WOULD HAVE pleased the Commissioner more, while awaiting the release of further funds, than to be left to run the Yamen as best he could without them and then return each evening at a reasonable hour to Government Row in order to check on the progress of his son, who was, day by day, shooting up hand over fist. The last thing, therefore, that he would have wished for, was another summons to the Inner City.

'What do you suppose she wants this time, Chow?' he questioned his First Secretary. 'Ought I, for instance, to make my will first?'

'A will is never a bad idea, Excellency. Not for someone in your position.'

'And what position would that be, Chow?'

'When in government, Sir.'

These were mere pleasantries, gallows humour. Making a will would have taken too long, and the delay might well have sealed his fate as the summons indicated that Her Ladyship wished to see him on a matter of utmost urgency. So it was in no time at all that he found himself approaching a magnificent mahogany gate—the Gate of Exemplary Achievement—and once more entering the hallowed precincts of the Inner City.

'Urgency?' thought Po Cheng, surveying the largely tranquil scene spread out before him. 'What urgency?'

He might well have been looking at a painting, at some idealized portrait of life at court. Two rival groups of palace ladies, all with identical beehive hair-dos and butterfly-wing eyebrows, were having a snowball fight, watched over by a number of court scholars, all in fur-trimmed robes and with their hands tucked firmly into their sleeves.

Urgent? So where, then, was the fire? Inside the Bright Hall, just as on his previous visit, the Lady Regent was sitting bent over her desk, writing furiously, and studiously avoiding taking any notice of the fact that she was no longer alone.

'Don't trouble yourself, Your Ladyship,' Po Cheng thought out loud. 'It's only me.'

'Indeed. Only you. But there's no need to sell yourself short, Minister.'

'*Minister*, Your Ladyship?'

'Why so surprised? Am I not entitled—and above all as a woman—to surround myself with people who can be trusted?'

'How very flattering, Madame. On the other hand, I've only just got my feet under the table at the Yamen.'

'In which case you ought to be able to get them out again without any great difficulty.'

So this was the urgent matter. He had been summoned there not to be asked but to be informed of his having received a promotion, and his desk in the Yamen—he could easily imagine—would in all likelihood already have been cleared.

'And ought a person not to know his own limits?' Po Cheng pleaded. 'To aim too high, although I cannot recall at the moment who said it, is to be as far off the mark as to aim too low.'

'Nonsense. Whoever said that was obviously not in government and was probably just lazy.'

'But even in government, Your Ladyship, must one not walk before one can run?'

'Why make government sound more difficult than it is? Didn't you yourself not long since remark on how every river eventually reaches the sea? And what more need one know in order to run Bridges and Waterways?'

THIS THEN WAS government, at least as practised in the Celestial City. Having become adept at steering the Yamen of the Southern Suburb, Po Cheng, now a minister, found himself assigned to Bridges and Waterways, where he was likely to be looked upon by those already in place there not as a helmsman but rather as an upstart, a mere stowaway. Hence, when first entering the ministry, Po Cheng used a side entrance, stole up a little-used staircase, managed to locate his new office without asking for any directions and barricaded himself inside it.

Government looked after its own. The new office was more spacious, had more bookshelves and offered him a panoramic view of the city. In addition, whereas he had formerly been on five hundred cash a year, his salary would now be twice that, he would have the use of a sedan chair, and their plain wickerwork gate, back on Government Row, would be replaced with one of cherrywood.

It surely behoved him, whatever his reservations, to set to work at once bringing himself up to scratch on those subjects upon which he would need to appear knowledgeable. He studied the books on the wall, taking down a slender, well-thumbed volume whose title—*Kinds of Bridges*—suggested that this was a book written for novices.

There were few things more pleasurable for a man of letters than to be lost in a book. Time, for as long as one read with full attention, stood still, and yet, in one's mind, one was on the move, covering new ground, plumbing new depths. Po Cheng had until then crossed bridges as and when he came to them, without ever giving a thought to how they had been erected or why they remained standing, and this was no doubt a common enough failing but it was one which he now needed to correct.

The author began with the simplest sort of bridge, the so-called 'swaying bridge', which could be constructed at little cost using bamboo cables. For use in the mountains, where people travelled for the most part on foot, it was likely to be employed for crossing dangerous crevices or spanning bottomless gorges, thus allowing essential goods to reach even the most isolated communities, while at the same time—with its lateral movement—deterring frivolous people from making unnecessary journeys.

Where wheeled traffic could be expected, something more substantial and as a consequence more costly was required. Hence the 'flying bridge', which in order to keep it in place had to be supported at either end by a firm abutment. Such a bridge was stable and long lasting and could be made to pay for itself by charging a toll, something which was only possible, the author warned, if the population was not just prosperous but also of an even disposition.

Human beings, the reader was assured, were inventive, endlessly so, and for bridging rivers which frequently flooded, another solution had been found, namely the ingenious 'pier-and-beam' bridge, for which sturdy supports had first to be securely anchored on the riverbed, as the failure of even a single one of these piers would result in the entire bridge being rendered useless. Such bridges were also susceptible to the notorious wilfulness of water, as when a river abruptly changed its course, leaving the bridge which had formerly spanned it looking very foolish indeed.

'Ah so,' sighed Po Cheng, 'as in the sad case of Li Ting.'

Sadder still, in the author's view, was when a bridge simply went out of fashion. Such was the case of the graceful 'camel-hump' bridge, which was still celebrated by painters and poets and much admired by foreign dignitaries, but was generally considered by people in a rush to be far too narrow to be practical and so of use only to vagabonds, wandering monks or farmers with just one cow.

Po Cheng could hardly have been in greater agreement. Were ancient bridges, even if now obsolete, not still good to look at? Why could one day of the year, for instance, not be set aside for the viewing of such bridges?

'Fashionable or not,' Po Cheng vowed, 'my own policy will be unequivocal. So long as I'm the minister in charge of bridges, it will be of *all* bridges.'

ONLY WHEN THE book on bridges had been replaced on the shelf from which it had been taken did Po Cheng notice that he was by this time starting to feel quite peckish. Just as in his previous office, there was a bell mounted on the wall within easy reach of his desk, and he therefore took this opportunity to ring it and then waited to see how long it would be before anyone appeared.

It took, in fact, no time at all.

'You rang, Excellency?'

'Well, well, Chow! What a coincidence—isn't it?—that we've both been promoted.'

'Orders are orders, Sir. And that's always one's best alibi afterwards.'

'An alibi? Let's just hope that neither of us, afterwards, has any need to produce one.'

Chow nodded in agreement and was already on his way to the door to search out a tasty snack of steamed buns when the Minister called him back.

'Just one more thing, Chow. Just out of curiosity, what befell the person whose place I'm taking?'

'An unfortunate accident, Excellency, according to the logbook.'

Perhaps it was best not to dwell on such things but the topic had now been opened. The former minister, a hitherto respected figure, had apparently gone into a public latrine, locked the door behind him, accidently thrust three fingers down his throat and subsequently died of asphyxiation.

An accident? Really? Po Cheng stood at the window of what had become his own office looking out over the bustling city spread out below. On his desk, the snack which First Secretary Chow had rustled up for him remained untouched. Soon it would be spring, the ice would melt and traffic would once more be clogging up the waterways, so this was not the time, Po Cheng judged it necessary to remind himself, to be dwelling on the failures of others. Far better to go on just as he had done at the Yamen, learn what he still had as yet to learn and take as his motto that lightning struck only those with secret faults.

二十四

24

NARRATION | HEAVEN'S ORDINANCES, EARTH'S
REVISIONS | THE FIRST STEPS OF THE CHILD ARE
TAKEN BY ITS PARENTS | HOW YU STILLED THE
WATERS | STRANGE CREATURES INDEED, AND ALL
UNDER ONE ROOF!

They would not, they were agreed, make the mistake of filling Wu's head with nonsense which he would later on need to forget. He could be spared, for instance, the story of how an ogre living under Magpie Bridge roamed the streets of the Celestial City at night in search of disobedient children to roast over her fire. Also the tale of how a boy who picked his nose had grown a trunk. Also accounts of a moon-hare who appeared whenever the moon was full, bearing gifts for children whose behaviour had been exemplary.

All the same, like all boys, Wu was hungry for stories and was before long refusing to go to sleep at night until he had

heard one. Sooner or later, in any case, there was a story
which he would need to know by heart, a story which
might on the one hand be discarded as false but which—as
occurred with many such stories—became true once
regarded as poetry.

Wu had already taught himself to crawl and so was no
longer confined to his cradle. When it was bedtime he
would thus crawl across the floor, climb into his father's lap,
curl up and listen—until his eyes grew heavy—with rapt
attention.

'What a clever little chap he is,' reflected Po Cheng, with
admiration, 'and what a responsibility!'

The story which he was telling his son, bit by bit, night
after night, was an account of the hero Pan Gu and of how he
had brought about, inadvertently, the Great Differentiation.
In the beginning, it will be recalled, the world was empty, it
contained nothing in particular, and it was not until Pan Gu
got to his feet that Heaven and Earth became separated,
Heaven being lifted and Earth pressed down.

Then Pan Gu, who was made up of what was to become
the Ten Thousand Things, commenced the first of his
perambulations. Walking north, he created North, and
turning back South, and so too East and West. Hence the
Five Cardinal Directions, the fifth of which, the Centre,
being the hero himself.

'Wherever he lay down to sleep,' Po Cheng related,
'today there's a plain. Wherever he stopped to relieve
himself, that left behind a hill or in some cases a mountain.'

When the hero, as he grew older, began to drag his feet,
riverbeds were formed. His thirst, in the meantime, had
brought forth rain and there was soon water in the rivers for
him to drink, and it was then that his urine collected and
formed the sea.

The rest followed after Pan Gu's demise. One by one the myriad things began to appear on Earth and the story could thus be extended indefinitely, for as long as there was someone to listen.

'At the very moment when Pan Gu ceased breathing,' related Po Cheng, not in order to frighten the boy but simply to inform him, 'his breath became the wind. The same wind which blows on Earth to this day, rippling water, rustling leaves, and upon which kites soar in the springtime.'

THE BOOK TO which the Minister next turned—simply to inform himself—was the *Book of Yu*. Yu the Great was celebrated as both a sage and an engineer, and he was credited with being the first person to have tamed a raging river, which he accomplished not by seeking to arrest its flow but by observing the propensities of water. The essence of water, he realized, was not just to flow but to overflow, and once armed with this knowledge he was able to utilize the floodwaters which regularly inundated the countryside, and so bend Nature, as it were, to man's will.

Yu, as it was often expressed, had tamed a dragon. By anticipating the seasonal surges of the river, he was able to transform its destructive power into useful energy; by means of a chain of ditches and a network of canals, he was able to provide farmers with water for irrigating their fields and merchants with a calm and secure waterway for the conveyance of their goods. In order to carry out his work, Yu had invented locks, sluice gates, winches, water marshals, a dredging machine and weather forecasts, this last by posting lookouts in treehouses with orders to report at once any anomalies observed in the behaviour of birds.

Po Cheng once more read with keen interest. The story chronicled the ceaseless struggle between human invention and the persistence of water. The human armoury was soon augmented to include marking cords, levels, compasses, balance beams, squares, awls, grips, shovels, picks and ramrods for compacting the soil. Then, with the wheel, came carts and wagons, allowing the soil excavated from an irrigation ditch or a canal to be hauled away and employed for the construction of dikes by women suitably equipped with wicker baskets, sandals and sun hats.

Yu the Great had been thorough and had left no stone unturned. Great works, he taught, did not come about merely by chance, nor was their continued existence to be taken for granted. Things, if left unattended, soon fell apart. The dangers, for instance, which threatened packed-earth structures were itemized as subsidence, shifting sands, earth tremors, underground streams, tree roots and burrowing animals.

The battle was never over. Nature never surrendered, nor was the power of water ever likely to be harnessed once-and-for-all. Anticipating correctly that the water level in canals would drop in the hot months owing to evaporation, Yu ordered hilltop cisterns to be constructed. Also, as canal boats did not propel themselves, he urged the planting of willow trees on the banks of the canals so that those who were conscripted to trudge its towpaths, pulling boats loaded with grain, gravel, wood, charcoal, paving stones or barrels of wine, would at least be able to do so in the shade.

BASED ON THE experience gathered when they were both employed, once upon a time, as teachers in the same two-room, thatched-roof schoolhouse in a place called Nettle Village, the couple agreed on a plan for their son based on the premise that every child was unique. Wu would not be rushed, nor would he be held back, not so long as he was headed in the right direction. Under this tolerant regime, the boy showed every sign that he was flourishing; he moved on from crawling to walking completely of his own accord and he was soon to be found waiting at the new cherrywood gate in the evenings for his father to appear, and more often than not with a book tucked under his arm.

'I was just the same at his age,' Po Cheng confided to Precious Pearl. 'I would go about with a book under my arm so that everyone would think that I could read.'

Rather than the fully illustrated children's encyclopaedia gifted to him by his 'Uncle' Lü, which Wu pretended to have outgrown, what he carried about with him now was a battered copy of *Multiple Perils Survived*, a volume of adventure stories, a present from his 'Uncle' Pang, a work which, as a result of its having been read to him so often, he all but knew by heart.

'I worry,' confessed Precious Pearl. 'He gets so excited when he hears those stories.'

'And what if he does, my dear? Isn't that just the sort of book, at his age, that's likely to excite him into learning to read?'

Excitement could in any case not long be avoided. Just as the couple were preparing for bed one night, a sudden commotion could be heard as someone wrestled with the cherrywood gate, which sometimes stuck, and this was followed by a frantic knocking at their door.

'Tell them to go away,' urged Precious Pearl. 'Who comes calling at this hour?'

'Who indeed?' Po Cheng agreed. 'But ought we not to find out?'

He had never before seen anyone looking so distraught. The poor woman must have come running through the streets all the way from the Blue Heaven Pavilion, as she was out of breath and barely able to string together a coherent sentence.

'It's him, Sir!' gasped the Widow Wen. 'Wang Tzu! It's scandalous! And to think that I saw the whole thing!'

Po Cheng led her inside and Precious Pearl shut the door to the street so that the scandal—whatever it was— wouldn't be spread all up and down Government Row.

'Now then, dear lady, what was it that you saw? And please keep your voice down or you'll wake up Wu.'

'Begging your pardon, Sir, but where else was I to go? I've come to report a kidnapping.'

The story then spilled out. Hearing loud voices coming from the entrance of the brothel, she had looked from a window and seen Wang Tzu in conversation with two coarse-looking individuals who she at once took to be gangsters.

'It sometimes happens, Sir. It's a doorman's job to turn such people away.'

A midwife, on the other hand, had to be prepared to turn her hand to anything. Just when she was thinking of getting a cooking pot from the kitchen and going out herself to give those two thugs what for, she saw all three men moving off together—the two gangsters with Wang Tzu in between them.

'Ah,' acknowledged Po Cheng, calmly. 'A possible abduction. And was there a note?'

'A note, Sir? Wang Tzu can no more write than I can read.'

'A kidnap note. If he's been abducted, you'll need to pay to get him back.'

'Good heavens!' cried Widow Wen. 'It's true that we've managed to save a little money, Sir, but that was intended for something else entirely.'

Was this whole thing not slightly ridiculous? Po Cheng and Precious Pearl, once the old woman had been sent back to the Blue Heaven to wait for a kidnap note, could not agree.

'As for me,' said Precious Pearl, 'I find such late-blooming romances to be quite touching.'

Po Cheng promised, as they were getting into bed that night, that if Wang Tzu hadn't reappeared by the morning, he would make a few inquiries. Strictly speaking, however, street crime in the Southern Suburb was no longer within his jurisdiction.

'Naturally, if a crime has been committed, then it will need to be investigated but not by me. It's just a pity, that's to say, if the old fellow was indeed snatched, that it couldn't have been from a bridge or a waterway.'

IT WAS NOT just the Widow Wen who was beside herself with grief over the disappearance of Wang Tzu, with whom she was clearly smitten. First Son Wu, when he was told, also took it hard, no doubt owing to the habit which he had of calling the roll, so to speak, of his uncles and aunts whenever he got into any sort of difficulty: *Uncle Wang, Uncle Pang, Uncle Lü and Auntie Wen!* Only the boy himself, had he wished to, could have said why he did this, whether it was a prayer, a litany, an incantation, a curse or some hitherto unidentified method of his own devising for calling up the reserves.

The boy's despondency, as day after day passed with no further news as to the whereabouts of his Uncle Wang, was painful to behold. He no longer pestered Precious Pearl to be allowed to feed the goldfish in the garden pond, or the canary, whose cheerful chirping must have seemed to him—in the continued absence of Wang Tzu—to be in very poor taste.

Po Cheng, when he could no longer bear seeing the boy so gloomy, then had an idea.

'Here's what we'll do. We'll have an adventure of our own, just the three of us. In fact we'll make a whole day of it!'

Precious Pearl was put in charge of the provisions, which included green plums and a large bag of cherries. First Secretary Chow had secured the necessary permission for them and they were duly met at the door of the Imperial Menagerie by the Head Keeper, who admitted them to that facility using a large iron key.

'Keep a close eye on your parents,' the official warned Wu. 'Don't let them wander off on their own.'

Wu, who was not accustomed to being talked down to, was about to object but Precious Pearl silenced him by taking out a handkerchief and pretending that she was blowing his nose. Had it not been for her quick thinking, Po Cheng noted, they might—all three of them—have been sent packing.

The first room contained 'guest' animals. According to the signboard on the wall, these beasts had either been brought to the Celestial City as gifts by foreign ambassadors or else had arrived as stowaways in the caravans of merchants. Visitors were invited, after viewing the creatures on display, to reflect on the backwardness of countries in which such unsightly animals had not yet been hunted to extinction.

The next room was for animals which had been awarded medals. They viewed a pig whose frantic squeals had saved a sleeping family from a housefire, a dog that had saved a child from drowning, a cat which had chased off a highly venomous snake and a parrot which—by mimicking the sound made by its owners when they were quarrelling—had tricked a would-be burglar into thinking that they were still awake.

A three-foot rudder, that day, steered the ship. Wu raced from room to room, as if determined to disprove the belief that it was impossible to see all that there was to be seen in the Imperial Menagerie in a single visit. There were rooms for animals which were known only from their bones, for those generally found in the bottom of wells, those said to wax and wane with the phases of the moon, those mentioned in *The Classic of Mountains and Seas* and those which could be cooked in their shells.

The final room housed but a single animal. It lay with only its eyes showing above the surface of its pool but its gaze alone was sufficient to stop the party of intrepid adventurers in their tracks and to send shivers down their spines.

Precious Pearl read aloud from the signboard bearing the creature's motto:

THE CROCODILE:
IT DOESN'T PUT ON A SKIN, IT GROWS ONE.

The adventure was over. Even if there had been another room to visit, what would have been the point of carrying on? Seeing just the eyes of that creature had brought their imaginations into play and what had for a time distracted them from their preoccupation with the fate of Wang Tzu had in the end returned them to it, and with a vengeance. Eyeing that frightful reptile, how could they help but be reminded that Wang Tzu, at that very moment, might be mouldering away, half-digested, in the belly of just such a beast?

二十五

25

GROWTH | HEAVEN ORDAINED IT, EARTH TENDS IT
| SCHOOLING THE SOVEREIGN | THE RISE OF WU |
A TRAITOR IN THEIR MIDST | WATER THE ROOTS
AND SHAPE THE BRANCHES: A FINE TREE ONE DAY

Undisturbed by the unexplained disappearance of Wang Tzu,
the seasons turned as always, following their usual course.
The easeful months of brightness were once more fading
into the dark and brooding months of winter, in accord with
Heaven's plan, as seconded on Earth by the Son of Heaven
with his perpetual changes of clothing.

In the Ministry of Bridges and Waterways, all that needed
so urgently to be done if the country was to prosper, sad to
say, still remained to be done. The various directives issued
by the Minister to the water marshals had largely fallen on
deaf ears, as most of those individuals, rather than waiting
any longer to be paid, had by this time deserted their posts,

making a mockery of the bold lettering carved into the façade of the ministry:

WHEN THE RAINS STOP,
RESTORE THE CANALS!
WHEN THE RIVERS FALL,
REPAIR THE BRIDGES!

'What will people in the future say of us?' Po Cheng was thus left to ponder. 'That we took no heed of what we were sworn to uphold?'

Willingness, the Ancients had taught, was the one essential in government. All of the cleverness in the world, without willingness, wouldn't boil an egg. Willingness alone, on the other hand, without any fuel for the fire—so to say—would not even warm the water.

Various documents left by his predecessor revealed to the new minister that funds alone were not all that was lacking and that there was in fact no such thing as adequate funding. What was meant to take a year never took less than two years, what ought to have required a hundred workers was likely to keep several hundred occupied, and whatever sum was allocated for a project was hence bound to be nowhere near sufficient.

'*One never sees*'—Po Cheng made a note—'*the true peak of the mountain from the plain below.*'

The situation, he decided, was desperate enough to warrant his informing a superior, which was to say, to his composing another memorial to Lady Yao. The first tethering of a dragon by Yu the Great, he first reminded Her Ladyship, while it deserved to be applauded, ought not to be taken as definitive:

We must remain on guard, Your Ladyship. One is never out of the woods. Years of neglect may well produce decades of decline. Nor should the infrequency of dragon-sightings be taken as evidence that such creatures are extinct … .

The time to consider posterity, he went on to say, was when one was still in office. What would be one's legacy? How would one be remembered? Did one wish one's name to be forevermore linked to a flood, a typhoon, a landslide, to the collapse of a bridge or to the disappearance of a ship which had been swept so far out to sea as to be unable to find its way back to land?

FAR MORE REWARDING than the long hours which he spent each day at the ministry was the time he spent in the evenings hearing from Precious Pearl about the progress which had been made that day by their son. Wu had already taught himself how to count and so was making inroads into an understanding of the world about him: he kept count of how many seeds he fed to the canary, of how many people he saw passing the house each day, of how many times he could hop from one foot to the other without falling over, of how many more days had to pass before he could start school.

'On the other hand,' reported Precious Pearl, 'he can also be irritating. He no longer wants gruel for breakfast because he thinks that it's making him fat.'

'Compliance isn't everything,' Po Cheng said, defending the boy. 'I didn't like gruel at that age either and I'm now on a thousand a year.'

Like his father before him, Wu was also fond of games, including such rowdy games as kickball, pass-the-plum and beat-the-blind-donkey. Children living on Government Row were no more gentle with each other than children anywhere else and Wu often returned home sporting bruises on his arms and legs and rips in his clothing.

'And why must you always be the blind donkey?' Po Cheng quizzed him.

'Because it's better to be a blind donkey, father, than to beat one.'

There was also a game that the three of them played together in the evenings, one which they called Examination Day. Precious Pearl would first search the boy for any hidden notes, so preparing him for the times to come when he was likely to be searched by hands far less tender than her own.

'All clear,' she would then announce. 'This one must really know his stuff.'

The Chief Examiner would then take over, beginning with material with which the boy was well familiar. How what was clear and bright had formed Heaven, for instance, and what was heavy and torpid, Earth. There could be no doubt that Wu had all the makings of a scholar, as there was nothing that he liked better than to be asked a question and to hear the answer come tripping effortlessly off the tip of his tongue.

'And what did the first people see when they arrived, candidate?'

'Flowing rivers, father, and ocean waves crashing on the shore.'

'And when they looked up?' the Chief Examiner prompted.

'They saw that the sky was full of lights, father.'

'And what did they make of the sun?

'They thought that the sun was a yellow bird, father.'

'And the moon?'

'They likened it, father, to a magic frog.'

'And to what did they liken the stars?'
'The bright manifestations of Heaven's will, father.'

ACCORDING TO LI Ting, rather than the Celestial City becoming more civil subsequent to the crackdown instigated by Marshal Yao, it was less so. In addition to the factions already present in the city, new groups had formed, secret societies made up largely of people new to the city: tight-lipped people who met in secret, did their work in secret and communicated with one another—when necessary—using secret codes.

'How unpleasant, Li,' the Minister agreed, 'but what has that to do with Bridges and Waterways?'

'Nothing yet but perhaps we too should take a few precautions.'

Once again, the fellow's time spent as a convict came in handy. Convicts passed most of their time plotting how they might escape and thus needed to be able to communicate among themselves without the guards knowing what was being said. For this purpose, the simplest possible code had been devised, one which in fact required no coding or decoding but was nonetheless unbreakable.

So it was that the next note which Po Cheng received at the ministry read as follows:

ADJUSTING ONE'S CAP,
BUT FORGETTING ONE'S TROUSERS.

What made the code indecipherable by anyone apart from its intended recipient was that the message was not contained *within* the note but was rather activated by it. Whatever the text, the message from Li Ting to Po Cheng was this:

Meet me tonight at the usual place, at the usual time.

The usual place was under Magpie Bridge and the usual time, after dark. If they were overheard there at that hour, it would be only by the rats which had their burrows in the mud of the riverbank. As for what Li Ting had dug up this time, it made clear the need for such precautions.

'Very well, Li, spit it out. I'm all ears.'

Even as First Secretary Chow had been keeping an eye on things inside the ministry, Li Ting had himself been keeping an eye on Chow. Growing more and more suspicious, he had followed Chow one evening when he left the ministry and hence his suspicions had been confirmed. Instead of going home or to a brothel or to a gambling den, Chow went from the ministry each evening straight to his desk in the Bureau of Proper Proceedings and Public Decency.

'To the headquarters of the Secret Police, Li? But why would he do that?'

'To write a report. The person known to you as First Secretary Chow, as it happens, is in reality Sergeant First-Class Chow, a graduate of the Forest of Clubs Police Academy and one of Marshal Yao's most trusted operatives.'

'But that's appalling! And just when I was starting to trust the fellow!'

All the same, why should he have been surprised? Had he not always suspected that government was a dirty game and one best played with one's fingers crossed behind one's back?

'So what should I do, Li? Dismiss the fellow and send him away in disgrace?'

'Or else, by doing nothing at all,' advised the former sub-prefect, 'you could turn this around and use it to your own advantage. If you know that Chow is a spy, and so long as he doesn't know that you know, then you have him right where you want him.'

FOR WU, IT seemed, the seasons could hardly turn fast enough. He had of his own accord moved on from mere childish games, games played simply for the fun of it. He was no longer the blind puppy, playfully chasing his own tail. No matter the activity in which Wu was engaged, it was now carried out with the firm expectation that he would emerge from it victorious.

For someone like Wu, as a result, the First-Level Examination was a mere formality. This first trial weeded out only those who were obviously unsuited to school and so could be set to work immediately digging holes, lifting weighty loads, marching in formation or treading a waterwheel. So what must the examiners have made with a candidate of Wu's age who, when asked which subject he hoped to study, had had the temerity to reply, '*Cosmology, Sir.*'

Wu had been looking forward to his first day of school with great anticipation and perhaps for the same reason that Po Cheng and Precious Pearl, as the three of them left the house on the big day, were feeling somewhat anxious. There would be, from now on, a sizable portion of Wu's life which would be his alone, a portion of his life of which they themselves would know only as much as he chose to tell them.

'You'll always tell us everything, won't you?' Precious Pearl pleaded.

'Of course I will, mother,' Wu replied, a bit too readily in Po Cheng's opinion. 'You're my parents, aren't you?'

They accompanied him only as far as the cherrywood gate, as this was as far as he wanted them to come. He would know the way to the school. Most likely—being Wu—the boy would have practised walking the route. He may even have drawn himself a map.

They stayed at the gate watching until Wu had reached the end of Government Row and turned off into the city beyond. For his first day as a student, he had insisted on wearing his favourite dog-fur jacket, along with a tiger-head cap which was far too small for him by this time and so no longer able to contain his unruly tufts of hair.

'If only he could have dressed more neatly,' Precious Pearl lamented. 'What will the teacher make of him, turning up like that?'

'You're right, my love. First impressions are important. But in addition to making a mark with the teacher, he'll also need to hold his own in the playground.'

二十六

26

Wu took to school like a frog to a well. School was his element, the place where he felt at home and where his voice could resonate, but he was no stranger either to the playground and was soon making excursions further afield with his new-found friends. Hence the scandal of their having been caught climbing onto a barrel and peering through a window of the Forest of Brushes Academy of Art in order to see who was posing that day and in how much disarray.

Boys would be boys, and Wu was also curious about the riverbank, where cricket and grasshopper fights were staged and beetle races held, with each of the competing insects being harnessed to a tiny wagon. Such escapades, Po Cheng was convinced, were essential, as not everything that was useful to know was to be found in books, nor could it be taught in school.

'Boys will be boys,' Precious Pearl merely remarked, 'and so will men.'

What did worry them were the times when Wu—for no obvious reason—suddenly became quite sluggish. Boys of Wu's age, they knew, were apt to experience sudden bursts of growth, which might from time to time have sapped his strength, but no such prodigious growth was evident. Wu's own explanation was that life was boring, especially in the classroom, where he was constantly being made to sit and wait while the others caught up.

'This won't do,' Po Cheng one day decided. 'One doesn't become sluggish simply by looking at snails.'

The shop was called the Good Physician Pharmacy and he passed it every day going to and from work. There was a gourd above the door and a sign in the window boasting that the establishment had been in the hands of the same family, and trading from the same address, for more than three generations.

Having entered the shop, the Minister found himself confronted by a wall taken up entirely with small wooden drawers. Surely, in one of those drawers, there would be something that would keep Wu moving at his hitherto accustomed pace. Equally reassuring—for someone making his initial visit to such an establishment—was the motto prominently displayed above the counter:

ABSOLUTELY NO CHEATING!
NOT EVEN OF CHILDREN OR THE ELDERLY!

The proprietor listened closely to Po Cheng's description of his son's strange lethargy, nodding now and again as if to signify that this was nothing out of the ordinary. He then began opening various of the drawers, taking from them a pinch of this and a pinch of that and placing all of these mysterious substances into a large stone mortar.

'It's best to be thorough,' he explained. 'A Spring Tonic might be cheaper but an All-Season Tonic will go right on working.'

After pounding the mixture into a powder, the pharmacist used a paper funnel to pour the contents of the mortar into a porcelain jar on which was painted the figure of a famously mischievous cartoon cat. The creature was standing upright, on its hind legs, and wearing boxing gloves, and the balloon above its head read as follows:

> IF IT'S TENDER, CHEW IT UP!
> IF IT'S TOUGH, SPIT IT OUT!

That was medicine for you. If the tonic had been intended for an adult, the Minister supposed, it would have come accompanied by an endorsement from a dragon-boat racer or an all-in wrestler. A medicine, clearly, derived its strength from being not one thing but many, an amalgam, a fine mix of the evident, the concealed and the fanciful.

THE MINISTER, WHEN he returned home from work in the evenings, no longer expected to find his son waiting for him at the cherrywood gate. Wu was more likely, at that hour of day, to be in his room, propped up in bed reading. The tonic which was supposed to have restored his vital energies had so far accomplished no such thing and what was more—the boy complained—it was giving him diarrhoea.

Someone was indeed waiting for him one evening at the gate. That someone was Precious Pearl and she was furious, beside herself and positively livid with rage. It was a disgrace, she declared, a travesty, an injustice of the highest order!

'I'll take your word for that, my love. So why not just tell me what happened.'

She was not exaggerating. Wu had left for school that morning with his homework having been done—as always —and his student satchel as ever bulging with books. Also accompanying him were his talismans: a pair of wooden dragonflies and a terracotta statue of a child riding on the back of a dolphin. But those charms, for once, had let him down.

'Just imagine,' said Precious Pearl, calmer now that there was someone to whom to tell this.

Just imagine the unfairness of it all. Hardly had he turned up for school that day, than poor Wu, who had been praised on his last school report for 'discernment-beyond-his-years', was sent home in disgrace, expelled for disturbing the class, excluded because his constant yawning was causing the rest of the class to yawn as well.

It was a very poor teacher indeed, Po Cheng agreed, who couldn't keep his own class awake, but all the same, wasn't it time to admit that a listlessness which failed to respond to a three-season tonic was a legitimate cause for alarm? Deciding that it might be time to call in a doctor, however, still left them with the task of deciding which one to call, given that Wu, from a very early age, had not been one to suffer fools gladly.

The book with which Old Gentleman Lü provided them—*This One or That One?*—commenced with a warning that one ought not, when choosing a physician, to allow oneself to be influenced by the fact that a particular individual was wearing a fine robe, as fine robes could be rented by the hour.

'But isn't that simply common sense?' remarked Precious Pearl.

'Indeed. But perhaps the author's mentioning it indicates his belief that common sense is not so common as is generally supposed.'

SO AS NOT to alarm the boy, they at first kept the matter to themselves. They read only late at night, only after looking in on Wu to make sure that he was sleeping soundly. It went without saying that they wanted the best for their son—as would any other parent of any other child—but how were they to avoid, when in pursuit of the best, doing more harm than good?

A physician of the first order, they learned, would begin by examining the orifices; then he would locate and assess the patient's deep and floating pulses, probe the five vital viscera and most probably end up prescribing an all-purpose restorative. As such a physician was poorly trained and never far to seek, it was customary to pay him only afterwards and then no more than half of what he had asked.

A second-order physician dug deeper. He noted the hue of the eyes, listened to the tone of the voice, sniffed the urine and the faeces, and observed the reactions of the patient to each of the five notes of the musical scale. His diagnoses included disorders brought about by sitting in a draught, bad dreams, excess toxicity or fruit eaten out of season. Being better trained, he was more in demand and could command larger fees, half being paid in advance and the remainder only if the patient showed subsequent signs of improvement.

Should the treatment carried out by a physician of the first or second order fail, one of the third order might then be summoned. This individual would appear on the scene empty-handed, as he arrived at his conclusions solely through close questioning, by means of which he attempted to trace any present ills back to such unfortunate events as having been startled by a sudden noise, having noticed a shadow crossing one's path, having encountered an ill-omened animal or having harboured unconfessed cravings. And here the author became quite animated in his critique:

> *Let the public beware! These fellows never dirty their hands, on top of which their fees are often excessive, which they attempt to excuse by claiming such high fees to be essential to the cure … .*

Were they any the less in the dark? They undressed for bed that night in silence, slipped beneath the bedclothes, extinguished the bedside lantern and took up their usual sleeping positions, with each accommodated to the posture of the other. In what they called their yin/yang formation, the body of one was moulded to the back of the other, the buttocks of the one to the fore tucked snugly into the lap of the one behind, with the knees of the latter similarly fitted tightly into the hollow of the knees of the former, each one of them thereby filling entirely the space left by the other.

'And what if it was us all along?' queried Precious Pearl, thinking out loud. 'What if we had not been quite so strict? What if we had allowed him to run around more? What if in the beginning, when he was being rambunctious and disobedient, we had not rebuked him but instead had praised him for his liveliness?'

THE FLUCTUATIONS IN their son's condition, while confusing to his parents, also gave them some reason for hope. While much of his time was spent in his room, there were still days when he went to the riverbank, not to view the entertainments offered there but to sit apart from them, at the edge of the water, folding paper boats which he subsequently released to the river, apparently not in the least disturbed to see the current catch them and carry them off downstream.

'One day, I keep thinking,' said Precious Pearl, hopefully, 'he'll get up in the morning, look in the mirror, see a shadow on his face and complain that he needs a shave.'

'All the same,' said Po Cheng, firmly, 'isn't it time, don't you think, that we ourselves took action on his behalf?'

The physician that they selected was a jovial fellow and Wu submitted without complaint to his crude poking and prodding. The boy's passivity, on the other hand, no doubt influenced the fellow's diagnosis, which was that what the patient was suffering from was an insufficiency in the blood. Wu, at the conclusion of the examination, had immediately fallen into a deep sleep and this allowed the physician to speak frankly.

'The healthy human body,' he explained, 'can be seen as a pleasant landscape in which everything essential to its maintenance is present, and in the appropriate measures … .'

The body's tubular conduits—the internal pathways which channelled the seasonal yin and yang energies to their appropriate depots—were to be imagined as a network of well-maintained canals, complete with locks and winding gear, water marshals and a steady stream of canal boats.

'Ah, in layman's terms,' thought Po Cheng. 'In terms understandable even to so simple a person as a mere Minister of Bridges and Waterways.'

Just as boats and barges were constantly on the move through the canals of a well-run country, delivering the five grains to their designated granaries—the fellow continued—

so too, within a healthy body, nutrients were continually being delivered to its five depots, restocking and refreshing the lungs, liver, heart, spleen and kidneys. Any blockage, therefore, by slowing the flow of nutrients through the bodily conduits, was bound to cause distress, just as any interference with the flow of grain through a country's canals was likely to lead to insurrection.

Analogy rode on the back of analogy. No region of a country had all that it needed or needed all that it had, and hence trade was essential. Similarly, within the human body, no organ produced all that it required or required all that it produced; hence, just as what permitted a country to flourish was its well-maintained canals, so too it was a network of free-flowing conduits which provided the human body with its vibrancy.

By now the fellow, although still having a jolly demeanour, was in full stride. Even as a country might come under threat either from subversives within or from enemies beyond its walls, so this was true as well of the human organism. The endogenous agents of disease—he proceeded to list—were vexation, grieving, pessimism, indifference, alarm, fear, fury, foolishness, idiocy and confusion; the exogenous vectors—the enemies lurking beyond one's walls —were then named as what burned, what bit, what infuriated, what frustrated, what came upon one from behind, rich food, humidity and, of course, warfare.

'What a sorry catalogue of woes!' Precious Pearl burst out, impatiently.

'So it may seem,' the fellow agreed, 'but one must not lose heart. Many a seemingly intractable ill has been put right, dear lady, simply by employing sound policies.'

As in the halls of government, so in the sick room, two distinct strategies were available, one for dealing with insurgency and another for warding off an invasion. Would it not have been a foolish general indeed—the genial but somewhat long-winded fellow pointed out—who thought it possible to quell dissent with a catapult or who attempted to halt the advance of an enemy army with a curfew?

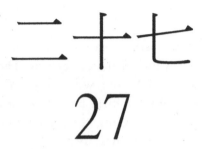

二十七

27

MORTALITY | HEAVEN APPORTIONS, EARTH APPEALS | WHY COMPLAIN OF DIFFICULTIES, WHEN ALL IS DIFFICULT? | DESPERATION | STILL ONE FOOT TRAILS BEHIND THE OTHER | AS BELOW, SO ON HIGH

Rather than the parents or the patient himself, it was the physician who first showed signs of becoming discouraged. The fellow had now lost—or put to one side—his earlier cheerfulness. Being unable to explain why his methods had brought about no change in Wu, he spoke instead of his former successes with cases of lethargy, cases in which he had merely altered the patient's diet, adding insects admired for their endeavour, the livers of animals known to have superior stamina or the eggs of fish so frantic to breed that they swam upstream in fast-flowing rivers.

It was, suggested the boy's Uncle Pang, when told of this state of affairs, time to move on.

'Assuming, of course,' he qualified, 'that you intend to leave no stone unturned.'

So it was that they agreed to submit poor Wu to the mercies of a cup-and-needle man. What did it matter how the thing was achieved, after all, just so long as the boy's conduits were put back in order and his depots duly replenished?

The individual arrived carrying a leather satchel and with a large scroll tucked under one arm. The scroll, once unrolled and pinned to the wall, was seen to contain a detailed diagram of the human body, laid out flat, revealing its vital viscera, its many joints, its myriad pressure points and its numerous meridians, these last being the non-material pathways which, in the diagram, seemed to be all that was holding the whole rickety structure together.

'And what a fine stone we've turned over this time!' Po Cheng couldn't help thinking.

So it began. One day would be for cups and the next for needles, one day for moxibustion and the next for acupuncture, to be repeated until the first green shoots of recovery appeared. Having hot cups affixed to his body unfortunately left the boy with unsightly welts, and the needles, he complained, while painless, nevertheless gave him bad dreams afterwards.

'We'll need to make it up to him once he's better,' Po Cheng suggested. 'For instance, hasn't he always wanted a skiff?'

'But aren't they dangerous?' Precious Pearl protested. 'Aren't boys always drowning on the river?'

'It will be a proper skiff,' Po Cheng promised. 'One that's perfectly seaworthy, not just a pot with an umbrella for a sail.'

What a pity that, in the meantime, there had been no further word as to the present whereabouts of Wang Tzu.

Would the presence of the ex-pugilist in his corner not have been a great boost to Wu and a further encouragement to him not to give up?

'An ex-pugilist who has never stuck to anything himself?' queried Precious Pearl.

'All the same, just imagine the prestige, when Wu returns to school, if he can boast of having as an uncle someone who's the doorman of so disreputable an establishment as the Blue Heaven Pavilion.'

WHATEVER IT WAS that had hold of Wu, it showed no sign of letting go, and worse still, it seemed to be tightening its grip. The boy's sleep had up to this point at least been peaceful but he was now troubled as well by raging fevers and these gave rise to restless and exhausting sleep, from which he was likely to awake confused and all but incoherent. Who or what—any parents of any child undergoing such an ordeal would have had to ask themselves —could have hated their child so?

Wu, whose eyes were still glistening with fever after one such troubling night, then announced the next morning that he had been thinking and had reached a decision and would they like to hear what it was?

'Of course we want to hear,' Precious Pearl instantly replied. 'We're your parents, aren't we?'

Her heart, like his, Po Cheng surmised, must be in her mouth, as they both waited to hear just what it was that their son had decided.

'I just want you to know,' said Wu, firmly, 'so that you can't say later that you weren't warned, that I won't be going back to school again after this.'

'But you liked school,' Precious Pearl reminded him. 'And you were doing so well.'

'But school didn't like me, mother, and I'm not going to take that lying down!'

So that was all it was. At least Wu was still going to the trouble of making plans for the future, and whatever those plans might be, Po Cheng was only too happy to play along.

'Ah. So you won't be attending school any longer. Well I can't say that I blame you but what will you do instead?'

'What I've always wanted to do, father. Become an actor.'

'An actor, is it? Living from hand to mouth? One moment the envy of others and the next, pitied by all?'

'But I might be good at it, father. Uncle Wang, at least, thought so.'

Po Cheng tried to remember if, when recounting his own adventures with the Small Fulness Theatre Company, he may have glossed over the trials and the hardships of a life lived perpetually on the road. Be that as it may, it was Precious Pearl who now took up the argument.

'An actor, Wu? Someone who can at best barely make ends meet? And who, in that case, will look after your father and me when we grow old?'

'Of course I'll look after you,' promised Wu, with his accustomed seriousness. 'I'll just need to find my feet first.'

'Just so long as you don't forget,' teased Precious Pearl. 'It's one thing for an actor to go hungry and not to have a proper roof over his head but that should never happen to old people.'

IT WAS NOT only in the city's markets or in its brothels or in the fairground on the riverbank that shady practices and shameful deceptions were to be found. No matter in which quarter of the city, there were also shrines and temples dedicated to the magical treatment of this or that feared misfortune through the agency of one or another deity, immortal or animal spirit. Availing himself of any of these surely fraudulent treatments was the last thing that Po Cheng would ever have imagined himself doing but what other possibilities remained?

'It's called the Temple of Timely Redress,' Precious Pearl filled him in, 'and Widow Wen swears by it. It deals only with cases of mistaken identity.'

There was a certain amount of sense to this, he thought. What harm had Wu ever done to anyone? What could possibly justify his having been afflicted by an insufficiency of the blood? Might it not be possible that a mistake had been made and that the misfortune suffered by Wu had been intended for someone else?

He dressed down for his visit to the temple. There was likely to be a goodly crowd ahead of him, awaiting admission, and would it not have been shameful of him to pull rank? Instead of his robe of office, he put on the patchwork robe in which he had first arrived in the Celestial City and which he nowadays wore only when working in the garden.

The queue, when he arrived at the temple, stretched right around the block. Administrative errors did no doubt occur from time to time but were Heaven's errors really this numerous? Or was it rather that no one, no matter how profligate or how negligent, was ever prepared to bear without complaint just what he or she might very well, in fact, have brought down on their own heads?

'Still and all,' he told himself, 'it's worth a try. It must, in the past, have worked for some.'

Once admitted to the temple, he was shown into an already over-crowded waiting room. The story which had brought so many to the temple was of an honest and hardworking magistrate who vowed not to retire from his post until every last injustice of which the government of his day was guilty had been put right. Death, however, caught up with him first, forcing him to leave many cases still unresolved and hence he had been appointed an immortal and lived on today, it was believed, with one foot in Heaven —as it were—and the other still on Earth.

There was certainly one miracle performed at the temple, Po Cheng noted. For each individual who was summoned to view the image of the Exemplary Magistrate, three more were somehow squeezed into the waiting room, thereby giving the impression that it had infinite capacity.

The viewer was not permitted either to linger or to address the venerable figure directly. Details of one's complaint would be taken down afterwards by a clerk. The immortal, as immortalized inside the temple dedicated to him, was shown seated at his desk, hard at work, so personifying the qualities to be expected in an ideal official: competence, confidence, compassion, concern and—perhaps inevitably—a modicum of self-satisfaction.

The clerk, once he had recorded the list of woes which had of late beset poor Wu, then suggested that, as his father, Po Cheng might want to make a small donation in the boy's name.

'All proceeds,' the clerk added, 'to go towards the upkeep of the temple.'

'Of course,' Po Cheng acquiesced. 'Why not?'

Why not? Could the immortal, being by definition of advanced age, be expected to work seated in a draught or beneath a leaking roof? How would he get through the stack of papers on his desk unless there was a cheerful fire burning, a lap rug around his knees, warm slippers on his feet and, for the best chance of a favourable outcome, a jar of spiced wine for company?

THERE WAS EVERY reason to believe, from the expression on the boy's face when they sought to wake him one morning, without success, that he had passed from life peacefully and not amidst the delirium brought on by one of his fevers. There would, mercifully, be no more of those fevers and for that at least they had reason to be grateful.

'Should we have talked to him about this, do you think?' asked Precious Pearl, who had knelt down beside Wu's bed and was smoothing his hair.

'Talked to him about death?' Po Cheng replied. 'How could we have? Since when have *we* been experts on the subject?'

Without waiting for her answer, he went out to the well for some water. As there was no need now to heat the water, they went to work at once washing Wu, with no need either for further conversation, each of them being shut off, enclosed within their own grief. Once they had dressed the boy, choosing to do so in the clothes which he had worn on his first day of school, his Uncle Pang was summoned, as Wu had now to be measured up for a second time, this time for a coffin.

They then cleaned the boy's room, which was to be left just as it was. On the wall—and there to stay—was what had been, during Wu's final struggles, his favourite motto:

TO THE HEIGHT OF THE MOUNTAIN
ADD THE HEIGHT OF THE TREE!

What Wu had understood by this was unclear, as he had never said and they had never asked. Wu, while attending school, had begun to spread his wings but only to find himself, subsequently, back under constant scrutiny by his parents and so badly in need of at least his own thoughts.

While life went on, it was by no means in the way that they had expected. They rose as usual in the mornings when they heard the boom of the Thunder Drum, dressed and ate breakfast, spoke of how each of them had slept the night before, glanced into Wu's room and saw that it was empty and hence were made to recognize that they were indeed awake and obliged to face another day.

All the same, on his way to work and often when crossing Magpie Bridge, Po Cheng was brought up short by the sensation that nothing of what had happened to him since the morning that he had been lured away from Nettle Village by the two recruiters was quite as it seemed. Might he not be caught up in some drama in which he himself was merely a player, acting out a role which had in fact been crafted elsewhere, by some hidden hand, by some devious mind?

He was brought down to Earth on those mornings by the substantiality of the Ministry of Bridges and Waterways, with its ceaseless comings and goings, and by the fact that the key in the pocket of the sleeve of his robe fitted exactly the lock on the door of his office.

In the evenings, rather than remain at home, in a place from which Wu was now absent, they went together to visit his grave. The site was on the riverbank, not far from where the boy once sat folding his paper boats. A simple stone marked the spot, engraved with the following simple farewell:

AT LEAST WE HAD HIM
FOR A WHILE,
BUT IT WAS SUCH A SHORT WHILE!

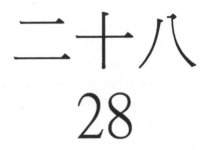

二十八

28

For the one, for Precious Pearl, weeds were still threatening
to strangle the peonies, there were still meals to be prepared
even if not for Wu, and clothes to be washed even if none
were any longer his. For the other, for the Minister, bridges
were still in need of repair, dikes still being undermined and
canals still springing leaks, all for want of funds. For neither
of them did grieving preclude work, or working grief.

With winter, once the grave had disappeared beneath the
snow, Wu's room became his shrine. Only two things had
been changed: the room could now be kept spotlessly clean
and Precious Pearl had taken down the scroll left behind by
the cup-and-needle man, complaining that its network of

finely drawn meridians bore no resemblance whatsoever to their son, as it made him appear as a mere puppet, at the mercy of so many strings.

'And after all that distasteful talk,' she recalled, 'of depots and conduits.'

'All the same,' Po Cheng ventured to point out, 'where would any of us be without them?'

Despite having one eye on the past, Pearl was nonetheless able to see ahead. When spring came, she proposed, in order to prevent grass from growing over Wu's gravestone, they could plant a flower garden around it.

'Wu was fond of flowers, don't you remember? He was always remarking on how nice the peonies looked.'

'He was also fond, my love, of telling us things that he thought we would want to hear.'

Whether or not one dragged one's feet, life went on. On his way to work one morning, Po Cheng heard the sound of a carriage coming up behind and he stepped aside to allow it to pass. But this was not just any carriage, it was the lacquered carriage favoured these days by the Lady Regent and it came to a halt just beside him.

'Ah,' he thought. 'So she must at last have got round to reading my memorial.'

The next thing he knew, he was inside, and the coach was once more in motion but not headed in the direction which he might have expected. He was not that morning, for some strange reason, on his way to the Ministry of Bridges and Waterways.

'You needn't be alarmed,' said Lady Yao in her usual, business-like tone. 'Something unfortunate has indeed occurred but to someone else.'

Wherever they were headed, the coachman was wasting no time. The bouncing of the carriage on the cobblestones made it difficult for the Minister to retain his balance, whereas Her Ladyship, who had put on a good deal of weight since they had last met, appeared to be sitting quite comfortably.

'These are troubling times, Minister, and it's a question of how best to redeploy one's forces.'

'But I'm perfectly deployed where I am, Your Ladyship. It's taken some time, I know, but I'll soon have a grip on things.'

'On what, for instance? Getting water to do what it would probably have done anyway?'

He realized that to argue any further would get him nowhere. Once her mind was made up, there was no shifting her, and regardless of whether or not she was asking for his own opinion on the matter, there was but one possible response.

'Whatever you think best, Your Ladyship.'

APART FROM THE Sky-Piercing Observatory, the tallest building in the Celestial City was the Jade Tower, a five-storey structure which housed the highest echelons of the government. Here one encountered, one above the other, the Music Bureau, the Census Bureau, the Department of Ways and Means and on the top floor of that imposing structure the office of the new Chief Minister, from where there was a view not just of the entire city but also of the countryside which lay beyond it.

'Ah well,' thought Po Cheng, resignedly, 'either one goes forward in government or else one finds oneself left by the wayside.'

With the job—as these were parlous times—came a new rank, the obligatory rank of Conveyed-by-Coach. What a surprise it hence was for Precious Pearl that evening when she saw that conveyance pull up at their gate and realized just who it was that was being delivered.

'Dear husband?' she greeted him, somewhat perplexed.

'The same, although now to be addressed as the Chief Minister, if you please.'

There was plenty for them to discuss as they stood together feeding the canary its evening ration of seeds. His new post would mean a substantial increase in salary, a front gate of glazed bricks, a purple robe with gold trimmings, a peacock badge for her to sew onto his cap and the right to add a second storey to their house.

'To show that we've arrived,' Po Cheng spelled out. 'Not even millionaires are allowed more than two storeys. It's the maximum permitted to parvenus.'

'And I suppose, dear Chief Minister, that people will be kowtowing to you in the street after this.'

'Unless they cross to the other side in time, or duck into an alley.'

None of this changed the fact that they were still in mourning. The pure joy which they might have felt at the good fortune which had come their way was tempered by the sadness that they felt at being unable to share it with Wu.

'Just imagine how proud that boy would have been of me,' said Po Cheng, wistfully.

'Or at least he could have said that he was,' remarked Precious Pearl, slyly.

She too, whether she liked it or not, was to have a new role. It would fall to her as the wife of the Chief Minister to champion the cause of the elderly, the infirm, orphans, the disturbed, the confused, the lonely and soldiers wounded in battle.

'While continuing,' Po Cheng added, 'with your duties as a Faithful Companion.'

This was a suggestion and it was accepted. That night, for the first time since Wu's death, instead of going straight to sleep, they made love. They still needed each other, still needed to embrace, and not only to console themselves for what they had lost but to fill a deeper need, one which had been in abeyance but not extinguished, namely the need felt by two, from time to time, to be one.

Precious Pearl afterwards fell asleep at once, whereas Po Cheng remained awake, troubled by the one thing which he had failed to tell her. Lady Yao that morning, just as he was leaving her carriage, had called him back in order to inform him in no uncertain terms of just what it was that would now be expected of him.

'One misstep, my dear Po, at a time like this, is one too many, so no more memorials. Your job, from now on, isn't to rock the boat, it's to steady the ship.'

EVEN IF THESE had not been perilous times, it would have been a daunting task. As the government's Chief Minister, he would be in charge of nothing in particular but responsible for everything in general; he would be answerable to the Lady Regent for what should have been done but hadn't been, as well as for what ought never to have happened but had. He would be the hub about which all else revolved and as such he would be the last to be praised when the ride was smooth but the first to be blamed when it was not.

At least he was not alone. He had only to ring the bell beside his desk in order to summon First Secretary Chow, not forgetting of course that behind this seemingly subservient public servant there lurked Sergeant First-Class Chow of the Secret Police. All the same the fellow was not a bad sort and could be counted on to sniff out what might otherwise have remained swept beneath some carpet.

His predecessor in the post of Chief Minister, Po Cheng thus learned, had been appointed solely on the basis of his father having held that post before him, and the son had proved far too weak. People had been allowed to get away with all manner of things, including theft of government property, which if not stolen outright was 'borrowed' and never returned.

'Sounds like the fellow was a sorry specimen, Chow.'

'The second generation often is, Excellency.'

The rest was sad but also sadly predictable. When informed that he was to be cast aside, that his services were no longer required, the failed official had gone off without a word, got hold of a sturdy rope and was discovered later hanging by the neck from a lamppost in Great Redemption Square.

Enough said? The mistakes of others, Po Cheng told himself, were there for one to learn from and if too much had been stolen in the past, then even more would now need to be clawed back. Not for nothing then the long, cold nights spent in the Celestial Harmony Lodging House poring over Lü's copy of the *Treatise on Iron and Salt*, which had turned out to have little to do with iron or salt but rather with the various ways in which they might be taxed.

Of all the branches of government, it was the Department of Ways and Means which needed to be the one which was most feared. Taxes, Po Cheng recalled reading, needed to be collected ruthlessly, with the fine for non-compliance being at least five times what it would have cost the culprit to have complied in the first place, for only then would the inevitability of taxes be accepted as being on a par with the predictability of death.

Various schemes had been devised in the past in the hope of increasing tax revenues, each of which had, after some initial success, proved to be counterproductive. Altering the calendar in such a way as to increase the frequency with which taxes could be collected, for instance, had resulted in a windfall but was also found to be confusing migratory birds, causing hibernating creatures to awaken early from their sleep and inducing silkworms to burst prematurely from their cocoons.

A similar scheme, one which sought to increase the take from duties and tariffs simply by moving the customs barriers further out into the countryside, had produced similarly worrying repercussions. Thousand-league horses, according to *Iron and Salt*, were no longer able to cover that distance in a day, eggs were soon being sold at nine to a dozen and the widening of the tariff net—as this left larger gaps—simply opened the way wider for smugglers.

Was this a losing battle? Had it ever been possible, in government, to bring revenues into step with expenditures? Even should taxes be paid on time and in full, there remained a further problem, namely the shameful debasement of the currency in which those taxes were paid. The longer that any currency remained in use, history taught, the less it was worth, as the populace exacted a tax of its own, with the wealthy removing a sliver of gold or silver from every coin that passed through their hands and the humble, a shaving of copper.

Just thinking about the task which faced him made Po Cheng's stomach rumble. Before he could ring for Chow, however, the fellow appeared of his own accord with a pot of tea and a good-sized helping of some truly delicious-looking buns.

'Ah, Chow, you've read my mind. What would I do without you?'

'It doesn't bear thinking about, Excellency.'

IT OUGHT TO have been impossible for anyone to have entered the Jade Tower unchallenged and to have made his way up the various flights of stairs to the office of the Chief Minister without coming under the gaze of First Secretary Chow but someone had, and he was waiting there for Po Cheng first thing one morning when he arrived for work.

'One of the door porters recognized me,' the old man explained. 'Recognized Mosquito Wang, that's to say. I took the liberty of saying that you were expecting me.'

It was indeed Wang Tzu, although he had all the appearance at that moment of being a mere tramp. His clothes were in shreds, his face was covered with bruises and his hair was long and matted. That anyone could still have recognized, in this unsightly individual, the up-and-coming young boxer that he must once have been, Po Cheng put down as being of a piece with the old fellow's strange practice of reappearing when and where he was—in actual fact—least to be expected.

'I came as soon as I heard about Wu,' said Wang Tzu. 'What a pity when these things happen.'

'It's good of you to come. But weren't you being held captive by kidnappers?'

Wang Tzu seemed amused by this suggestion. Held against his will? When outnumbered by only two to one? The pair of 'gangsters' whom Widow Wen had seen that night outside the Blue Heaven Pavilion had not been kidnappers at all, they had been boxing promoters and they had come there, he explained, to make him a proposition. They had it all worked out, the time was right, he was sure to make a fortune and with any luck there would be a little something in it for them as well.

'And what use would you have,' inquired the Chief Minister, 'at your age, for a fortune?'

'I have a use for it alright, as will be revealed in due course.'

The proposition put to him had been that he should make a comeback, climb back into the ring, but not, as before, with Bulldog Ma. His opponent, this time, was to be a bear.

'An actual bear?' queried Po Cheng. 'With teeth and claws?'

'With its claws clipped,' Wang Tzu clarified.

He then paused, fished about in the remains of what had once been a quite decent set of clothing and produced something which, once it was unfolded, turned out to be the following poster:

ONE NIGHT ONLY!
MAN AGAINST BEAST!
WANG VERSUS BRUNO!

There had been no time to lose, no time to explain to Widow Wen that he wasn't leaving her or being abducted but was going off of his own volition with those two gentlemen to find a bear, train it to box and then start raking in the money.

'But instead of a fortune'—Po Cheng indicated the old rascal's battered face—'you seem to have come away with a good hiding.'

'In *addition* to a fortune,' Wang Tzu corrected.

Fitting gloves onto the bear and teaching it to box had been straightforward enough, as bears were by nature pugnacious. Nor had it been difficult to attract a crowd, as what else was there to do in the countryside in the evenings? Nor had Wang Tzu, even at his age, found it hard to outsmart the animal and give it the slip for the contracted six rounds.

'What the brute never learned, unfortunately, was that at the end of those six rounds, it was meant to throw in the towel.'

二十九

29

Winter, that year, had been dragging its feet. Despite the
New Year having been welcomed with the usual rites and
excesses, there were still immense icicles hanging from the
eaves of the houses, buds had as yet to appear on the trees,
and small birds, during the coldest hours of the night,
continued to fall frozen from the sky. Facts were indeed facts,
Po Cheng was prepared to concede, but surely that was no
reason to lay the blame for everything untoward that
occurred at the door of the government.

Any number of communications were now reaching his
office which the Chief Minister could well have done
without. Along with the usual complaints concerning late

payment for services rendered to the government, there were reports of new acts of dissent on the song terraces and in the drinking dens of the city, where some were blaming the Lady Regent herself for the worrying persistence of winter, as she had yet to set a date for the resumption of the Spring Examinations.

'Never mind, Excellency,' First Secretary Chow assured his superior. 'Measures are already being taken.'

'Ah, measures. But why not simply reinstate the examinations?'

'In such parlous times? Who, then, could guarantee the results?'

'But must one not make allowance, Chow, for mere youthful high spirits? Students, since time immemorial, if left with too little to do, have got up to mischief.'

'Mischief, Excellency? When did you last look out of your window?'

The First Secretary had a point. Someone had gone to a great deal of trouble—late one night and no doubt with the aid of a ladder—to vent his frustrations on a public building:

Q: WHY DOES THE OX TILL THE SOIL?
A: SO THAT THE HORSE MAY EAT GRAIN!

Mere youthful high spirits or something worse? In either case, why had the offending material not simply been painted over? In answer, Chow pointed down to the street, to where a very shady-looking individual indeed was standing in a doorway pretending to read a newspaper. In fact the fellow was there to take into custody anyone who paused long enough to read what was written on the wall.

'It's an old trick, Excellency. It's known, I believe, in police circles, as the beneficial use of bad things.'

Further troubling news came from Li Ting, based on conversations which he had overheard in the Green Monkey Tavern, an establishment long-known to be the headquarters of a veritable brotherhood of habitual lawbreakers. The tunnels which they used for entering or exiting the city—and which their fathers and grandfathers had used before them—were now being used by strangers, by unfriendly types who once inside the walls immediately vanished, as if the city itself had swallowed them up.

Po Cheng's thoughts went back for a moment to those adventure stories of which Little Wu had been so fond, stories in which—if the hero had wished to enter a city without drawing attention to himself—he would have slipped in through one of its gates hidden under a load of vegetables or of firewood or of fodder, or simply walked in behind a flock of waddling ducks or honking geese.

WHAT HAMPERED THE Chief Minister, as he attempted to steady the ship of Lady Yao's government, was not knowing where to begin. With the bills, for instance, which had been run up during the Grand Tour but still not settled? With the tunnels of the smugglers? The debasement of the currency? The unpaid salaries of the government's own employees? The lack of respect for public buildings? What, in short, most required his urgent attention, and what could—with the least damage to the country—be put off till another day?

Precipitant decisions in government, history taught, had in the past left the door open to unforeseen consequences; delay in reaching a decision, on the other hand, would increase the likelihood of one's being overtaken by unfortunate events.

What overtook the Chief Minister was his receipt of a dispatch sent from the South by an individual identifying himself simply as 'The Woodcutter'. The calligraphy, with its neat, squared-off characters, nevertheless belied his claim to be a mere woodcutter, revealing him instead as a middle-level government official who had for some reason felt it necessary to use a pseudonym.

His report was on the activities of General Ma, Bulldog Ma, the legendary bandit-chasing general. Ma, oddly enough, and upon no other authority than his own, had declared an amnesty for bandits, for the very scoundrels with whom he was meant to be at war. Any bandit willing to switch sides and to demonstrate that willingness by capturing and bringing in some unrepentant fellow bandit, would be presented with a pardon, issued with a bedroll, fitted out with a uniform, taught to salute and added to the payroll.

'So,' Po Cheng concluded from this, 'unsatisfied with a mere brigade, the Bulldog's decided to recruit his own army!'

And what might the ramifications of this turn out to be? What would Ma want with an army? Or was Po Cheng being deliberately naive? What would *anyone* who had successfully passed the Military Examination want with an army?

The note which he received shortly afterwards from the Bright Hall was equally troubling. In it the Lady Regent placed the blame for no spring bulbs having yet appeared on General Ma's not having as yet sent off his contracted Spring Tribute of bandit heads:

How is it, Chief Minister, that everyone else can manage? So many teams of horses or lines of dancing girls, so many cartloads of charcoal or bricks, so many sacks of frogs or grass snakes or freshwater clams ... . Need I go on?

There was no need for her to go on, as worse news still was on the way. Instead of a lacquered box containing the agreed number of heads, what arrived from the South, from the headquarters of General Ma, was a wagon carrying two coffins which between them contained the corpse of 'The Woodcutter', who had been sawn neatly in half at the waist. And, as a final insult, a note had been stuffed into the poor fellow's mouth:

I WAS SENT OUT AS ONE,
I COME BACK AS TWO!

WAS HE OR was he not to continue as the hub about which all else revolved? Lady Yao's instructions could hardly have been any clearer and he would have only himself to blame, Po Cheng realized, if he should lose his nerve along the way. He thus took the precaution of looking up the exact definition of a punitive expedition.

'*A limited military action in answer to an affront,*' he discovered. 'So how hard could that be?'

After that, it was just a matter of rolling up his sleeves and deciding which book to take down from his office bookshelves. The volume which he chose—*Preparing for Victory*—was a primer on warfare and as such it began with the pronouncement that the only thing more heinous than sending an army off to battle was to send it off to battle poorly prepared.

As he read, he made notes. Were the country's catapults, for instance, up to scratch? Would their range be sufficient? Would there be wagons available to take them to the front? Soldiers, after all, could simply be marched into battle but heavy artillery needed to be hauled there.

There would also need to be transport for the field

forges, the field kitchens and field mills for the grinding of the five grains. What chance, unless the horses were well shod and the men well fed, of a rapid advance, a convincing feint, a faultless flanking movement or—if the worst came to the worst—an orderly retreat?

An entire chapter was devoted to the importance of rope. Rope was essential for purposes as diverse as the putting up of tents, the crossing of rivers, the tying up of horses, the securing of captives and the raising of flags. Production would therefore need to be increased, the price of hemp controlled and all unnecessary, non-military uses of rope forbidden.

Drilling was sometimes mocked—the author freely admitted—but was nevertheless indispensable. Battles were fought on battlefields but they were won or lost on the parade ground. Men and horses alike needed to know by heart the battlefield commands and to recognize their associated drumbeats. Whatever the strength of the enemy and however difficult the terrain, a well-disciplined army would move as one, as though under the control of but a single will, as conveyed by the drummers.

The final chapter dealt with the inevitability, even in victory, that there would be casualties. For this reason a cohort of 'useful girls' should be recruited. These ought not to be prostitutes, the author clarified, but simply cheerful young women with pleasant faces, pleasing voices and soft hands for the dressing of wounds. Hence those who were wounded, or even maimed, would return home afterwards having experienced not just the brutality of warfare but also moments of tender care.

IT CAME AS something of a surprise to the Chief Minister and to his wife, when they took their places in the Bird's Eye Pavilion, to find that they were being greeted with applause from the crowds lining the street below. Were people really so fond of war, the couple asked each other in low voices, or had they just come out to enjoy a parade?

'Ought we to wave?' whispered Precious Pearl. 'Or might that not lead to our being accused of drawing too much attention to ourselves?'

'It's a dilemma,' Po Cheng agreed. 'If we don't wave, we run the risk of appearing stand-offish.'

Spring had arrived at last, drying out the roads and putting leaves back on the trees, and the entire city appeared to have turned out to watch the Imperial Army set off on its punitive expedition. And what a roar greeted the appearance of the Black Scorpion Battalion, the vanguard battalion, keeping in perfect step beneath a banner displaying its eponymous animal and the battalion's somewhat boastful slogan:

ALWAYS TO THE FORE, WHERE ELSE?
AND IT PACKS A MIGHTY WALLOP!

The sudden roar had startled pigeons from their cubbyholes in the city walls; for a moment they circled in formation in the sky above, until a second roar sent them flying off in utter confusion, every bird for itself. The second battalion, the Red Snake Battalion, was famed for its quick strikes, its rapid changes of direction and its equally uncompromising motto:

THOSE WITH POISON, STING;
THOSE WITH VENOM, BITE!

The Chief Minister drew his lady wife's attention to their alignment: left-handed men on the left and right-handed men on the right, thus leaving nothing exposed and nowhere for an enemy to penetrate.

The third battalion, the White Tiger Battalion, was the hinge on which a battle might well turn. The members of this elite force could not only march tirelessly but also trot, run, climb, abseil or swim, according to the circumstances. Any gap could thus quickly be filled, any hole plugged, and its popular rallying cry would have strengthened the resolve of many a small boy before a spirited game of kickball:

AGAINST TEN THOUSAND,
BE LIKE TEN THOUSAND!

The reassuring cadence of soldiers marching in perfect unison was then interrupted by the creaking of wooden wheels. These were the shock troops, an armoured division consisting of row after row of iron-skinned carriages on which powerful crossbows had been mounted; these impregnable vehicles, with their crews of strong-armed archers, rolled past behind a banner sure to strike fear into the hearts of even the most valiant enemy:

THE DOGS ARE OFF THEIR LEADS!

This left just the rear-guard, the beloved Grey Fox Battalion, the final posting for veterans, for men with many a victory already under their belts. What had they not done already, not seen, not suffered, and yet here they still were, marching as best they could under a motto which combined—in Po Cheng's opinion—a lingering cockiness with a truly heart-warming modesty:

ALWAYS READY FOR WHATEVER IT TAKES,
BUT ALL THE SAME KNOWING ONE'S PLACE.

30

HOSTILITIES | HEAVEN'S VIGILANCE, EARTH'S VAGARIES | HOT PURSUIT | FIRST ROUND TO GENERAL MA | A NIGHT AT THE THEATRE | THE MORE SENSE IT MAKES, THE MORE ONE FEARS FOR ONE'S SANITY

Hardly had the Imperial Forces departed the Celestial City than the Chief Minister found himself beset by doubts. Had he given it sufficient thought? Had it really been necessary to send all of those men off to battle, and if so had they been properly provided for? Each of the would-be combatants, besides bearing arms, also had in his possession a sun hat, a rain cloak, suitable footwear, a cup from which to drink, a plate off which to eat and a pair of chopsticks. What preyed on Po Cheng's mind, however, was the possibility that the entire enterprise might nonetheless founder in the end because—despite his endeavour and attention to detail—he had failed to foresee the unforeseeable.

Essential to the success of even a limited military operation would be the maintenance of a secure line of communication. Orders would need to be sent from the capital to the government generals and news of their having been carried out successfully received back in the capital. General Ma and his bandit-chasing troopers, now augmented by an unknown number of those very bandits, would need to be defeated not just on a distant battlefield but also on the street corners, in the wine shops and in the teahouses of the Celestial City itself.

That there was an enemy within as well as outwith the walls of the city was confirmed by Li Ting. Among the crowds turning out to watch the departure of the troops loyal to the cause of the Small Son of Heaven and the Lady Regent, there had been a number of individuals—according to Li—whose intention had been not to cheer on the government troops but to count them.

'Ah, a head count! The things that go on these days, Li, and right under one's nose!'

'Because that's just where one is least likely to look,' Li Ting postulated.

The fellow was a real bloodhound. Having once got a whiff of something, he followed the scent doggedly, no matter where it might lead, and once he got his teeth into the thing he didn't let go. He worried it until the feathers flew.

'So who are these people, Li? These agitators? And what do they want?'

'It's hard to say. They look like everyone else. They blend in. All that's known for sure—and it's the reason for their being called agitators—is that they're here to stir the pot.'

'An interesting expression. By stirring a pot, does one not seek to prevent anything from sticking to the bottom?'

'Or else to scrape loose what's already stuck there.'

Po Cheng enjoyed these discussions. If anyone was likely to understand the difficulties which he himself faced or the doubts which he was harbouring, then was it not Li Ting, who had in the past been first a government official and then a convict and was now something in between?

'So these agitators, Li, what's the best way of dealing with them? To send them back to school so that they can learn some manners?'

'If you're asking what history teaches, it's that many different measures have been tried in the past, each of which was once the preferred measure of a government which has long since gone the way of all governments.'

THE PROGRESS OF the Imperial Army, according to the dispatches which each day reached the capital, had so far been truly exemplary, exceeding that of all similar expeditions in the past. The morale of the soldiers, moreover, could not have been higher, and such was their joy at being on campaign that they spent their evenings, after the last meal of the day, dancing. How odd then—the Chief Minister was left to muse—that the moderate months of spring had been replaced by the searing months of summer without the government forces having as yet reached the garrison town in which General Ma was known to have his headquarters.

Hence the following missive from the Bright Hall:

Was this not meant to be a lightning strike, Chief Minister? So when did it become death-by-slow-slicing?

Po Cheng chose to ignore this. From the window of his office, he could look out over a city which, for all its magnificence, was also a hotbed of vice, greed, cheating, concupiscence, misery, poverty and need. Might it not be argued that, as in a forest, an occasional conflagration was to be welcomed as it would clear away the undergrowth? Would it not, in a city, on the other hand, be the clapboard hovels of the poorest of the poor which would be the first thing to go up in flames?

Although the Imperial Army had as yet to catch sight of any enemy soldiers and much less to have engaged any, the first casualties were now being reported. In addition to blisters, which could be put down to each man having been issued prior to his departure from the Celestial City with a new pair of boots, there were—in order of ascending frequency—cases of hay fever, sunburn and homesickness.

The Lady Regent, after receiving her copy of the report, was quite scathing:

> *Homesickness? Are they not grown men and fully armed? Someone ought to ask them why they enlisted in the first place if their homes were all that wonderful.*

What irritated the Chief Minister were the highly questionable requisitions which he had begun to receive. For winter caps when it was not yet autumn? For more arrows when not a single arrow had as yet been loosed at an insurgent?

'They might be shooting at rabbits,' the First Secretary suggested. 'Or it might be a case of optical illusion.'

'Optical illusion, Chow?'

'When a soldier goes too long without seeing the enemy, Excellency, he starts to see one behind every tree.'

EVEN TAKING INTO account that First Secretary Chow was playing a double game and was in reality a policeman assigned to keep an eye on the Chief Minister, the fellow was not really such a bad sort and he had, without even being asked, managed to get hold of a military map and pin it up on the wall. Any time that a courier arrived with a new dispatch, Po Cheng could thus consult the map and so form a picture in his mind of just how things stood. At the same time—without Chow's knowledge—he would be indulging in an optical illusion of his own, one in which he saw his son Wu standing beside him, gazing wide-eyed at the map as his father explained its various conventions.

'Notice the bridges, my boy. Can you remember when I was in charge of them?'

'Of course I remember, father. And in charge of waterways as well.'

'Very good. And how did I tell you that a bridge was calibrated?'

'By the number of warriors in full armour who can be marched over it abreast, father.'

What the map along with its daily amendments revealed was that the end was now near. The Imperial Forces had at last reached the garrison town and encircled it and had now only to tighten the noose. In his mind's eye the Chief Minister could see the government forces creeping silently ahead through tall grass, while behind them the wagons transporting the catapults would be creaking forward inch by inch.

How could this end except in victory for the government? How could a makeshift army on the periphery hope to hold its own against the inherently superior force of a concentrated centre? All the same, Po Cheng spent that night at his desk, not wanting to miss any courier who turned up in the middle of the night. News from the besieged garrison town, after all, even if conveyed by a relay of fast ponies, would already be at least three days old by the time that it reached the capital.

The news, when it did arrive, was mixed. It was not particularly good, that was to say, but it might have been much worse. The town had not been defended, as there was no one left there to do so, and the same went for Ma's headquarters, which was not only deserted but had been completely stripped of its supplies, its records and its furnishings, leaving the government generals—who would no doubt see the taking of Ma's headquarters without a fight as a victory—without anything on which to sit.

So now what was to be done? A punitive expedition had been organized at great expense but Ma remained at large and the campaigning season would soon be at an end. Ma and his insurgent army could simply vanish back into the landscape, knowing the autumn rains would soon enough wash away their tracks.

Po Cheng did his sums. Even should the Imperial Army be summoned back to the Celestial City immediately, autumn was likely to find it still in the field. Ordering it to carry on with its pursuit on the other hand, as even the most urgent communication would take a further three days to reach the government generals, meant that Ma would be able to count on at least a week's head start.

What a quandary! Whichever way one turned, the prospect appeared bleak. One was left with no recourse other than to remind oneself that tomorrow would be another day, and in fact, when the Chief Minister—who had not been to bed at all that night—looked out of the window of his office, he saw that it already was.

THE INVITATION HAD arrived at a somewhat inconvenient time but how could he ignore it? Better for history to record that the Chief Minister, despite the raft of serious matters with which he had been grappling, had put those aside long enough to attend, accompanied by his wife, the first performance in the capital of the recently reconstituted Small Fulness Theatre Company. The address on their invitation was that of a rather run-down edifice which a now-faded signboard identified as having once been *The Forest of Blows Boxing Academy*.

The fellow had come full circle, and the banner prominently displayed at the entrance showed that he still had no scruples when it came to quoting reviews yet to be written about events which had yet to take place:

IT REACHES NEW HEIGHTS!
IT PLUMBS NEW DEPTHS!

It was Widow Wen who was taking the tickets, and Po Cheng was for a moment transported back to those carefree days on the road when his only concerns had been dog bites, flea bites, bedbugs and convincing Wang Tzu to cough up a firewood fee so that the company could have hot baths.

The play to be performed was *The Ladies of Plum Village Get Their Day in Court*. Wang Tzu was again to play the Visiting Magistrate, with the same five actors—Tiger, Bear, Monkey, Deer and Owl—making up the jury. The remaining roles were to be played by actresses—or at any rate would-be actresses—spirited away from the Blue Heaven Pavilion.

To represent the village catalpa tree beneath which the drama was to unfold, a broom had been 'planted' upside down in a bucket. But what was missing, Po Cheng pointed out to Precious Pearl, was the stool on which he himself had sat, in his role as the court clerk.

'I'm sure it's nothing personal,' she replied, sensibly. 'Why pay someone an actor's salary just to sit and take notes?'

The story, as taken from his own notes, was of how easily people who knew nothing of the world beyond their own boundary stones could be deceived. It was a story which, even on a second hearing, left him feeling by turns angry, despondent and more than a little ashamed. Others in the audience, to his surprise, seemed to find the play amusing, perhaps because one of the girls from the Blue Heaven kept forgetting her lines, so leading them to believe that they were watching a comedy. Poking fun at country people, after all, was the stock-in-trade of the city's most popular playwrights.

All in all, the performance was admirable. Wang Tzu made clear his own dismay at the laughter but did so in character, by repeatedly calling for *order-in-the-court*. This the audience took in good spirits, and afterwards, when the cast members were taking their bows, the poor girl who had repeatedly fluffed her lines was cheered to the rafters.

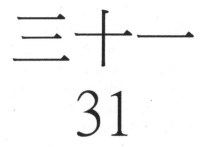

31

ATTRITION | HEAVEN'S DESIGN, EARTH'S DODGES |
IT MIGHT NOT BE TRUE BUT IT'S TIMELY | A GAME
OF CAT AND MOUSE | A BIRTHDAY BOY | EARLY
THIS YEAR, THE WILTING GRASS OF AUTUMN

What was to be done? Was mere happenstance to dictate the future course of events? Naturally the populace ought to be kept informed by the government, even with regard to distant occurrences, but this had to be done without creating alarm, and hence the practice generally employed by governments with something to hide. Hence, misdirection.

And so it was that news of the capture of General Ma's abandoned headquarters had been made public throughout the Celestial City beneath a heading strongly suggesting that final victory, after this, would be a mere formality:

REBELS NOW ON THE RUN!

But were they truly on the run? Ma appeared to be making no effort to cover his tracks, nor did he seem to be in any hurry, being instead content to remain just far enough ahead of his pursuers to ensure that his patchwork force would be safely beyond the range of the government crossbows.

What further confused matters were the gifts which he left behind for those whose task it was to run him to ground: large earthenware jars of still-cool spring water for instance, assorted snacks and—to mark the first day of autumn—a small flock of sheep which the government cooks soon converted into a platter of succulent kebabs.

The Chief Minister's response to this was to convene what had by now become popularly known as his 'war cabinet'. He summoned, that was to say, his First Secretary.

'So what do you make of it, Chow? Is this the behaviour of someone in his right mind?'

'It's the behaviour of someone wishing to conceal his true intentions, Excellency.'

And was that not what they should be doing as well? Had the art of war not been defined, in the past, as the art of deceit? The art of misdirection, but carried to an extreme?

'These are thorny matters, Chow. Is one ever fully aware of one's true intentions? And if not, then what is the meaning of deceit? Is it not just one's own dark arts, when employed by someone else?'

The Lady Regent, meanwhile, had weighed in with a measure of her own. The individual hitherto known as General Ma, she decreed, had been stripped of his rank and was in future, in all official documents, to be referred to as Warlord Ma:

See that the word gets spread, Chief Minister. Let's just see how the insolent fellow manages to take this in his stride!

Getting word of his demotion to Ma would not be easy, as the established line of communication between the capital and the Imperial Army was by now in tatters. Various individuals, under cover of darkness, were placing trip lines across the roads used by the couriers and it had yet to be determined whether they were doing so out of sympathy with the insurgents, out of a dislike of the government as presently constituted or simply because they objected to having their sleep disturbed during the night by the sound of a galloping horse.

BRIGHT SUMMER, THE season of growth, expansion and rival armies in the field, had abruptly given way to Brooding Autumn, the season of harvest and lengthening shadows, but still the Imperial Forces were in the field and still in pursuit of the newly designated Warlord Ma. In the Celestial City, while the Chief Minister continued to deal with requisitions for more rope and yet more arrows, the Lady Regent was busy arranging for the festivities which were to take place to celebrate the anniversary of the Little Luminary's accession to the Peacock Throne:

> *Of course it's not the real anniversary, Chief Minister, but why stand on ceremony? These are vexing times and are we meant to take them lying down?*

Why stand on ceremony? Why be dictated to by the calendar? The ruler was a boat, the people were the water and the same water which could float a boat—Her Ladyship argued—could also capsize it. Hence the people needed to be given the impression that things were moving forward.

'Which is all very well,' Po Cheng supposed, 'but what sort of gift is likely to be appropriate for someone whose anniversaries are determined not by history but by reasons of State?'

The invitation specified that his presence was required not in the Bright Hall, as previously, but in the Throne Room, and the scene when he arrived there, with his present under his arm, was much as he might have imagined it: the still-diminutive figure of His Small Highness was perched somewhat tentatively on the huge, velvet-upholstered Peacock Throne, where he was being fussed over, and quite outrageously so in Po Cheng's opinion, by a bevy of butterfly-browed palace ladies.

Seeing who was now approaching the throne, the palace ladies retreated, backing away in unison, like ballerinas, balancing on the tiptoes of their tiny feet. The Chief Minister kowtowed, clumsily, and by the time he had risen to his feet again, the boy was reaching out impatiently for his present.

'It's already wound, Your Highness. You need only to pull on the cord and see what happens.'

He had not forgotten the boy's fondness for all things bizarre. It was a monk, a wooden monk, a clockwork monk, and nearly life-size.

'Alms! Alms!' pleaded the monk, thrusting out a begging bowl.

The boy's face lit up with joy. He wanted the thing wound up again at once.

'Alms! Alms!' persisted the automaton.

By this time everyone was watching and not least the Lady Regent.

'Again!' the boy indicated.

What Po Cheng had failed to take into account, when choosing that particular gift, was that there was a stage in every boy's life when he took great pleasure in being deliberately irritating.

'Alms! Alms!'

A hasty departure from the Throne Room was impossible. Not even a chief minister, when the Peacock Throne was occupied, was permitted to turn his back on it. Even the head of the government, for the sake of protocol, was obliged to employ the clownish, side-to-side shuffle which had over the centuries led courtiers to believe—like the proverbial crab—that only they could walk straight.

AUTUMN WAS SOON well entrenched and when not required anywhere else the Chief Minister took long walks back and forth within the narrow confines of his office. With the dropping temperatures, more substantial rations were going to be necessary if the Imperial Army was to remain in the field, along with warmer clothing and heavier blankets for the men, and for the officers, thicker quilts. And how long would it be before people began to notice that for every cabbage despatched to the South, to an army which had as yet to confront a single insurgent, there was one less cabbage for sale in the market stalls of the capital?

He was also reminded, during his perambulations from one side of his office to the other, of the motto which he had seen prominently displayed in the Throne Room:

CHEERFUL IN SUMMER, CAUTIOUS IN AUTUMN, THOUGHTFUL IN WINTER, AND YOUTHFUL IN SPRING!

Of course it was politic for the moods of the ruler to mark, and be consonant with the changing of the seasons but were they truly essential to it?

All in all, the more time that he spent considering the situation in which he found himself, the more ludicrous his position seemed to be. Was he still in charge of anything?

Did it matter in the least what his opinions were? Any instructions issued from the capital, as things were, would reach the government generals far too late to be of interest to anyone apart from historians or antiquarians.

These gloomy ruminations were cut short when First Secretary Chow suddenly appeared with what at first glance appeared to be a miserable excuse for a child in tow.

'This creature was behaving strangely, Excellency. She sneaked into the building through a window, to be exact.'

'Good work, Chow. Leave her to me. I've dealt with her type before.'

He knew that face, that frown and those wretched clothes. He had—to cut a long story short—once hired her to row him across a river.

'So tell me,' he said when they were alone. 'Why didn't you use the door like everyone else?'

'Because the monk told me not to. He said to be discreet.'

'Ah,' thought Po Cheng. 'A monk again. I must have monks on my mind.'

'So this monk,' he said aloud, 'did he by any chance have a name?'

'Why wouldn't he have? He said to tell you, if you asked, that his name was Jade Verity.'

BY WHAT WAS, no doubt deliberately, a round-about route, they arrived eventually at what would have once been a quite elegant teahouse.

The paint on its elaborate latticework façade, where it was not chipped off completely, was badly faded but it was not hard to imagine the clientele of such an ornate establishment, the men in elaborate headwear and the women with their faces half-concealed behind their elaborate fans.

'You're to go straight in,' ordered the little boat girl.

As the door was half off its hinges, the Chief Minister didn't stand on ceremony but simply climbed in through the gap that was left. He sensed, despite the fact that he had never set foot in such a place previously, that he was on familiar ground. His having been taken to this particular teahouse was thus not to be put down to coincidence. Was coincidence after all—in rational thought—not considered to be an explanation of last resort?

The so-called 'monk' then came forward out of the half-light and offered him her hand. This was indeed the person who he had first known as Jade Verity and then later, in a different setting, as Madame Ma.

'It was good of you, Chief Minister, to be so prompt.'

'I couldn't help myself. Curiosity got the better of me.'

And suddenly he knew where they must be, even if not yet the reason why she had chosen it as the site for their meeting. It was here—to the Early Spring Teahouse—that Lady Yao and her brother had been brought as children, fresh from the countryside, to be introduced, on the floor above, to the sordid side of life in the Celestial City.

'The sooner we get started, Chief Minister, the sooner that your curiosity will be satisfied. How much do you know about this place?'

'Just what everyone knows. That Lady Yao and her brother, as children, were brought here in a dog-cart.'

'Then allow me to amend that. In actual fact, there were three siblings … .'

She had been the youngest, the runt of the litter, so to speak. For her it had been a great adventure, first a ride in a dog-cart and then her first view of a busy city, with all manner of people constantly on the move, coming and going, but somehow managing not to collide.

'But we had not been brought here, of course, to join in the fun. We were merely wares.'

The two eldest siblings had been taken at once to the floor above the teahouse but she herself, as she was too young even for the most jaded appetites, had been made to work in the teahouse kitchen, tending to the cooking fires and scrubbing pots. Each evening, however, from the floor above, she could hear the sound of music and peals of laughter.

'I made a nuisance of myself, I'm afraid. I pestered and I pestered. The girls who worked on the floor above did a dance each evening for their gentlemen callers, a dance called "Crossing at the Ford", and why couldn't I join in as well?'

'Ah, at the ford. And you didn't know at the time that that dance was notorious?'

'There were any number of things which, at the time, I didn't know.'

It wasn't, properly speaking, a dance at all. The girls simply lined up and stepped forward as one, lifting their skirts as they did so in order to show off their pubic hair.

'I got what I deserved, I suppose,' conceded Madame Ma. 'I was still a child and I could be quite insufferable when I didn't get my own way. So there I was, humiliated, the only one in the line with nothing yet between my legs for the gentlemen to stare at.'

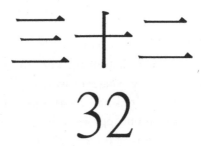

32

SCHISM | DISHARMONY IN HEAVEN, ADVERSITY ON
EARTH | CROSSED DESTINIES | A GOOD TIME TO BE
TAKING PRECAUTIONS | NEVER RELEASE A TIGER
TO THE JUNGLE, OR A DRAGON TO THE OCEAN

Anyone noticing them on the riverbank that evening would
no doubt have concluded that there was nothing suspicious
about it, that they were merely paying a visit to the grave of
their son and would perhaps be tidying up while they were
there in order to prepare the grave for winter. To encourage
just such a belief, Precious Pearl was carrying a watering can
and Po Cheng was wearing his patchwork robe, which he
now put on only for gardening. Perhaps he ought to have
known better than to attend a meeting with the wife of
someone designated as an enemy of the State but might she
not—for all he knew—have slipped into the capital in order
to negotiate the terms of her husband's surrender?

At the grave, as they weeded the small flower garden which Precious Pearl had planted, they could speak without fear of being overheard.

'Please don't keep me in suspense,' pleaded Precious Pearl. 'Had she come to surrender or hadn't she?'

'She most definitely came to negotiate but the subject of surrender never came up.'

At first the three siblings had stuck together and looked after one another, one toiling in the kitchen of the teahouse and the other two doing whatever was required of them on the floor above. Out of this had come a plan, namely to put to use what their own unhappy experience had taught them and go into a similar sort of business themselves.

'And are you sure that Wu should be hearing this?' interrupted Precious Pearl, indicating the stone beneath which he lay.

'No one ought to hear it but keeping it a secret would be even worse.'

At that point, according to Madame Ma, fate had intervened. One morning, when she went out into the alley behind the teahouse with a basket of ashes from the kitchen stoves, she found a man standing there urinating. He was not in the least handsome, not with his laughably crooked face, but her heart nevertheless leapt and her reason told her that she had best act fast.

'Carry on,' she had told the fellow. *'No need to be shy. And would you like to see a dance? Would you like to watch me cross a ford?'*

Hence her first encounter with Bulldog Ma. Although she had known little about prize fighting, it was obvious that someone who lost all of his fights was unlikely ever to become a champion and that it was up to her to set him on a new course. She would be his, she therefore promised, but only on the condition that he pass the Military Examination, which after all consisted of little more than archery and leaping over obstacles.

> *'And after that, my love, I could cross the ford for you every night.'*

THE NIGHTS WERE closing in and the first snow flurries were in the air when the Chief Minister next took shelter under Magpie Bridge, where he found Li Ting, as always, ready with his latest report on the minutiae of life in the Celestial City, on those matters which it would not have been possible to observe from the top floor of the Jade Tower but only by someone strategically placed below, someone who was able to move unnoticed among those who spread the gossip and repeated the rumours which to a large extent made up everyday discourse in the capital.

Li, forever curious, had managed to overhear rumours, he reported, concerning a strange monk who had recently visited the capital but had, during his stay, never entered a temple or a monastery.

'Ah so,' the Chief Minister replied, somewhat uneasily. 'A monk on a spree, perhaps?'

'If so, he was misinformed. He was seen entering a brothel which was shut down years ago.'

How complicated things were becoming. It was no secret that girls had often been delivered from that brothel to the Inner City, to share the couch of the ageing but still childless Emperor, and that in the end it had been not some nubile novice but a somewhat more shop-worn beauty who had turned out to be, against all the odds, seemingly just what the Son of Heaven had been waiting for. So, in due course, the Emperor had his heir, the elder Yao sister had a title and the younger sister had become an embarrassment.

Po Cheng turned his mind back to the matter at hand.

'So no one knows for sure, Li, what that monk might have been after?'

'No one who's prepared to say, at any rate.'

There was also unsettling news coming out of the Inner City. The Little Luminary had installed the mechanical monk on the Peacock Throne and was carrying on endless whispered conversations with it. What had been intended as a mere toy, had become a confidant.

'And what next, Li? One shudders to think.'

'And rightly so,' agreed Li Ting. 'Boy emperors grow into emperors in the same way as tiger cubs grow into tigers.'

Alone afterwards, standing atop Magpie Bridge and listening to the water rushing past under him, Po Cheng filled in for himself a few more pieces of the puzzle. The younger Yao sister was true to her word and had married a mere foot soldier, whereupon Lady Yao had him promoted overnight to the rank of general and then sent the poor fellow, along with his wife, to the nethermost corner of the Empire to chase bandits.

That much was evident but not where he himself fitted into this family history. Why had he been summoned to that teahouse of ill repute? Why, in government, was nothing ever straightforward and—given that it was not—how could one be expected to get anything done?

'Just do what you're paid to do,' had been Madame Ma's instructions, *'no more and no less. The duty of any functionary is to continue functioning, to turn up faithfully for work, to shuffle his papers and to await the verdict of history.'*

ALL MANNER OF opinions were now being expressed on the walls of the Celestial City under cover of darkness and with utter disregard for propriety. One morning, in full view of the parade ground on which new recruits were being put through their paces, lest any reinforcements should later on be required, the following scandalous notice was found to have been painted:

Q: WHO IS IT WHO FIGHTS THE BATTLES?
A: AND ON WHOSE CHESTS ARE THE MEDALS PINNED!

What one faction had begun, others were soon copying, including factions which supported the Lady Regent, even if they had little sympathy for those individuals who served under her. Hence the Chief Minister, to his dismay, saw that he too was being pilloried:

Q: AND WHEN A SWIFT STEED WAS CALLED FOR?
A: ONLY A LAME DONKEY CAME FORWARD!

What more was he meant to be doing? Did he not spend hours each day, when not pacing or staring out of his window, studying the map on his office wall and keeping it, as best he could, up to date? Warlord Ma and his insurgent troops had continued to lead the Imperial Forces on a merry chase across a far-distant and lacklustre province, much of which—Po Cheng could still well recall—was left a vast wasteland owing to a river having mysteriously changed its course.

'Or maybe it wasn't so mysterious,' argued Li Ting, who had formerly been the sub-prefect of that unhappy province. 'Think about it. Ma, when he arrived in the province, would have needed a proper headquarters and a town to support it, as well as fields and orchards and some way of watering them.'

'So you think, Li, that he was clever enough to divert a river?'

'Probably not. The fellow's no fox, nor does he need to be, as he's married to a vixen.'

Meanwhile, a new line of communication was in place. A series of spindly legged, hilltop watchtowers had been erected, by means of which messages could be transmitted during the day using smoke signals and at night by coded drumbeats. While fine in theory, the towers still left much to be desired, as the high winds of autumn played havoc with the smoke signals, and what was conveyed by the drummers was often distorted or drowned out completely by thunder.

Was there anything which wore one down so much as having nothing else to do but wait for news upon which it would be—by the time that it arrived—too late to act? How not to become discouraged, dispirited or downhearted? How not to imagine oneself slumped over one's desk with deadly spiders crawling out of one's mouth, seated in a public latrine with one's fingers down one's throat or strung up by one's own hand in Great Redemption Square?

THE SCHEME WHICH Lady Yao came up with in order to boost the morale of those in the capital who were losing patience with the prolonged pursuit of Warlord Ma and his ragtag army, had in Po Cheng's view but one thing to be said for it. In government, even the most ludicrous action ordered by the ruler was preferable to having nothing at all to do, and what choice did one have, as a mere functionary who wished to appear as if he were still functioning, than to carry out even the most ridiculous exercises, if ordered to do so from above?

First of all a wagon had to be located which had not yet been commandeered by the army, along with a horse still strong enough to pull it, a drummer, a street vendor and as many unshaven, unkempt and generally disreputable-looking individuals as the wagon would hold. Not wishing to become too closely associated with what he considered to be a hare-brained scheme, the Chief Minister summoned his First Secretary.

'Get onto it right away, will you, Chow? As for those men, get them out of jail if you have to.'

No sooner said than done. Chow, as a policeman, knew exactly how to ask favours in such a way as to make clear that he wasn't prepared to take no for an answer. Hence the cast was soon assembled and the show could commence.

'Good work as always, Chow. If you ever want a commendation, let me know.'

'Heaven forbid, Excellency. In times like these, one is well advised to keep one's head down.'

So, as requested by Her Ladyship, the show was on the road. Up one street and down the next was the order of march, led by a drummer obtained from the Bureau of Music, whose task it was to draw the public's attention to what was to come. What came next was what had until then been a hay wagon but was now packed with individuals who had been rounded up from here and there and not least from the city's drinking dens. Finally, following closely behind, was an erstwhile leek-and-cabbage vendor, a strong-lunged fellow, hired to cry to the rooftops his curious and unaccustomed wares:

Captured enemy scum! Captured enemy scum!

三十三

33

STALEMATE | HEAVEN'S AUTHORITY, EARTH'S
INSOUCIANCE | IGNORE IT AND IT APPROACHES,
REACH FOR IT AND IT FLIES | DECEPTION | THEY
DON'T SEE A FOREST FOR THE TREES

All was not well, most certainly it was not well. The Chief
Minister's face darkened as he poured over the latest
communiqué from the front, and this despite the boast of
Lady Yao's hand-picked generals that the end of the affair
was now near and victory imminent. To this point the chase
had taken place over open ground, with the government
troops able to see the glow of the insurgents' campfires in
the evenings, but the rebels' flight was now about to be cut
off by what was shown on the map as being an impenetrable
forest.

'Unfortunately, Chow, there's one thing that their maps
won't show them.'

The Chief Minister could recall as if it were only yesterday how—as a fugitive himself—he had arrived at that forest of closely growing trees and found the only passage to be on the faint trails left by animals. Subsequently, however, had he not heard the sound of trees being felled? Had a certain individual, still known at that time as General Ma, not been constructing a road?

'A military road, Chow. One wide enough for an armoured carriage or a supply wagon, but not one inch wider.'

'How curious then, Excellency, that it should not show up on the army's maps.'

'That's just what I've been thinking, Chow.'

Perhaps it was not yet too late. The government generals could be forbidden to enter the forest, no matter how tempting it might be to do so. Whether or not the order arrived in time, the Chief Minister would at least have done the best that he could under the circumstances.

The order, unfortunately, was returned unsent, along with an apology. The line of communication between the government of Lady Yao and the forces sent to defend it— sad to say—had been severed. A coordinated effort by individuals sympathetic to the rebels had resulted, over the course of a single night, in every second hilltop watchtower having been burned to the ground.

Where there was no news, rumours abounded. The channels of communication employed by the insurgents were various and were said to include not just word of mouth but the barking of dogs and the cackling of chickens. News from the South still reached the capital but only through the secret smugglers' tunnels which undermined its walls; hence it reached the ears of the Chief Minister only after having been recounted in the Green Monkey Tavern and there overheard by Li Ting, who passed it on, in due course, under Magpie Bridge.

The military road had been but slightly camouflaged and so must have been too good to resist. Fully convinced that this was the endgame and that the insurgents were now within their grasp, the pursuing generals finally called for speed and just when caution would have been the wiser course.

'Those with ribbons already pinned to their chests,' remarked Li Ting, in an aside, 'were no doubt making room for one more.'

A forced march, the first of the campaign, had brought them to an abandoned boxing camp and it was there, in the heart of that dense forest, that the road abruptly came to an end. Even more surprising to the pursuing forces was that an enemy which at daybreak had been only a half-day's march ahead, was now nowhere to be found.

'Amazing indeed, Li. So how was it done? How did Ma get his own forces out of the way just in time?'

'By disbanding them. Having marched his men to the boxing camp, he then sent them off in pairs, in all directions, each trooper accompanied by a former bandit. Who better than a bandit, after all, for slipping through cracks, and who better for following a bandit than a bandit-chasing trooper?'

TO TURN AROUND the Imperial Army in the confined space of a dense forest was no simple task, as this required the felling of more trees, and it was then discovered that no axes had been brought along, only the hatchets with which the cooks had been provided for cutting firewood. So it was that by the time all of the carriages and wagons had been reversed and were pointed in the right direction for exiting the forest, it was too late. What had previously been a firm road had been reduced by the autumn rains to a mere muddy track; a farmer, no doubt at the orders of Warlord Ma, had then driven a herd of cattle back and forth over it, thereby transforming it into a quagmire.

So what choice had there been other than to agree to a Winter Truce? The Imperial Forces were to remain right where they were, camped out in the forest, in return for which Warlord Ma would keep them supplied until the spring, at which point, once the roads had dried out again, the government generals would be free, if they so wished, to launch a Spring Offensive.

It was a shameful truce and the Chief Minister, when on his way to work in the mornings in his ministerial coach, sat with his head bowed, attempting to appear as humble and contrite as it was possible to appear in so grand a conveyance. Whether or not it was fair to blame an official for what he had been powerless to prevent was a consideration only for the official in question, not for anyone with something to throw at him.

Once within the privacy of his office, rather than dwell on the unfairness of his situation, Po Cheng turned his attention back to the bookshelves on the wall and what caught his attention this time was a modest work, *Veritable Discourses*, which had somehow found its way among the many and more imposing volumes of *Statutes Currently Pending*.

The *First Discourse*, which was indeed concerned with first things, began with a truly far-reaching analogy: in the same way as a myriad of musical works had been composed using the same five notes of the musical scale, the author claimed, so too had the Myriad Things been fashioned from the same five essential elements.

In addition, just as the musical notes formed a scale, so

the essential elements aligned themselves in accordance with the following protocol:

METAL CUTS WOOD
WOOD ENCLOSES WATER
WATER WETS EARTH
EARTH PUTS OUT FIRE
AND FIRE MELTS METAL.

The author was obviously fond of music and perhaps was even a musician himself. Just as each of the essential elements, wherever it occurred, could be identified by a distinctive quality, he continued, so each of the musical notes had its own distinctive tone, whether sounded on a flute, pipe, xylophone, bell, zither or whistle and so awakened in sentient beings joy, sorrow, playfulness, expectation or remorse.

It was an old trick, Po Cheng recalled from his earlier readings, that of putting two and two together in order to come up with five. Just as the five musical tones corresponded to the five emotions, in the author's view, so too the five elements gave to the Myriad Things, respectively: refinement, endurance, flow, inertia and combustion.

And again, just as a musical composition was fashioned using more than one note, so too were the Myriad Things made up of more than one element. All came about through admixture, a little of this and a pinch of that. All had been put together from the same five elements, albeit combined according to altogether different specifications.

And this, the anonymous author concluded his *First Discourse*, was what enabled things to cohere. Like called to like. So, in the case of music, a single rhapsody could evoke in one person expectation and in another remorse. And so too—among the insects—a breed of caterpillar which when eating green leaves turned green and when eating yellow leaves, yellow.

WARLORD MA, IT appeared, was keeping to his word. Caches of food had been left in the forest for the 'guests', who were also supplied with axes, animal skins, needles and thread, and a postal service of sorts which functioned for the sending of letters home, although not for receiving any back. Behind these seemingly conciliatory measures, however, the Chief Minister saw clever calculation. Would it still be possible, he worried, when winter was over, to rally the troops? Who would wish, by then, to bite the hand which had been feeding him?

Dark clouds were gathered above the Celestial City, reminding Po Cheng of the lament of a poet whose name he could no longer recall but whose lines hit the nail squarely on the head:

> WHERE HAS IT GONE,
> ONE'S CHILDISH JOY,
> AT THE SPECTACLE OF
> SOFTLY FALLING SNOW?

Where indeed? Already news had reached the capital of the first casualties—of men who were missing fingertips or had lost noses, lips or ears and so would never again touch a woman tenderly, smell her perfume, join his lips to hers or hear her sighs. Such carnage, and none of it down to enemy archers or to swordplay but only to frostbite!

A battle was meanwhile raging right there on the Chief Minister's doorstep, a battle which might go down in history, he imagined, as 'The Battle of the Brushes'. No wall was spared, nor any mercy shown. Warlord Ma was portrayed as an ape with a cap on and Madame Ma as a snake on four legs. In answer, the Lady Regent was shown crossing a ford with her skirt hoisted up to her waist and the Chief Minister characterized as a foolish sage whose notion of fishing was to sit beside a stream with a frying pan waiting for a fish to jump into it.

Nor did Precious Pearl escape unscathed. The likeness of the person named as Pricey Pearl was not unflattering and neither were the accusations levelled against her completely unfounded. She had once worked, according to the posters, as a show-all girl in an establishment calling itself an academy of art, in which establishment she had repeatedly defrauded the public by never, in fact, showing all.

Nothing was any longer sacred, as even the late Emperor was held up to ridicule. The poor old fellow was depicted lying naked on his couch and being examined by a physician, while a number of clearly displeased palace ladies looked on. And it was the physician's diagnosis which supplied the caption:

It's an obvious case, your graces, of a short rope for a deep well.

What gall! But at the same time Po Cheng could not help but admire the skill of it, the efficiency, the manner in which —with a few strokes of a brush—the manhood of one emperor had been put into question and doubt cast on the paternity of another.

BEFORE STARTING ON the *Second Discourse*, which the author had warned would deal with matters which it was far easier to pronounce upon than to understand, Po Cheng first cleared his desk of all remaining government business, sent Chow out for some steamed buns, removed his sandals, loosened the sash of his robe and rolled up his sleeves.

In order to succeed in any endeavour, according to the *Second Discourse*, even one so simple as laying one stone atop another to construct a wall, one needed to be aware that everything which existed—even a stone—was in perpetual motion. What went around, came around. What entered through the door, later flew out through the window. What was not on its way somewhere was on its way back and was therefore likely to encounter, somewhere along the way, the turbulence of its own wake.

The author paused to give examples of the absurd behaviour which could result when affairs were left in the hands of those with little or no knowledge of the true nature of the Myriad Things or of their preferred pathways:

1 *Draining a pond to catch a fish*
2 *Sowing beans to get hemp*
3 *Mending with a broken needle*
4 *Travelling East to go West*
5 *The compass survived but not the ship*

There were no exceptions. Nothing stood still, how could it? What drove the Myriad Things was the force which drove the entire Cosmos, the never-exhausted force generated by the never-ceasing commingling of yin and yang.

'Yin and yang,' Po Cheng recalled, with amusement, from his days as a schoolboy. 'One pushes and one pulls, and vice versa. Now she's on top and now he is.'

Hence the turning of the heavens, the progression of the seasons, the sprouting of a seed, the bud bursting into a flower, the snake sloughing its skin, the male crocodile bellowing on the riverbank. For everything there was a season and hence a time when the wind was fair and a time when it was likely to be anything but.

In his *Third Discourse*, the author promised, he would take on the topic of 'time' and demonstrate that time was more than mere duration. In the meantime, the reader was left to ponder the following temporal anomalies:

1 *A poor beginning produces a fine outcome.*
2 *A note plucked on a zither sounds on a lute.*
3 *Holding to the past, while living in the present.*
4 *Bringing up the past to discredit the present.*
5 *The teeth fall out, the tongue flaps on.*

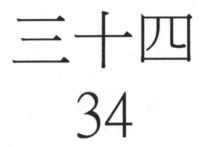

三十四

34

PERTURBATION | HEAVEN'S SCRUTINY, EARTH'S BLUSHES | STUDENT PANG SETTLES UP | DANGER FROM A RETURNING ARROW | THOSE IN A NEST FEAR THE WIND, THOSE IN A BURROW DREAD THE WATER

The notes which the Chief Minister was now receiving from the Lady Regent indicated someone who—to say the least—was no longer sure of her position. Why, she demanded, were things being allowed to slide? Were weeds not flourishing and was it not for want of a hoe?

Instead of people being praised for their restraint, aberrations are now being applauded, abominations celebrated and people being admired for having no shame … .

The Chief Minister replied to her tirades with what he hoped history might regard as calm reason:

Troubled times, Your Ladyship, have often in the past given rise to heroes. All the same, one must be prepared for others to come forward as well … .

The news, as overheard by Li Ting, was not all bad. Yes, the Imperial Army was trapped in a forest but what had been a mere boxing camp had by now been transformed into a full-blown military encampment, complete with a parade ground, a mess tent and log cabins for the officers. Spring, on the other hand, remained a long way off and for how long—Po Cheng had to ask himself—could someone who had never aspired to being a circus performer continue to juggle with more than one ball?

First thing every morning, he read the report prepared overnight by the Court Astrologer on the current state of the heavens. An early spring would be indicated in the heavens should the Jade Archer be detected making an early approach to the couch of the Splayed Maiden.

So why not a bribe? Why not offer Ma a generous pension, along with a release from his tribute obligations, so leaving him free to continue pursuing bandits, should he so wish, on the weekends, as a mere recreation? But how, on the other hand, was such a generous offer to be funded?

A note reached him, in the midst of all this, from his old friend Student Pang, saying that he had now given up all hope of ever passing an Imperial Examination and so had moved out of the Celestial Harmony Lodging House. He gave no forwarding address, simply closing with a poem:

TWO FRIENDS,

THE ROAD DIVIDES,

A PARTING OF THE WAYS

Po Cheng set himself the task of reading between the lines. Pang was a fine fellow, one who had always held that the world ought to be a far fairer place than it was, and would he not then be likely to prefer, on principle, any possible future government to whatever one was already in place?

Po Cheng peered from the window of his office, wondering if Pang might still be somewhere among the crowd in the street below. These were difficult times, turbulent times, when some were saying one thing and others saying just the opposite. Just the sort of times, Po Cheng speculated, when someone like Pang might truly come into his own.

WAS IT SOLACE that he sought or was it distraction? Was it not odd, in either case, that someone who had by now come to despair of his ability to influence events on Earth should nonetheless busy himself reflecting on those of the Cosmos? What drove the constant movement of the Cosmos, Po Cheng was reminded in the *Third Discourse*, did not act alone but in tandem.

First to emerge from the primordial sludge had been the yang, the male energy, whose obvious inadequacy, when acting on its own, had called forth the yin, the female energy, and so to this day the invocation spoken over a new-born infant by the midwife:

HEAT FROM THE SUN, DEW FROM THE MOON!

Where yin wasn't, yang was, and vice versa. Yin was the dark, the shade, the soft, the still, the yielding, the cloudy, the concave, the low-lying, and whatever yin lacked, yang supplied. Hence they were able to work in concert, neither encroaching on the other; whenever one advanced, the other one withdrew, turn and turn about, and hence they left no gaps.

Yin sought to conserve, to complete, to concentrate, to consolidate, while yang strove to create, to expand, to develop, to inflate; from this collaboration had come about the turning of the heavens, the succession of the seasons, the phases of the moon, the stations of the sun, the rise and fall of tides, the cycles of insects, the migration of birds and the swerving of a school of fish.

'*And,*' the author added, provocatively, '*the swerves of time.*'

What prevented motion from being a mere change of position—namely the push-and-pull of the yin/yang energy, the very energy which accounted for motion in the first place—also prevented time from being mere duration. Only a blockhead would ever see time, the author claimed, as simply one thing after another.

Time was not well-behaved. No matter how time was calibrated, whether by means of shifting shadows, the steady drip of water, the burning down of a candle or the slow slippage of a column of sand, there remained an aspect of time which was not being measured:

> *Consider the morning hours when one must rush to get to work on time. Are these of the same length as the evening hours, when work is over for the day and one's sole concern is to find a wine shop which in order to compete for customers has lowered its prices?*

Time was not a current, it was a tide. Time, like motion, was subject to the unceasing interplay throughout the Cosmos of the yin/yang energies. Time could fly or time could drag.

Even foreigners were aware of this attribute of time and they sought to measure it by employing a pendulum, causing it to swing perpetually between two points which they called Tick and Tock.

QUITE PROBABLY, HE reflected, he had no one to blame but himself. His rise had perhaps been far too swift, leaving him with insufficient time to learn along the way the many things that one needed to know in order to master the art of governance. Perhaps a more pedestrian pace would have brought him to the same place in the end, but better prepared. What a pity then that while immersed in time from the moment of one's birth until the final instant of one's life, one was like the proverbial fish which—as was popularly believed—was the last to see the water.

Meanwhile new rumours were surfacing. The Imperial Army was required by the Winter Truce to stay put until the spring, and given the state of the roads it could do nothing else. No restrictions, on the other hand, had been placed on the insurgents, who had in any case already been disbanded, and it thus came as a most unpleasant surprise to the Chief Minister, to say the least, to hear that they were already regrouping.

Putting aside for the moment any further doubts as to his fitness for the post that he held, the Chief Minister at once summoned his First Secretary.

'So what are we to make of this, Chow? Could it be true?'

'Someone clearly wants us to think that it's true, Excellency, or else word of it would never have got out.'

'So it might be just a feint?'

'Or that might be what they want us to think.'

Upon leaving his office that evening, Po Cheng noticed a new poster and by the time he reached Government Row he had noticed dozens of them. The original would have been cut into a block of wood, after which rubbings could have been taken, for distribution throughout the Celestial City, so that wherever one looked, there it would be: the image of an insurgent with sharply chiselled features leading a small child by the hand towards a brighter future.

Precious Pearl had seen the same poster and heard the same rumours. The insurgent forces had no carriages or wagons, only a miscellany of carts and sledges for transporting their supplies, and so were little deterred by ice or snow. At that very moment, if the rumours were to be believed, an army of fur-clad semi-barbarians was on the march, heading for the capital and with Madame Ma herself pulling the lead sledge.

'Which is why,' said Po Cheng to Precious Pearl, not being able to think of any way to break this gently, 'I must now send you back to your family.'

'Because I've been a bad wife? Because I was sometimes remiss and failed to kindle the morning fire or to light the evening candle?'

'Of course you've been a good wife … .'

'And have you ever found, upon returning home, any hair but your own on your hairbrush?'

'Certainly not. But regardless of how this fiasco turns out, it's likely that I'll get the blame.'

'And where would anyone as industrious be found to replace you?'

'In the interregnum between one government and the next, my love, good sense is by no means certain to prevail.'

'Or anyone else who always comes when he's called?'

'There's that, I suppose, to cling to.'

'Or with such an attractive wife?'

SUCH LOYALTY! THE Chief Minister lay in bed beside his wife for some time that night without being able to sleep. How fortunate, despite his many failings, he mused, to have so staunch a companion. Once she had drifted off to sleep, however, he slipped from the bed, lit a lamp, put another log into the still-warm stove and sat down beside it to read another chapter of the *Veritable Discourses*, the fourth of which dealt entirely with the subject of music, which the author referred to now as the emissary of time and now as time's ambassador.

Music, like speech, the author speculated, may have come about by accident. Just as the cries of animals gave rise to human speech, so blowing into a hollow reed had led to the flute and beating on an empty pot to the drum.

What does it mean, in that case, to say that music is time's emissary? Is it not obvious? Where else if not from music did human beings learn of the importance of timeliness?

Timeliness. The sounding of just the right note at just the right moment. And was it not this which had allowed human beings to advance, leaving behind the ox to earn its keep by pulling a plough, the family dog by guarding the house and the cat by chasing mice?

And in what way might music also be said to be an ambassador? Is it not the role of an ambassador to report back on the affairs of the people among whom he has been sent to live, and by what better than by their music are said people to be judged?

Hence the need, in a well-run state, for a Bureau of Music, so that whatever was undertaken took place in an orderly fashion, in the manner of a country dance in which the inherent urge to be in motion was shaped by a longing for pattern. As an example of how music might be used to keep the populace in check, the author cited an ancient rule-of-thumb:

IF THE PEOPLE ARE FRACTIOUS, RETUNE THE PIPES;
IF THEY APPEAR LACKADAISICAL, RECAST THE BELLS.

Accuracy was essential. A *shang* note needed to be the same note whether sounded on a *shang* bell, produced by the *shang* string of a zither, by the *shang* pipe or by the *shang* bar on a xylophone. Like called to like, and music, if both timely and precise, would resonate throughout the Cosmos. So a single note, properly played, might simultaneously calm water, soothe the liver, delight the dog, be heard on Mars and please the East.

But what could do good, the author warned, could also do harm. Hence a single discordant note—whether coming from a cracked bell, a poorly tuned string or a careless sing-song girl—could cause Earth to shudder and Heaven to cringe.

三十五

35

ADJUDICATION | HEAVEN FOREVER, EARTH FOR
NOW | TOO LATE, ALAS, TO CLOSE THE PASSES | A
SUMMONS | A RECKONING | A CLEAR CASE OF
GUILTY IF CHARGED

He would be unable to complain later that he had not been
warned. There was something ominous that morning in the
tolling of the Thunder Drum as it sounded to awaken the
Celestial City. Po Cheng, all the same, rose as usual, paid his
accustomed morning visit to the latrine, donned his robe of
office and put away a hearty breakfast of gruel, papaya slices
and freshly delivered steamed buns. Whatever was coming,
he calculated, it was surely best to confront it with a full
stomach.

Not wishing to alarm his wife unnecessarily, he then sat
patiently as Precious Pearl—after plucking out a few white
hairs—tied his topknot. This was most certainly no time to

be giving the appearance of someone who was ageing or world weary or a figure from the past.

'All done,' Precious Pearl reported word for word just as she always did. 'The old devil's every bit as handsome as ever.'

His coach was waiting where it was meant to be waiting. The insurgents, in that case, must not yet be at the gates. All the same, according to the coachman, Lady Yao had fled the capital during the night, taking along the Small Son of Heaven, while leaving behind her brother, Marshal Yao, to tie up various loose ends.

There was as yet no sign of panic in the streets, no more so at any rate than there was bound to be when so many people in so many walks of life all set off at the same time for work. Upon reaching the Jade Tower and alighting from his coach, the Chief Minister nonetheless found himself confronted by an individual who appeared as if from nowhere to block his path.

'Whatever it is,' said Po Cheng, firmly, 'not here and not now. But perhaps if you could come back in a few days' time … .'

'For shame!' replied the fellow, indignantly. 'What sort of way is that to treat an old friend?'

'Ah! Those pilgrims that time! You were wearing a saddle on your back, hoping to be forgiven for having murdered your horse.'

Unfortunately, the pilgrim said mournfully, things had not gone well for him. The others had soon abandoned him, complaining that he was keeping them awake at night by talking in his sleep.

'Ah, in your sleep,' sympathized the Chief Minister. 'And how would it be possible to defend oneself against such a charge?'

Then one night when he was sleeping—lying alone in a ditch beside the road—someone had stolen the saddle. Seeing no point in going on after that, he had spent what little remained of his travel funds on strong drink.

'So when I heard about your own good fortune,' the fellow concluded, 'and your high position, I just naturally thought … .'

'And quite right too,' agreed Po Cheng. 'It's not every day that one hears such a sad history.' Having reached his office, the Chief Minister at once summoned his First Secretary. 'There's a fellow waiting downstairs, Chow. Find something for him to do, will you? It ought not to be anything too complicated and he'll need to be kept away from alcohol and from horses.'

HISTORY WOULD DOUBTLESS have the last word, Po Cheng had to accept, but did that mean that he must remain silent? Might he not, by anticipating history, get in a word or two of his own? Otherwise, was he not likely to go down in history as someone of signal incompetence, whose sole accomplishment was his having found his way into government in the first place? It was with this in mind that he took a sheet of rice paper from his desk and headed it as follows:

A TALL TREE INVITES THE WIND

WHY LEAVE HISTORY to the historians? Why not give his own version of events? Celebrating one's successes—this was called—and blaming one's failures on the times. But was the title which he had chosen not somewhat too assertive? And might people not imagine the author as being someone of superior physical stature?

He balled up that first sheet and took out a fresh one.

Why dwell on himself at all? Why not take the opposite course and proceed like the landscape painter who included in his work only a minuscule rendering of himself, seated at his easel, unobtrusively, in a bottom corner of the landscape? Why not offer the public a reflection on the innermost workings and practices of government which would leave behind, in the mind of the reader, the figure of a conscientious official dutifully seated unobtrusively at his desk?

Time for a new start, and for that a new title was required. A more modest title. One which would capture, in a single phrase, the aforementioned innermost workings of government. Po Cheng scratched his head, he chewed for a time on the wooden end of his brush and then it came to him:

ONE DAY OF FISHING,
TWO DAYS SPENT DRYING THE NETS

He sat back in his chair, already imagining that a book with that title on its cover was being sold in the streets from pushcarts, by women wearing colourful aprons and matching headscarves. He might even have got down to work eventually on what would surely have been an excellent book, had First Secretary Chow not appeared in the doorway.

'What's the occasion, Chow? Isn't it your job to *prevent* me from being disturbed?'

'Begging your pardon, Excellency, but I'm here in another capacity.'

So saying, the First Secretary, in his other capacity, produced a set of wooden wrist clamps. The Chief Minister put up no resistance and they were soon on their way down the stairs to the street and the police coach, which would no doubt be waiting.

'It's nothing personal, Excellency, but orders are orders.'

'Of course they are, Chow. One must always call things by their names.'

He could hardly blame Chow for doing his job or for doing it well. Nor was the job of the Secret Police any great secret, as it was enshrined in their motto:

SUPERIOR MEN MUST BE WATCHED;
THE REST NEED ONLY BE MOVED ON.

LITTLE HAD CHANGED since his last visit to the erstwhile boxing academy and more recently the home of the Small Fulness Theatre Company. The same work was still being performed—'The Ladies of Plum Village'—although not on that particular day, as the police notice on the door made clear:

PRIVATE FUNCTION!
PERFORMANCE CANCELLED!

The stage was still set as before but the benches on which the audience had sat were now stacked against the wall. More ominously still, there were no actors present, only a single individual who had taken possession of the seat intended for the Visiting Magistrate. A lone oil lamp lit the scene but it was nonetheless obvious, even in the half-light, that the interloper was wearing a mask.

'Do please take the stand, Chief Minister. No one else has turned up to testify in your favour, so this shouldn't take long.'

The fellow's voice was quite soft, surprisingly so since he could be none other than the brother of the Lady Regent,

Marshal Yao, the dreaded head of the Secret Police, who had been left behind by his sister to tie up loose ends and who had chosen to fulfil this charge wearing as his disguise for the day what must have been the most ludicrous mask that he could find, namely that of a grinning baby.

Once Po Cheng had taken his place, Marshal Yao redirected the lamp so that only their two faces were illuminated, or rather the face of the one and the false face of the other. An awkward silence followed, ending only when the former water marshal cleared his throat impatiently.

'Do, please, Chief Minister, be so good as to begin.'

'Me?' Po Cheng held up to the light the wooden blocks by which his wrists were restrained. 'Why should I begin, given that I've been brought here against my will?'

'Because ... .' The fellow hesitated, as if he himself were somewhat less than certain as to how to proceed. 'Because the sooner that you get things off your chest, the sooner this will all be over.'

'Ah, a confession. To save you the trouble, I suppose, of having to read out any charges.'

'And to save you, my friend, the trouble of having to deny them.'

HOW MUCH LONGER did they have? How long before the city fell? How long before the capital was overrun and there were bands of fur-clad and bearded semi-barbarians playing kickball in the statue gardens of the Inner City?

Po Cheng took his time, confessing to every shortcoming that he could think of but stopping short of mentioning his meeting with Madame Ma.

'And that about does it,' he no doubt wisely chose to conclude. 'I can see now where I went wrong but I knew no better at the time.'

Marshal Yao had not interrupted, nor had he made any notes. And what, Po Cheng thought, if their positions had been reversed? Would the Marshal have admitted that his reason for going about masked—as many were now claiming—was to hide the fact that his resemblance to the Little Luminary was far less likely to be that between an uncle and his nephew than that between a father and his son?

The fellow at this point produced a jar of spiced wine and two bowls, both of which he filled to their brims.

'Just to show that there are no hard feelings,' he explained.

The strangeness of all this gave Po Cheng pause. This did indeed somewhat resemble a theatrical performance, one in which he himself was a mere player acting out lines which had been scripted for him by someone else. Which in turn suggested that there might even yet be a final twist to the tale, a miraculous escape of some sort, perhaps through some hidden trapdoor.

Otherwise how was this farce likely to be brought to a close? Unhappily, no doubt. With the less than competent Chief Minister being carried off at the end of the final act feet first. And already the small oil lamp which had lit the scene in that makeshift theatre was behaving oddly, suddenly getting brighter, seemingly, of its own accord.

'So this is how it concludes?' Po Cheng addressed the baby-faced Marshal Yao. 'With a choice of poisoning, asphyxiation or the noose?'

'Not necessarily, my friend. Each to his own taste. If you can think of a better way to end these proceedings, let's hear it.'

三十六

36

ENLIGHTENMENT | HEAVEN'S WAYS, EARTH'S
BYWAYS | DAY FOR NIGHT | STEADY AS HE GOES.
SEEN WITH HIS EYES OPEN | SCHOOL DAZE | IT
PAYS TO CONSULT A SUBORDINATE

Schoolmaster Po, after a brief moment of confusion, realized that he was no longer in the Celestial City or on trial for his life but back in the countryside, stretched out on the bank of Nettle Creek. His head hurt, his throat was dry and the bright light which he had taken to be that from an oil lamp was in fact that of the morning sun.

He took a drink from the stream and washed his face.

'What a poor show!' he recalled. 'I failed even to congratulate the bride.'

He must have cut a poor figure indeed in the eyes of his students but what was done was done and the sooner that he was back in the schoolhouse and chalking that day's lesson onto the blackboard, the better.

'And did I or did I not,' he tried to remember, 'get around to dancing with Miss Ling?'

Only when he reached the first house in the village did his thoughts go back to the dream which had kept him occupied for what must have been the greater part of the night. It was the house, as well as the place of business, of Tailor Chan, and hence the notice displayed in its front window:

THE FOREST OF HATS HABERDASHERY!

Things came back to him in a rush. Tailor Chan, although no doubt perfectly competent, was known to take meticulous measurements of any female client who entered his shop, even if she had come in only for gloves or a scarf or for needles and thread.

And did this not explain the presence in Po Cheng's dream of Director Chan, of the Forest of Brushes Academy of Art, who had taken so much care over the positioning of his models?

'What strange games the mind plays,' reflected School-master Po, 'when let off its lead.'

Wedding decorations still draped the residence of the Ba family, none of whose members were as yet likely to be stirring. All the same, Po Cheng gave the house a wide berth. Suffice it to say of so powerful a family that there was nothing which occurred in Nettle Village, by day or by night, which was so private or so personal as to be entirely free of their influence.

He encountered no one else in the street, no other living creature, not even a dog or a chicken. Not even Granny Wen had got up yet, Granny Wen the village snoop, who at that hour was normally to be found at her window, keeping an eye out for anything worth passing on later to Headman Ba.

Leaving behind the inoffensive little house—which concealed behind it an unlicensed wine shop—Po Cheng's mind was drawn back to the dream and the goings on between Wang Tzu and the Widow Wen. What a fine sleight of hand that had been: *Granny* Wen was not a widow, never having married, but it was common knowledge that she had for years maintained an off-and-on relationship with a travelling salesman called Wang.

And speaking of Wang Tzu, there he was, still standing guard on the porch of the schoolhouse. The schoolmaster paused to remove the football scarf that someone had placed around the neck of the statue and to wipe off the rouge from its cheeks. Boys in Nettle Village, he reflected as he did so, had not ceased to be boys, nor girls to be girls.

THE MIDDLE SCHOOL classroom was just as he had left it on the day before, with the desks in neat rows, the blackboard wiped and the books all properly arranged on their shelves.

Once again he was struck by the ingenuity of which one was capable in a dream, for were these not the very bookshelves which had accompanied him in the course of his dream, following him, as it were, from office to office?

The sound of footsteps on the porch warned him that he no longer had the schoolhouse to himself. He thus sat down at his desk and took out the day's lesson plan so as to appear to be busy.

'Knock! Knock!'

'Ah, Miss Ling. You're just the person that I wanted to see.'

'Indeed, Colleague? And for how long would you have simply sat waiting for me to appear?'

'For as long as it took, Miss Ling. I'm in no condition this morning, I fear, to chase anyone down.'

The same khaki shirt, the same baggy trousers as always. She slid herself into one of the students' desks—which left her long legs protruding out the front—and looked up expectantly.

'So what is it then, Colleague? Are there inspectors headed our way?'

'Nothing so drastic. In fact you may well think that it's an imposition … .'

He was feeling his way. It was he, as the senior teacher, who had hired her to fill the vacant post in the Minnow School and it had never occurred to him before now that she might be someone in whom it was possible to confide.

'It's a dream that I had last night, Miss Ling. A quite elaborate dream, as it turns out, and not all that easy to remember. But perhaps if I undertook to tell it to someone else … .'

'By all means, Colleague. It's not an imposition. Everyone has dreams but how few people, these days, are prepared to put their name to one.'

'All the same, one would not wish to give offence. In a dream, that's to say, certain matters may surface which are customarily kept under wraps.'

'And is that not all the more reason to recount them, Colleague?'

He wasn't sure. Ought he not to have thought this through more thoroughly before opening his mouth? What if she took things in the wrong way and ended up regarding him as some sort of sexual deviant?

'Let's be clear,' said Miss Ling, who must have sensed his sudden reticence. 'What I may not yet have experienced, I'm nevertheless sure to have read about, so could we not make a pact?'

'Ah, a pact. An excellent idea. So what is it that you propose?'

'Just this, Colleague. That you tell the dream and that I'll listen without taking offence, just so long as you promise to tell all.'

A PACT WAS a pact and he kept to it. Certain details resurfaced during the telling that he would have preferred to keep to himself but Miss Ling, for her part, never flinched. Their friendship—along with their courtship and marriage —she took in her stride, listening with mild bemusement. Only after the birth of Wu, when his early promise had been cruelly curtailed, did her smile vanish, her face having become contorted with unquestionably genuine grief.

'That poor child!' she recalled, with moisture welling in her eyes. 'His poor parents!'

It had happened only a few months earlier. One of the students in that very school had suddenly and mysteriously sickened and been sent away to a hospital, where he had died a short while later of what the doctors diagnosed as leukaemia.

He had to move on quickly. The day's first students had arrived and were milling about on the porch, clowning, making the most of their last few precious minutes of freedom. It was far from easy, under these circumstances, to do justice to a dream which had been so comprehensive, with tentacles extending out in so many different directions.

Miss Ling, when his recital was complete, took out a handkerchief and blew her nose.

'And do please dry your eyes, Miss Ling. It won't do for you to be spotted by the students leaving the Middle School classroom in tears.'

The first subject that day was Civics. On the dynamics of

a well-run country, one in which the ruler took heed of the needs of his subjects and received in return their obedience. In preparation, even as the students were starting to file in, Schoolmaster Po chalked the following slogan onto the blackboard:

WHEN PLANNING FOR A YEAR, PLANT GRAIN;
WHEN PLANNING FOR TEN YEARS, PLANT TREES.

The students, once at their desks, and once they noticed that something had been written on the blackboard, at once took out their notebooks and began to copy it. It would be, the schoolmaster recognized from his own days as a pupil, something on which to hang one's cap. If asked by one's parents afterwards what one had learned in school that day, one would be in possession of a ready answer.

They took their time, as was only to be expected. Civics was not a subject likely to arouse much enthusiasm and least of all on that particular morning, when a goodly number of those bent over their notebooks were likely to be experiencing their first hangovers.

'Now then,' the schoolmaster addressed his class. 'A brief review. Who will be so good as to remind us of how government was once defined?'

A single hand went up, that of a small girl with an eager face.

'Me, Sir!'

What took Po Cheng by surprise was not her eagerness, for she was always the first to raise her hand, but something else entirely. He nodded, signalling that she should proceed.

'Government, Sir, was formerly defined as excellence in practice.'

How had he failed to notice it immediately? What a

curious thing the mind was, with its endless store of tricks. Why had he not recognized, when he came across her asleep under a bridge, that the little boat girl of his dream was, in fact, also his most promising student?

WHILE NO DISCUSSION of the foibles of the government presently in power in the country was permitted, Schoolmaster Po nevertheless found it possible—by recounting histories of how other governments had failed disastrously in the past—not only to hold the interest of his pupils but to get across to them the difference between good governance and a mere struggle for power. All the same, it was a relief to get that first lesson over with: it was not a new practice—reviewing the past in order to understand the present—but it could be fraught with danger.

Mathematics was more straightforward, as both the students and the government recognized its importance. Similarly, although the government might be wary, biology had come to hold increasing interest for the students and at an increasingly early age.

He could hear, once his students had been dismissed for the day, the sound of Miss Ling tidying up after her little ones. Some, rather than returning the toys with which they had been playing to the toy box, would hide them away before leaving, thus ensuring that they would be the first to get their hands on them again the following morning.

'*Tiger cubs into tigers,*' reflected Po Cheng. '*Little devils into big ones.*'

He took his time putting things back in order in his own room. Miss Ling customarily popped her head in before leaving for the day and he wondered what her opinion of him would be now that he had revealed himself to her as someone not quite so stolid as she might have imagined.

'Knock! Knock!'

'Ah, Miss Ling. Calm has been restored in your realm as well, I presume.'

'Reasonably so, Colleague. Apart, of course, from that dream of yours. It's been going round and round in my head all day.'

'My apologies. Isn't it odd what one can come up with when one's not in one's right mind?'

'No harm done. Life itself is odd. What could be more outrageous, for instance, than a bridegroom turning up on his wedding day pulling a milk cow along behind him on a rope?'

Far from being offended by his dream, the schoolmaster was thus relieved to discover, she seemed intrigued by it and even considered it to be true to life.

'Besides which,' she added, 'what *is* one's right mind?'

'And are you therefore of the opinion, Miss Ling, that one ought to attend to one's dreams?'

'Indeed. And perhaps even, while the dream is still fresh, write it down.'

'Now you're pulling my leg, I fear.'

'Not at all. Were you not, in your own dream, about to write a book?'

'And how far did I get with that? Not far at all, as I recall.'

Undeterred, the Minnow School teacher approached the bookshelves which when school was not in session doubled as the Nettle Village Public Library. What she took down was a much-thumbed copy of *The Mustard Seed Garden Manual of Art*, a work purporting to contain all that a painter ought to know about his craft or a connoisseur with regard to his collection.

'If I may be so bold, Colleague, this might serve as your guide.'

With the book now open in her hand, she approached the blackboard. Just as a fine plant might be contained within the tiniest of seeds, she pointed out, or a wealth of knowledge within the pages of a single book, so a superior person might imagine an entire world without having ventured more than a few steps from home.

What she had meanwhile copied onto the board was the following:

THERE ARE MANY WAYS
TO ACHIEVE EXCELLENCE IN PAINTING,
AND ALL ARE ELUSIVE.

'A worthy motto for anyone,' agreed Schoolmaster Po. 'Albeit somewhat daunting.'

Nonetheless, just as in the dream, he began to picture a book with his name on it circulating far and wide, from one end of the country to the other, and before long groups of curious individuals would be turning up in Nettle Village in order to view the schoolhouse in which the book's author had once taught.

'So let me get this straight, Miss Ling. This book of mine, assuming that I am somehow able to write it, will be called *My Magnificent Mustard Seed Garden Dream*?'

'Best to write it first, Colleague. Put pen to paper, as they say. And then, afterwards, we could go to work on the title.'